R-Evolution

Evolution Series Book 1

R-Evolution

By Kenny B Smith

Teapots Away Press©
HTTP://www.teapotsawaypress.com

ISBN-13: 978-1-948643-00-9

ACKNOWLEDGMENTS

Edited by: Suzy Buckmiller and Kayla Wellisch

Cover Art provided by: Dracon Studios
Artist and Graphic Designer: Raleigh Smith

To Jonathan – For your unending support and
love throughout this entire process.
To Dominique – For your enthusiasm and
excitement over this entire venture.
To Xander – For your curiosity and eagerness to help
no matter what you have going on.
To EssieLee – For your cute smile and reminding me
we all have a light inside that can be shared with others.

Elva – your support and love never went unnoticed.

IN THE BEGINNING

The room was chilly as a stream of air wisped through the ventilation into her room. *The bed was too close to it,* she thought. But her parents wouldn't allow her to move it. They claimed it was the only way to get her moving early in the day. Stretching, she grabbed her garments and put them on. The same white, brown and gray outfit she wore everyday. Sometimes it didn't stave off the chill. The concrete under her feet felt cold. She wondered if her predecessors ever covered it to keep it warm. But no, they hung rugs and tapestries on the walls for insulation.

As she drifted through her doorway, her mother sat, quietly, in the only chair with stuffing. The only comfortable chair in the bunk.

"Good morning," a smile spread across her lips.

"It's too early in the day," moaned the girl.

"You are supposed to say too early in the morning. Remember your assignment?" reminded her mother.

"Ugh, I don't know if it's morning. I don't even know if the sun is up. What does the sun even look like? I have never been outside this underground concrete cell," lamented the girl.

"Oh dear. You are too smart for your own britches. I promise, one day soon, you will go outside. When you're a little older. When you get done with your lessons. And

1

when you do, you must try and sound like a topsider, just in case," explained her mother.

"Or an escapist. Do we even keep the same hours as the sun? How can I adjust my speech and thinking if I've never been outside?" she asked.

"Well, today, I get to show you pictures. And special papers. Today, you will learn our story," her eyes twinkled. "Would you like to hear it?"

Her mother rose and floated across the room. She looked so graceful grabbing the heavy leather bound book off the shelf. The girl often thought her mom could have been a dancer if circumstances were different. If her ancestors hadn't decided to cower and hide underground in the bunkers, allowing the Germans to march onto their great country without resistance. Anger contorted her facial features.

Looking up, her mother's piercing blue eyes read her expression. "Oh little one, today you will learn the entire truth. I have borrowed this book from the historian. It will help you understand," she sat back down and patted the stuffed chair. "Come dear. Sit and I will show you."

The girl looked concerned. *They've never allowed me to sit in the comfortable chair. This must be important,* she thought, moving hesitantly into the offered seat. Her mother's smile softened her anxiety over the change.

As she curled into the chair, the smell of old, wet leather pierced her nose. The spine creaked a little showing its age. Thin, musty sheets of paper were bound inside the cover. Running her fingers over the rolled corner of the first page, she found it turned her fingers black.

"Careful dear. These are fragile," protested her mother.

Jerking her hand back, she looked at the tall dark print screaming at her from the page.

GERMANY SHELLS BRITAIN
DEATH TOLL UNDETERMINED

SHIPS SUNK IN GULF OF MEXICO
WAR CABINET CONFIRMS U-BOATS ARE IN THE AREA

ARGENTINA SIGNS ALLY TREATY WITH GERMANY
THE REICH ARRIVES IN SOUTH AMERICA

REPORTS OF NEW BOMBS SWEEP SOUTH AMERICA

NEW YORK HIT BY BOMBS WITHOUT PLANES

NEW TECHNOLOGY MEANS ALL CITIES WITHIN REACH

TEXAS HAS FALLEN TO GERMAN-ARGENTINE FORCES

PUBLIC WANTS ANSWERS FROM WAR CABINET

SEE LOCAL OFFICIALS FOR SURVIVAL PLAN

She leaned further into the book with each passing page. Lines of tiny text blurred her eyes as she tried to read everything before the page turned. Flipping the pages gingerly, her mother explained each headline and what it meant. These old thin sheets were called newspapers and this is how news traveled before they moved underground.

As they turned to the last page, mother frowned, furrowing her brow. "The local governments were given the location of these bunkers. We had a very smart president once. His name was Roosevelt. He saw the turmoil starting in Europe and decided he would start a secret public works project to build these bunkers. It was the same time they built the interstate highway system, which I'm sure no longer exists."

A heavy handed knock interrupted the conversation before she could ask any questions. Mother quickly and quietly shut the book, hiding it back on the shelf. *Why is mother hiding this book? Are these things something I shouldn't be taught?* the girl wondered. Approaching the door, she spied her mother waving her hand behind her back. The signal to go to her room and not come out. This was par for the course as far as she was concerned.

Who was at the door? She knew she had to be patient to find out, if she ever would. Low whispering voices echoed through the main space, then the door opened with a whine and closed with a thunk.

"D darling," her mother called. "Erack is waiting for you in the quarantine room. Perhaps you should go play with him for a while."

D shot out of the room, rounding around the corner and out the door so fast her mother felt like she was a blur. Skipping down the halls, she couldn't wait to see him. Erack was her only friend in the entire bunker, but they could only meet in the quarantine room. She asked her mother once what quarantine meant, but her mother danced around the answer, refusing to explain.

She saw Erack through the window. Then pushed open the heavy glass door.

Erack looked at her sharply. "Kid, I don't know what kind of pull you have," sighing heavily.

"Not sure what you mean. Besides, you are not that much older than me. And you act more like a kid than I do," she replied, smiling sweetly at him.

He did not return her smile.

"What's the matter?" she asked.

"I was in the middle of something, but I always have to drop everything to meet you here," Erack lamented.

"Oh, I thought you lived in here. In the quarantine room," D looked at him earnestly.

"Um, no. You are the one stuck in quarantine," he snapped. "I mean, no one out there even knows you exist."

D tilted her head at him as the words echoed around her head.

"Why aren't people allowed to know I exist?" she asked.

Kenny B Smith

STRANGERS

Fresh air. It was invigorating. D filled her lungs with it, closing her eyes, taking in the warmth of the sun. The musty smells she had become accustomed were nowhere to be found. everything underground smelled a little damp and sterile. Topside it was all sweet smells. With every breath, colors painted themselves behind her eyelids. She envisioned what could make such a great set of scents and why they could not experience them more often.

Here she was able to leave the bunker behind. Her simple scouting mission left her by herself with her own thoughts. Topside was one of the few places where she felt at peace. With herself and her surroundings. In this place, she felt in tune, a term described by her ancestors. Maybe that's what she was all the time...in tune. Others saw it as a threat. She could feel somehow they didn't trust her. Felt they saw her as dangerous and different. D didn't want to be dangerous or different.

Birds chattered and took off behind her. Her eyes flew open, hand on her weapon, poised to fire. Looking around, she took in her surroundings again. Something had changed. The birds felt content a moment ago but fled their nests, suddenly startled. Had she lingered too long? Her trainer warned her about basking too long in the sun, but it was always so tempting and felt so nice.

A small herd of deer popped their heads up. She felt their sudden alertness, each with their piercing gazes looking hard toward the abandoned bird perch, ears twitching to find the noise. They stood perfectly still in anticipation and agitation. She was never sure how they stood so still and alert. Perhaps she should be studying their movement to better assist in her training. Or perhaps to make her a better hunter. She liked hunting more than scouting anyway.

She breathed in the crisp air bringing her brain to a focus. A cool wind wisped past her ear. Holding in the chill, she forced herself to be still and listen. **Crack!** The deer gracefully skipped away despite their hurry. An animal familiar with these parts would not have broken the twig. The sound gave away a human step.

When she arrived, she neither saw or felt any sign of humans here. And as she watched, there were no overwhelming feelings she generally associated with being around other people. Maybe being topside dulled her sense of her surroundings. Perhaps she felt too comfortable. Either way, she missed something and it could cost her.

The ruins ahead of her were now silent, eerily so. The lack of movement unnerved her. Leaving her hiding spot now would expose her to whatever was out there. She raised her weapon and scanned the area ahead of her. Checking the sky for planes first, then the ground. Standard procedure, which helped to calm and comfort her. And yet, she found nothing. Frustrated and mentally kicking herself, she attempted to regroup.

She focused on the sight of the disruption with her ears. Was it an echo? If so, which direction? *Focus! Focus! Focus!* she screamed to herself allowing it to bounce around her brain. Listening again, she heard rustling. They were now moving through the tall grass. Eyes shifting, for a moment, she would have sworn this person was invisible. Holding her breath, ears perking up. More rustling. Then she heard it. The echo off the concrete and metal behind her.

Realizing she was standing with her back to whatever was there, she spun quickly, weapon ready, scanning the new area in front of her. The original bird perch was situated near the watering hole. The path proved to be the most insightful, as she located the broken twig. A more careful examination revealed footprints behind the twig coming to an abrupt halt. Even they heard the sound, knowing it had revealed their location, causing them to dive for cover quickly.

The shuffling sounds continued, more slowly as they attempted to stay undercover. She checked her camouflage, assured they hadn't seen her. They were hiding out of instinct or perhaps information they were given. The Germans taught their people nothing went unnoticed. German officials assured everyone in their cities they had listening devices everywhere, even in the wastelands. But these were not stories or lies. D's bunker encountered many of them while setting up small farms topside. However, they had no issues when they interfered with the devices or dug them up. So the assumption was for an unknown reason they were no longer monitored. Which worked out in the bunker's favor. They developed their own technology with them.

Looking up, she realized her attention drifted too long. She held up her finger to gauge the direction of the wind. Tall grass moved in the wrong direction. She poised herself to fire, but a feeling of fear and despair washed over her with such force, she needed a moment to recover. Shaking her head, clearing her mind, she remembered her orders for situations like these. Before she could fire, she needed to establish how big the party was, who they were with and why they were here. Swaying grass would not yield those answers.

Could kids have gotten out of the compound and

followed her? Or sneaked out? Kids under twelve were rarely left alone but many teens were often left to their own devices. Too many years underground had given them leeway to secret entrances and exits and private spaces long since forgotten to the adults. There were always a few clever enough to wander decently far from their home. The temperature ruled this out first. Most would not be equipped with her all weather gear. And many would not travel out this far in this chill. Although some would not know better, they would not have made it out this far as all preferred to take a leisurely pace if they escaped topside.

They could be escapists from the city. The direction they came from would suggest this. While this group appeared possibly untrained, the scenario didn't appear to fit. Despite her prodigy level in training, they would not send her out alone to pick up kids, let alone on her first solo mission. Most escapists were under the age of eight traveling in a group of a dozen or so. While this was a rendezvous point, it was against protocol to send someone out alone on a recovery mission. No one informed her of the possibility. She was unaware of any recent transmissions alerting them of another group of escapists coming their way.

For a moment, she considered outcasts. They may or may not be trained or traveling alone or in a group. They knew so little about topsider outcasts, she felt they were used as characters in fables to keep them from sneaking out of the bunker. It didn't deter many. And she highly doubted anyone could survive out here alone for long. To her, this possibility did not seem credible.

This left one idea, Nazi Germans. The Reich ruled the roost here and she knew they had listening devices out here. Perhaps they heard her over one. Maybe they were scouting, looking for areas to expand. But their actions appeared careless. Assuming they would be better trained for stealthy approaches, she checked again for back up in the skies. Seeing no sign of planes, she considered this option again. Maybe the officers were trying to sniff her out. They acted untrained to fool her into giving away her position.

Her mind had wandered too long again, causing her to lose focus. The sounds stopped and the grass swayed with the wind again. Was she tracking a ghost? She would kick herself if she was tracking a herd of some kind. The noises couldn't have been her imagination. Something had spooked the animals enough to get out of the area. Animals were the first warning system. Their instincts were pure.

For a moment, she scrambled. Scanning the area vigorously, looking for any sign of the intruder. Then, she stopped, looking at the area near the path. A smile formed on her lips. Her work was complete before this had all started. The gap in swaying grass was a result of an old concrete foundation, probably for a shed or small house. It was still mostly intact and would make the perfect place to hide and wait it out. The group probably stumbled upon it, assuming it was harmless.

However, she had laid a glass trap on that foundation when she arrived in the morning. She would know soon who was out here with her. The S.S. uniforms had been made impervious to high-speed projectiles, but not things that cut like glass or knives, forcing close combat if you wanted to survive. The Luftwaffe and Intercontinental Bombs ensured the Germans saw little close combat fighting.

Escapists would cry and not know what to do. Animals would likely scurry out into the open to see what bit them. Teens would kick themselves for not deducing there would be a trap in the first place and most likely start cursing one another. Nazis would nurse their wounds and try to escape the trap with the least amount of sound possible. By now, she firmly convinced herself outcasts did not exist.

Dropping her weapon, it had become her turn to wait.

Loud shrieks shook the air, scaring more birds off branches, causing them to screech in disapproval as they took flight. She saw the tops of heads bob up and down. Adults and children alike began to filter back to the path. Bloody and hurt. Cradling arms and knees and other wounds. Her trap was effective.

But they were not soldiers, not escapists, not teens, not animals. They were dressed in rags, made more so by being cut up in the glass. Not deadly, just a bloody sight. They were pouring out onto the path virtually right in front of her, about a dozen or so. She looked them over and over again as she no longer needed her sight to count them or see them. They whispered. Watching them made her feel a little uncomfortable, like a voyeur.

The group scrambled to recover from the shock, trying to reinstate rank and file. They ranged from early teen to adult. She couldn't grasp why they would bring teens with them. It made no sense. How had they arrived here? How long had they been traveling? There were a few blonds in the group, but most were adults that weren't master race. Had they gotten lost trying to send these children to them? Was it an emergency escape?

Even though her training told her these circumstances required immediate reporting, she couldn't wave it in as the communicator was on the other side of the ruins. She needed to make a decision with no standing orders in place. How she proceeded rested in her own hands. She felt the panic rise in her throat at the idea. If she messed this up, they would never let her go on another solo mission.

Trying to convince herself to kill them made her sick to her stomach. There was training for this. Their trainer tried to make it feel as real as possible. And they took them out hunting live game. But somehow, animals felt different than other humans. Making her feel unable to follow orders if necessary. This group hit her particularly hard. There were children with them. That felt unethical. She assessed the likelihood they were trained soldiers. But again, they had children. They made stupid moves, didn't check for traps and weren't dressed for any cold weather. They were untrained. But none of this gave her cause to kill them.

She put her listening enhancer into her ear, turning her head to the group to extract any quiet conversations. The downfall of the device was one could not watch and listen at the same time. All she could hear were curses and whimpering. Her head was craned for so long, her neck began to cramp. Relentless, they finally began talking in hushed tones.

"This was a trap set for soldiers by soldiers. From the looks of things though, this area is uninhabited. We have possibly stumbled into someone else's territory and I guarantee they will not trust us or our intentions," said a male voice.

"You don't know that for sure Jaren," said a female voice.

"Tend to the children," Jaren replied gruffly.

"We could be miles from an actual colony. That trap could have been set by outcasts or it was laid years ago. We don't know if there is anyone even close to here," said another male voice. This one sounded younger.

"We know nothing about this area," Jaren said.

"We don't know anything about any area above ground, at least not with any certainty," interrupted the other male.

"We need to be more careful. Much more careful," replied Jaren.

She turned her head to face them when they appeared to pause. Putting faces to voices was difficult with her rudimentary technology, but she was glad she had it. She could see a woman tending to the injuries of the younger party members. Removing glass pieces, she had an orange bag with a medical symbol on it. The scout recognized it immediately as standard issue for compound medical personnel. The bandages looked familiar as did the liquid in the vial she was using.

There was an older man and a younger man exchanging what appeared to be a heated conversation. She assumed the older one was named Jaren. Pulling out her log book, she quickly jotted down the notes in her special code. The discussion was becoming more heated and she reluctantly turned her head to hear what was worth such a conflict.

"We wouldn't have survived if we had listened to you!" the young voice said in a hushed and terse tone. "If you hadn't followed us, you wouldn't be able to try and be in charge. You have no right to make decisions here."

"The intel was good," Jaren insisted. "You know the intel was good Xayres."

"How can you still believe the intel was good if it got the rest of us killed?" Xayres asked, trying to control his volume. "The intel cannot be good and wrong at the same time. How could you have overlooked the contradictory report? You chose which intel to pay attention to and look where that got us," he threw his hands up to illustrate the current location. "We're not listening to you anymore because you have blinded yourself to the truth." His voice was trembling and rising. "It's your fault she's gone! You're fault they're all gone!"

"SHHHHH!" the woman hissed. "You're scaring the children." She looked around quickly and continued, "And the animals."

Fearing Xayres had given away their position again, Jaren slapped his hand over Xayres' mouth, pulling him to the ground. They could not risk him shouting a response at the woman. No one moved but she could hear a light struggle. An occasional adult head popped up like a gopher to check their surroundings, gauging when it would be safe to speak or move again.

She noted in her log they sounded like escapists, possibly from the city in the east. She debated again whether to reveal herself, kill them all or continue to collect information to figure out who they were. They didn't seem to be too much of a threat except they couldn't keep control of themselves or one another. That provided opportunities for attention from unwanted places.

She grumbled at her options. Killing them would be too messy and if city soldiers did stumble upon their bodies, it would give away that there was another force in the area. Besides, this was an escapist rendezvous point as well and she didn't want to send the wrong impression. It would be premature to reveal herself before they managed themselves. She sighed and turned her ear back to the group. One could never have too much intel.

"Listening to you will get us all killed," Xayres hissed. Jaren had apparently released him after a short tussle on the ground.

"Shouting like that will get us all killed," Jaren hissed back.

"Both of you knock it off," said the female voice. "What is done is done. We can't keep arguing about it. We need to move on and find a safer place to be. This area could well be inhabited and since we don't trust strangers, it is safe to assume anyone here wouldn't either. And with you guys yelling like that, they are more likely to kill us than take us in. We pose a direct threat to them."

"Ra'Ella is right," said Jaren.

"What would you suggest then dearie?" Xayres spat at her.

"I don't know. What I do know is you need to calm down Xayres and Jaren, you need to get it through your thick skull that you're no longer in charge. Now we are a completely democratic group. We will all be informed and we will all decide. Working together will help us thrive. Right now, we cannot be working against one another."

"But he ignored the intel. How can we trust him even in a group decision? His voice still carries a lot of weight with this community," Xayres pleaded.

"There is still no indication they found the bunker," Jaren insisted.

"No indication. We were attacked. There is no indication? What are you talking about there is no indication?" Xayres spewed incredulously.

"They must have used some technology that we didn't know existed," Jaren pressed.

"Maybe we would have had a better idea of their technology if we hadn't been restricted from coming above ground. You were the one who insisted we didn't ever leave the bunker. We needed more than just our sensors and information from the network. For all we know, we were sitting ducks for years," Xayres said.

"That would require a traitor on the inside and there was no indication..." Jaren started.

"Maybe there is no sign of a traitor because the person responsible for keeping us safe from traitors is the traitor. You know, the one who selectively decides which information to listen to and disseminate. That person would have ample opportunity to remove anything incriminating them before passing that information on to others," Xayres argued.

"This is a pointless argument," a younger female voice joined the conversation. "We must choose now. We have people waiting for us to scout this area and make decisions. Right now, we are jawing off and wasting precious time. Xayres, we all lost a great deal, but you need to stop trying to blame someone. They had us out-manned. They're not spending their lives in hiding. They're not in the dark. They took us by surprise and no one could have stopped that even if we had information. You need to grieve and move on. Let it go."

"I don't know how to let it go. There's nothing left that she loved, that I loved. I don't know why I am the one here and she is the one who had to die." Xayres lamented and it sounded like he was starting to cry.

"You're still here. She loved you. She sacrificed herself for you. You are younger. Her time was much more limited than yours. She thought you had more to give than she could. Embrace that. Prove her right, not wrong," the young female said.

All she could hear now were sniffles. He was crying. Now she knew their bunker had been raided. They were all that was left and there was a camp of more survivors somewhere. This could be a show for her benefit but she still believed they had no idea she was there. They had obviously not been topside in a very long time.

The sun was starting to drop toward the horizon. The group went silent. D turned her head to see them looking glumly at the ruins. All these events had obviously taken their toll on them. As they picked up their supplies to move, she shifted, remembering she was right in front of the closest entrance. When they passed her, she could have touched every one of them from her perch.

Nightfall well set before D felt she could move. The chill becoming unbearable. Even in her cold weather gear, her fingers were starting to stiffen from the signs of possible hypothermia. Rolling over and stretching, her muscles protested as did her lungs. She must get back in time. They needed this information and if she was late, most possibly wouldn't believe anything she said. Knowing this prompted her, pushing herself to her feet.

Her breath was the only sign she was here. Moving swiftly under cover, she trotted around the ruins and onto the open space. This area was mostly traveled at night for protection, fearing she'd hit this stretch too late, quickening her pace to a hard run. Her chest protested as she pushed to her limits.

By the time she reached the door, she was beyond out of breath. It took all her strength to stay standing long enough to put in her code. Her fingers twitched and shook as they grazed over the alphanumeric code unique to her and her assignment. The panel buzzed at her with red flashing lights. She growled at it. Her outdoor gear would not keep her warm enough or protected enough in these temperatures.

Looking to the sky, she surveyed the moon. Was it past clocked midnight? If so, her code would be invalid. Maybe she tapped in the sequence incorrectly. It was cold and she was shivering from the temperature and exhaustion. Clouds from her mouth floated on the air every time she exhaled.

Closing her eyes, she steadied herself through breathing and training. Slowing her responses would stop her shaking. She eyed the moon again. It was close to the cut off and she was wasting time. Her body was responding to the training. It loosened and relaxed. She closed her eyes. Sweat dripped down her forehead. Shifting her weight, trying to refocus. Holding her breath as she tapped the pad again. Her lungs protested, begging for release. Finally her lungs forced the air free. The panel lit green, releasing the door.

It swung open as she struggled to move inside. Trying to close it, the weight was too much for her weakened body. The clock on the wall read 0002. Two minutes past clocked midnight. She struggled with the weight of the door while trying to figure out how the code worked. The door wouldn't budge. She dropped to her knees. Her pack fell to the floor. It had unlatched while she sprinted back home and she hadn't noticed.

"Hands on your head!" a male voice shouted.

Someone pushed the door out of her hands. She heard it click. Two men stood over her but they were blurry. She was starting to lose consciousness. The world spun around her. If this was the way they would act when she came back late, why did they allow the code to work? She tried to keep her thoughts straight as she limply lifted her hands on her head.

All she wanted was to turn in her log book and get some sleep. Today felt long and emotional. But she knew that after she turned it in, there would be a long list of questions from the council. Even more so once they actually knew what was in it. Then action plans and maneuvers would follow. Her notes guaranteed that. Her head hurt. The spinning increased. She couldn't think as she reached for her log book.

One of the men shouted at her again, moving to face her.

"Damn D! What took you so long?" he said.

"We figured you were dead, or worse," said the one behind her.

They smiled at D, relieved she was okay. It would be difficult to replace her. They tried to help her to her feet unsuccessfully. All she could do was reach for her log. Fumbling around in her bag, one of them knelt down to help her. They managed to get her log book out.

"Taz, I need to see them. Immediately! There's been a change," she mustered between pants before the world went black.

The men watched for a moment, unsure if she was okay. Her body convulsed violently causing them to panic. One ran shouting down the corridor while the other regained his composure, turning her on her side to ascertain if she already swallowed her tongue. Then proceeded to keep her from doing so.

"Oh, she will kill me for putting my fingers in her mouth," he whispered to himself.

They followed her all the way to the med bay but were met by the council's private guards and allowed to go no further. Turning over the log, they returned to their post. Slowly, as the sun rose and the hours passed, the council began to gather in the bay, waiting for her to wake.

NEW MISSION

Her eyes burst open. D tried to sit up, head aching. Why couldn't she move? She didn't panic. She felt in control, but her ears were buzzing and her vision blurry. The straps were most likely for her safety. D had a nasty habit of throwing herself off the med bay table.

"Doc..." she whispered, "How long was I out?" she asked.

"Unfortunately, not long enough D," Doc answered. ""You need to be more careful. Your body has limits. Running like that in the cold air. You're not trained for that. None of you have been trained to do that."

"Had to get back before midnight," D croaked. "So, I guess I keep inventing test programs for myself."

It hurt D to laugh, but she couldn't help herself. As she lamented the pain, she felt something shift in her ear. Her listening device was still in it, but she couldn't reach it to turn it on. She found her arms were bound to the table. A look of confusion spread across her face.

"Doc, a little help here," her vision was starting to clear and she felt the need to sit.

"Nope. I'm trying to keep them from noticing you're awake. You must rest and allow your body to recover," Doc pleaded. "I know you're young and you think you're invincible, but really, you need time."

D had noticed the whispers in the background. Struggling against her bonds, she loosed them just enough to turn on her ear piece. Turning her head, the voices were familiar. The council now gathered in the corner, attempting to have a private conversation. Doc eyed her suspiciously.

"Careful D. They are serious right now," Doc said.

"So, how many times did I throw myself off the bed before you strapped me down?" D asked winking.

She felt the tension around the room. These were strained talks and now more than ever, she needed to know if her feelings of distrust were justified.

"Oh, well, maybe four times," Doc replied. "It's good this isn't your first time here or you may have hurt yourself even more than you did."

"What are they talking about?" D asked even though she already knew the answer.

"You know what they're talking about. You just want to draw attention to yourself. So hush and behave for once," Doc scolded. "Teens...I don't know why I even have to bother..." her voice trailed off.

"So you'd rather I just lie here silently until they leave?" D pressed.

Doc's voice had an edge to it D was unfamiliar with, "They've disrupted this bay all morning. They should be in chambers, but no, they're here waiting for you to wake up. What in the world did you see out there? That stupid log has been a thorn in my side since you got here." Doc roughly rearranged her pillow and sheets. "Now do what I tell you. Shut up and lie still."

D closed her eyes and did as she was told, pointing her listening device toward the corner of the room. They were discussing her and she wanted to know what and why.

"If this is accurate," a woman said. "Then she needs to take our troops back. This needs to be met with full force."

"I am the military advisor. I know we cannot have the

element of surprise without the darkness and the sun is well up. And she almost died not eight hours ago. We can't send her back out there, regardless of whether that group is on the move," said a deeper voice.

"Besides, the log says they had no idea she was there. There is no risk. They don't know we're here. But there is a risk if we go back out there," said Trey, head of the council.

She only knew a few of them by name. Footsteps shuffled in her direction. Closing her eyes, she hoped they hadn't seen her awake. Anxiety washed over her, making it difficult not to react. Doc pulled herself away from the table to intercept them.

"She is not available and you are not waking her. She needs rest. Leave her be until she comes to on her own. That's a medical order," Doc said forcefully.

D always admired her ability to say exactly what she needed with nothing extra. She didn't waste breath. Doc arrived back at her bedside as she heard steps moving away. The anxious feeling went with them and now D felt a tension she couldn't describe.

Someone else approached the table. This man looked thin, but she knew he had a slender, muscular frame. His blue eyes could pierce her even if she couldn't see them. She'd know his figure anywhere. Although she hadn't heard his voice mixed into the hushed conversation, she knew he must have been standing and listening intently, as it was his job. She felt his hand caress her ankle. His influence calmed her somehow, made her less suspicious.

"Erack, why do they want to send me back out so quickly?" she asked him.

"I don't know. It doesn't make a lot of sense to me. Then again, I haven't been fully read in yet either. I think they're waiting to talk to you before they declassify info," answered Erack.

Doc hushed them, eyeing the conversation across the room suspiciously.

"No matter what they want, you need to rest," Doc hissed. Erack smiled as if to agree. "Now pretend you are still asleep until they decide to leave."

"I was never very good at acting," D replied, watching Doc's forehead crinkle above her almost black eyebrows.

Doc sighed, turning to Erack, nothing but seriousness in her green eyes as she rolled them, "Honestly, you're one of her commanding officers. Can't you order her to can it?" she motioned toward D.

"At the tender age of 17, she thinks she's invincible. She's not much for following orders either," Erack mused quietly, shaking his head. "Especially from me. Maybe because we're so close in age."

Doc pursed her thin lips, causing her brow to furrow. "I don't think it has anything to do with the age of the person giving her orders, Erack. We'll just go over there and figure out what the big deal is. She certainly can't tell us, especially now she knows it's still eyes only classified information," Doc mused.

"Didn't he just tell you I'm not so great at following orders?" D winked at Doc, a grin from ear to ear.

"That is not a smart idea D," Erack warned. "They may just leave you out there for good."

"I for one want to know what brought them to be in my space for the last four hours," Doc said.

D looked from one to the other, assessing their moods. Doc was tense and annoyed, possibly frustrated. She could feel it pulsing through every word and movement. Erack was fearful, not wanting her to get caught sharing information. Something told D Erack already knew everything, but she pushed the idea he'd lied to her aside.

Pausing only long enough to appear to have thought about it, she began relayed the events of her mission. She moved to emphasize the oddest points, discussing her thoughts about them at length. Erack stood and listened, grabbing random tools and only walking away to fetch things for Doc. She walked away from the table repeatedly, causing D to pause her story, only to resume when Doc returned.

The more she told them, the more Doc found it difficult to hide her confusion, fear, and amazement at the events. She was starting to give them away. D enjoyed the feeling of causing so much intrigue. But the meeting in the corner began to die down. They knew she was awake.

Suddenly, a sea of faces surrounded D, leaning over her, peering down from all directions, making her dizzy. Feeling tense and hurried, the pit of her stomach began to tremble. Where was this feeling coming from? As she tried to straighten her view, she felt distrust, confusion and exhaustion, all in an overwhelming fashion and all at once.

She tried to sit up, forgetting she was strapped to the table. Her head slammed into it with a force loud enough they all heard it. Her stomach churned. Her complexion greened, a vile color usually unseen with her darker skin. But she knew it must be ever present as Erack rushed to release her straps and Doc flew back to her head with a bucket. Her throat burned as the contents of her stomach emptied into the bin. Erack moved around the table to assist.

Doc started pushing everyone back. "Can't you see she's still struggling. Step back. All of you!" she yelled.

D sat up. The motion caused another release of her rations. Hoping it was the last bit left in her stomach, she tried to steady herself. Erack set the bin on her lap and snatched a rag. She waved it away, unaware she was covered in muck. A nurse appeared with crackers and seltzer water. Both were also waved away, but they were left on the tray next to her bed. As the nurse turned, Doc handed her the bin and motioned for a fresh one. The onslaught of feelings faded into one of shock and awe. Then as the group backed away, it dissipated even further. D was excited about the reprieve. The room stopped spinning.

D croaked, "What the hell do you want?"

Immediately, the overwhelming cacophony of noise ripped through her brain. Everyone spoke at once. Some started to raise their voices attempting to speak over one another. Squeezing her eyes shut, she covered her ears, feeling her ear piece. It was still on. She clicked it off quickly, which only served to reduce the volume but not the actual noise. Now her gut felt frenetic and she tried to push it all away. Focusing on her training, breathing slowly, maintaining heart rate, but it was still all too much. Before she could stop herself, she screamed.

Silence. The beeping of med bay monitors and the gentle hum of electricity running to machines hard at work were the only noises breaking through. She opened her eyes. Doc scanned her head. D saw her deep concern. The group had taken many more steps away from the exam bed, and with them again, the wave of overwhelming emotions. Erack was still at her feet, shock all over his face. Flopping backward, she laid down before the room could start to spin again.

Trey cleared his throat loudly, in the way he always did when he was uncomfortable and wanted to shift the attention in a room. Stepping forward cautiously, D saw him out of the corner of her eye.

Doc stepped between them again, her hand looking abnormally small on his chest. "Go slowly. One at a time or all of you will leave," she said sternly.

Trey nodded. Doc went to check on the other patients in the ward. It was this moment D realized she was in a private room. Probably requested by the council in response to the eyes only status on her log. She released a long drawn out sigh. Turning her head, she saw Trey with her log book in his hand. He motioned as if asking for permission to speak. She gave a weak nod.

"Is everything in this log accurate?" Trey asked.

"Yes, to the best of my knowledge, which apparently

has gaps, based on your conversation," answered D.

She was beginning to feel the exhaustion. His distrust of her log made her agitated. The overwhelming tension and distrust from the rest of the group only served to aggravate her own feelings of frustration and anger.

"You were listening to our conversation? How?" said a woman on the council.

"Kaya, I am sure she just means..." Erack started.

D pulled the listening device from her ear and set it on the table next to the crackers. Erack looked surprised. The shock wave washed over the room.

"Eavesdropping is not a good habit. And in this particular instance, it could be treasonous," Kaya scoffed.

"Oh, be indignant later. It's your fault you didn't make sure it was removed before you congregated in here," snapped D.

She felt Erack's hand on her ankle again, but this time it wasn't gentle. He squeezed her tightly. His silent warning. She let out another exasperated sigh.

"Look, I'm tired. Can we get on with this?" D asked.

"We don't take orders from you, young lady," Trey rebutted.

"Well, seeing as you were all eagerly awaiting my consciousness and you admitted yourselves this is a pressing matter, we should probably make this quick," replied D.

All this back and forth was wearing on her nerves, which were already shot. She usually had more; she must be tired. The control on her reactions slipping with every interaction.

"So no embellishments? No omissions?" asked another councilman.

"Nothing forgotten?" asked another woman.

Although they were proceeding, she saw it as a superficial attempt at sounding less like they didn't believe her and more like the events were unbelievable. Somehow she knew their true intentions. This was part of being in tune with her surroundings.

"Of course. I follow my training course in making my log into a riveting story that no one can put down," replied D sarcastically. Erack's grip tightened a little more, causing a small wince at the pressure. It did not sway her response. "Because we all learned a great story is so much better than the facts of the situation. And I surely aim to please." She threw out more sarcasm, agitation rising in her tone, "I mean, you question everyone's logs so thoroughly and repeatedly, right? You wouldn't single me out in any way at all," throttling out of control and unable to catch herself, "Wait! You don't question other's reports like this, do you? So why do I get to play twenty questions?"

One councilman started to open his mouth. Trey raised his hand to silence all responses and call for a private conversation. None of them left the room though. All determined to keep D and what she knew among only them. They reconvened in their corner. D tried to pull herself back together, not understanding where this was coming from completely. She knew they distrusted her but shocking them like that might cost her everything she had.

"What was that D?" Erack whispered tersely. "They're going to decommission you if you don't knock it off."

D picked up the listening device, placing it in her ear. Erack's eyes grew wide as she placed her finger on her lips. The council repeated words like classified and eyes only and another mission and false logs. Doc returned and D motioned for her to be quiet. Doc continued her scans and when she was done, she joined Erack at the foot of D's bed.

As D listened, an unexplained feeling of dread and fear filled her stomach. It was slow at first but the more she listened and the more they said, the deeper the feeling crept. Then, when she turned her head to look at them for a moment, complete disgust filled her head space. Anger, fear, frustration. It was becoming too much again. She closed her eyes, turning her head back so she could listen again.

Reviewing all her movements in her head as she waited, hoping it would calm her down, she wanted to know why they felt afraid, why she felt afraid. But they didn't give her enough time to regain her composure because doubts of their intentions began bouncing around her head.

Trey turned to look at her, "You realize everything in this log is eyes only until you've been debriefed?"

D opened her eyes but didn't flinch. She waved her hand in a dismissive way, never taking her eyes off the ceiling.

"Young lady," Trey persisted. "Officer!" his voice rose.

"Why would you send me so close to the city on a scouting mission? What aren't you telling us?" D asked, slyly removing the device from her ear while she turned her head and attempted to sit up again. "Were you hoping to hear some of this information?"

"D. Stop it! That's an order!" Erack commanded, his grip on her ankle tightening again. This time, he didn't notice until she wrenched it free.

She glared at Erack, "Well, you know more than you're willing to give. Then again, we always knew you were better at following orders than I have ever been." She moved from Erack to the council. "Are you planning missions to enter the city?"

"D, we talked about this," Erack's tone was urgent.

"So have we," Trey stated. "You certainly ask too many questions. You know there will almost always be details concerning your missions that we do not tell you, for the greater good. That's how these things work."

"I think everyone needs to calm down," Doc began to move between them again. "We're all getting a little out of hand in here. D, I understand your need to know and Trey, I understand your position as well. How about we find a way to meet in the middle? Why don't we discuss what has the council all up in arms in a nice way so D can rest? It's becoming more and more apparent that she needs it." Doc covered for her.

"Fine!" D folded her arms and harrumphed like a defiant toddler.

"D!" Erack's voice commanded attention.

D unfolded her arms and breathed in deep. "I will behave," she relented.

"What is it exactly, that needs clarification from D?" Doc continued to mediate.

"Just these names," Trey pointed to her open log. "Are you absolutely certain these are the names you heard?"

"I can't be certain I spelled them correctly. But I know those are what I heard. I only heard three names. So there wasn't an overwhelming amount of information to forget or omit," D replied, trying to stay calm.

"So Jaren, Xayres and Ra'Ella are the only names you heard?" Kaya asked.

Doc looked stunned as the color drained from her face. D tapped her foot to redirect her attention, looking expectant.

"I thought we all decided they were too close to the city to be above ground," said Doc.

"Yes, we did," Kaya said.

"Now I understand. D, why didn't you..." Doc couldn't finish the statement. She could only look at D. Confusion swept over D as she watched Doc carefully.

"I hadn't gotten to that part of the story yet," D's tone softened in response to the look on Doc's face. She tilted her head toward the council. "We got interrupted."

Erack's lack of surprise stirred up the tension in her chest again. "Of course you already knew," she said, giving him her look of disapproval.

"Someone had to decode your log D. Of course, I read it," responded Erack. "But it was eyes only and you know that means not even I can really discuss it without permission. Not even with the person who wrote it."

His logic, no matter how sound, frustrated her, "So you would rather play me for an idiot?" she sighed indignantly, refraining as she promised. "Yes, those are the only names. Doc, do you know something?"

"D, please let us ask the questions," insisted another council member.

Erack grabbed a chair for Doc as she exhibited difficulty standing. After she was secure, Erack resumed his post at D's feet.

"D, will you take us back to them?" Trey asked.

"No! Absolutely not! She needs to recover." Now Erack moved between Trey and D. D noticed how small his frame looked against Trey's. Everyone looked small in relation to Trey.

"You have her logs, her surveys, her direction and her time. You can send someone else," Erack insisted.

"Erack, I understand your concern but it will take too long for someone else to retrace her steps. We need to get there quickly. She is the only one," Trey responded calmly.

"He's right," D said, sitting up. "If the sun's up already, they've already headed back to the camp to get the rest of their people. I don't know how far away that was." D pushed her exhaustion back and tried standing.

"I'm not sure it's a good idea for you to stand yet," Doc interjected waving carelessly only half paying attention. "Maybe..." she walked off without finishing the thought.

"Doc has to go with her and knows it. She can monitor D's condition in the field. This may be fruitful for research on training practices," Trey said.

"Why would Doc go with me?" D asked, stumbling to get her balance on weak, fatigued legs.

"You'll take Tallin too," Trey ignored her. "And a few other soldiers just in case."

"Why are they coming with me? Why aren't we going

out with a full complement of soldiers?" D pressed more firmly.

Tallin moved to the front of the group and spoke for the first time, "Because we have to confirm your information. Doc and I are the only ones who can do that. Doc is Xayres' cousin. Jaren is my brother. But my brother and I had a falling out before I left the bunker and I am in no hurry to see him again. So I am not going," Tallin turned toward Trey. "As I have already stated. The less I see of him the better."

D was more concerned with Doc than Tallin and his apprehension. Doc's usual poised demeanor had deteriorated into confused mumbling. It was rare for Doc to be lost in her own thoughts while tending to others. She was obsessively playing with a pendant she had pulled out from under her collar. D had never seen it before. Kaya walked over and placed her hands on Doc's shoulders, coaxing the pendant out of her hand and back into its hiding spot.

"They found them," Doc murmured, face contorted and wrinkled with extreme concentration. "They were attacked. The precautions didn't work. We need a new plan."

"What do you mean Doc?" D asked cautiously.

Doc looked at her blankly. D couldn't make sense of it all and found herself feeling Doc's pain and confusion. She noticed Erack's voice rise as the disagreement with Tallin continued in the corner. For a moment, she drifted to see why they created such a commotion. Then forced herself back to Doc. She needed more information.

Her voice barely above a whisper, D leaned in to hear her. "When Four was attacked, the Reich gave away the position of the city, by accident I'm sure," Doc started to explain. "The network decided Five could no longer go topside. They were too close to the city. It wasn't safe. That was ten years ago." Kaya gently shushed Doc. "They found them even though Five no longer went top side. Was it just luck or..."

Doc's voice was drowned out by Erack and Tallin's argument. D couldn't hear another word. The shouting in the corner had become too loud to ignore. As she turned her head, she noticed Tallin was red in the face and Erack fumed.

"What are you so afraid of?" Erack struggled to maintain a steady tone.

"I'm not afraid. I don't see a need to risk my life. Anything could happen out there," Tallin shouted back.

"That sounds like someone who has something to hide," responded Erack.

D watched as Trey tried to move between the two of them. They continued to shout at one another. The longer she watched and listened, the more contemptuous she felt, but she couldn't explain why. This was not her fight and she had no stake in it.

"Erack, you have no right or place to judge my decisions," Tallin screamed.

"I'm not questioning your decisions. I am challenging what you are giving us for reasons," Erack reasoned.

"Gentlemen. This is not how this should be handled," Trey tried but found himself struggling to stay between them.

"Looks like whatever you're trying to hide is going to come to light," Erack chided.

"I'm not hiding anything. I just hate my brother," Tallin replied.

"Enough to put us all at risk by not going to confirm it's him or to condemn any survivors because we can't verify who they are?" Erack asked.

"We haven't heard from them in weeks. They could be impostors. What if they are impostors?" Tallin spat back. "I am not willing to risk my life for impostors!" he growled.

Suddenly, Doc came to life, as if someone had flipped

her switch. "It's not like we're marching into the lion's den. We would be stealthy...careful," she argued back, caution with every chosen word. "I am willing to risk it for survivors. Why aren't you? And I want an actual answer Tallin."

"Because he has something to hide, that's why," Erack shouted, trying to dodge his way around Trey.

Tallin held Trey by the back of his shirt, ensuring Trey stayed in front of him, keeping Erack at bay.

"He's not willing to risk us finding out what he's hiding. Trey, I've told you for a long time we shouldn't trust him," Erack persisted. "He's always acted a little suspicious."

"Erack, calm down. This is not your decision to make," Trey boomed at him.

"I've got nothing to hide," Tallin screeched. "Who are you to question my behavior?"

"The only person who will question it. That's who," Erack screamed back. "Why are you acting this way if you have nothing to hide?"

"I'm not hiding anything," was all Tallin would answer.

D had given up on standing and was now leaning precariously against the examination bed, unsure whether her legs would work correctly. Pursing her lips together, she released a whistle so loud it reverberated off the walls for what felt like hours. The room went silent as everyone took care to cover their ears from the high pitched sound. Trey sighed in relief as the two men stopped squirming to maneuver around him.

"Great, it's settled then," she shouted, shocking herself with how well she could hear her voice. She hadn't realized there was no longer a reason to shout. She continued in a more regular tone. "If you have nothing to hide, then you should have no problem coming with us Tallin. We leave as soon as Doc gets my legs working," she swung herself back up on the bed. "Doc!" she called. "Doc!"

Doc was mumbling to herself again, but at the sound of

her name a second time, she snapped back into focus again.

"Yes...yes. Just let me run a few more tests. Then you'll be ready to travel again, I suppose. I still want you to take this time to rest," said Doc, motioning for her to lie down.

BROTHERS

They made their way around the ruins in the daylight. It was warmer today than yesterday. But the air was still crisp and clear. D took a moment to breathe it in, allowing her a chance to steady herself and disguise it as appreciating the outdoors. Because she was still weak, the trek had taken longer than she wanted and Tallin made it even more difficult. The sun was dropping close to the horizon by the time they arrived at the ruins which left little time for tracking.

D went to work, checking for footprints and other signs of a large group passing through the ruins. She found it almost immediately by the entrance she was watching the previous day. Shaking her head at their inexperience, she wondered if deciding never to go topside had given them too much of a disadvantage in protecting themselves and others.

Signaling for the others to follow, she carefully traced the steps inside. This group was dangerous, not because they had skills, but due to their lack of survival skills. She easily found them in plain sight making food over a fire. *How could these people have survived this far?* she thought.

They easily took a hidden perch to observe them carefully.

"Doc, how long had it been since you last saw your

cousin? Do you see him there?" D asked.

"No, do you see the man who called himself Xayres down there?" replied Doc.

"Actually no. I don't see any of them. Maybe they're smarter than I gave them credit for. The big boys are hiding while the expendable ones are in plain sight. That's how I would stay safe anyway," D stated flatly.

"Can we get this over with please?" Tallin whined.

"For someone who didn't want to be here in the first place, you seem in an awful hurry to meet your brother again. It will be easier if we go in after sundown. Then we can take them by surprise and minimize resistance, or the chance for them to shoot us. You were very clear about not risking your life for these people," D said, signaling to two other soldiers in the party. "I'll go down and see if I can get them to cooperate. So hunker down Tallin, we've got a few hours. I suggest taking this time to re-hydrate and eat," she chucked packs of rations at them.

As the last flicker of sunlight fell below the horizon, D slowly made her way to the sentry's post. The other officers would watch her closely and only intervene if necessary. One sentry appeared to be on duty on this side of the ruins. She would need to assess his abilities.

Noticing the increasing clouds and wind, she kicked herself for not paying closer attention to the rising storm. Now they were downwind and if the sentry had any skills, he may be able to smell them.

Watching the sentry closely, she tossed some rocks behind him. He didn't turn toward it. Then she threw a few more. Still no response. He either didn't hear it or thought being a sentry meant holding still. Either way, he would not smell them either.

She crept up behind him. Then she noticed him flinch a little. The hair stood on the back of her neck. This may be a trap. Stepping softly up behind him, at this last moment, she decided to talk instead of knocking him out. Back up was right behind her and if they were from a bunker, she didn't want to risk any ill will.

"You're actually pretty good at this. Silent. Creepy almost," the sentry said aloud as if to answer her thoughts.

"If you knew I was here, why didn't you stop me?" D asked.

"I knew you were somewhere, but I couldn't figure out where. The echoes out here are not so great and I don't like to chase my tail unnecessarily," the sentry replied. "So just make this quick. You won't get any information out of me."

"Make what quick?" asked D.

"My death and the deaths of all the others," said the sentry.

"If I wanted you dead, I could have killed you hours ago. Besides, why would I bother getting this close to you if I was just going to kill you? I mean, have you seen how far blood splatters?" replied D.

"Yes, I am actually aware of how blood splatters. I saw a lot of it when you raided our bunker," the sentry was seething.

D moved cautiously around the sentry to get a better look. He sat next to an old entryway to a concrete building. She moved into the doorway, leaning against the one side still taller than she was. Her legs were screaming for her to release them from their pain. This was the only solution she could find.

She looked the sentry up and down. Dropping her weapon to her side, she spoke carefully, "You think the Nazis would send one person out here by themselves...alone? You're funny. That makes no sense. They only send in ground troops when the bombing is done. Or at least that's what we would expect, I suppose."

"I suppose you would know. Maybe you guys are ticked you didn't get the information in the bunker and you want more," he still refused to look up at her.

"Do I look like S.S. to you?" her question forced him to

look up.

He eyed her suspiciously. Then he stood. Sitting had masked his bulky frame. But he wasn't very tall. He looked from her hand to her weapon, which still hung at her side. Although her stance looked casual and unassuming, he approached cautiously, tripping a little over the pieces on concrete in front of the door. She smirked and chuckled at his ineptness.

Her smile must have comforted him a little because when he reached the doorway, he grabbed her hood, managing to knock it off her head. She snatched his wrist, gripping it hard enough to make him wince. As he dropped to his knees under her grip, he caught his first glimpse of her.

Black hair and chocolate brown eyes gleamed in the light of the moon. Her skin looked like it would have been dark if not for a life underground, but it wasn't pale. Still darker with more pigment than most. He gasped at the sight of her. What should have been a compliment immediately rubbed her the wrong way. She threw his hand back at him, exhaling a snort of disgust. Cradling his wrist, he stood up again.

"I've never seen one up close, but if you are a Nazi, you've disguised it very well," the sentry awed.

"Again, not a disguise. If I were German, why would I bother to approach you or gain your trust if my goal was to kill all of you?" D reasoned.

He leaned back carefully, considering her logic with which he could find no flaw. The look on his face went from awe to puzzled to full confusion.

D continued, "Besides, I had ample opportunities to kill you all yesterday and I didn't take them."

"Yesterday?" he repeated.

"Yes, yesterday. When Jaren, Xayres, and Ra'Ella came here scouting," she said, scanning his face for any sign of comprehension or even digestion of the information. "They fell into my trap or rather, crawled onto it. Cut them up pretty bad too," explained D.

"I suppose if you wanted to know where we all were, you would have waited until we were all back together. But then again, I have seen no mercy in my limited dealings with the S.S.," said the sentry trying to make sense of the situation.

"You've only dealt with them when they've raided your bunker," remarked D.

"Yes, twice now. I was one of the few survivors out of number Four," he lamented.

"Then you have more experience with their brutality than most," D sympathized.

"So, what do you want?" the sentry asked.

"Aside from being home at this moment. Not much. Just go get Jaren and Xayres and Ra'Ella and bring them out here. I have some people who want to speak with them," answered D.

"And if I refuse?" inquired the sentry.

She saw the fear in his eyes long before she felt it. He had a great duty trying to protect his people after all that happened to them and he allowed someone to get this close.

"Then, I'll knock you out like I was going to originally and go in there myself. But I will take my extra soldiers and they are much more trigger happy than I am. Any resistance and they are not opposed to shooting anything that moves. I imagine that is not ideal for you," replied D.

"Well, let's see if you're telling the truth. I'll go get them and you go get your soldiers. Then we'll go toe to toe," the sentry was snide.

He stepped passed her through the doorway gingerly and walked across the open area to a concrete structure that was mostly intact. When he reappeared, he had two men and one woman with him. They approached the doorway. D laughed heartily and they all started to smile, until she abruptly stopped, showing her level of dismay. Her gaze made them fidget uncomfortably.

One held out his hand, grabbing her elbow to shake. "My name is Xayres. You called for me," he said.

D yanked out of his grasp and stepped down out of the doorway a few paces.

"Do you think I am stupid? Oh, you thought I was lying," smirked D.

"What do you mean?" asked the woman.

"I asked you to bring me specific people and I expected you would comply," said D through clenched teeth, raising her weapon.

The refugees began to move toward the doorway. D gave a warning shot just above their heads. They froze, raising their hands.

"I had hoped it wouldn't come to violence. I was really hoping to get my verification without these issues," she sighed and waved her hand. It was the signal to her troops. "Now bring me the people I asked for," she insisted.

"He did," D heard the familiar voice behind her.

Turning, she saw Xayres, gun trained on her. "I am right here and Ra'Ella is over there and Jaren, over there."

Not wasting a moment, he signaled with one hand. D found herself laughing again.

"So, Ra'Ella is over there?" She pointed and out of the brush came Ra'Ella. "And Jaren is just that way?" She pointed in his direction at which time, he also came out from his cover.

Both were disarmed and held at gunpoint. D snapped at the sentry.

"Give me your weapon and Xayres, I imagine you will give me yours. You have no idea how many men I have out here and it's obvious we are better trained," she smiled.

The sentry and Xayres lowered their weapons as she gathered them. Only after the weapons were secure, D gave the signal to release their bargaining chips, gathering them close together.

"Just get it over with already," whined the sentry. "Why all this posturing?"

D lowered her weapon and signaled for the others to do the same. Then she pulled out some rations from her bag and offered them to her captives. They appeared confused by her behavior. Before she could offer an explanation, she heard footsteps pounding down the pathway. She raised her weapon.

Doc bounded into the small clearing, arms raised and open, without consideration for her volume, "XayXay! I am so happy you're okay," sweeping him up in an embrace before he realized who she was, knocking the wind out of him and almost toppling him over the others. "Sorry. It's just such a relief that it was actually you." Doc was out of breath.

She released him. The stunned look swept off his face as he recognized her.

"Enridoc!" he exclaimed. "It's a relief to see you Doc."

"I thought everyone called her Doc because she is a doctor," D commented.

"Nah, it's because when we were little, no one could actually pronounce her name. I always assumed she became a doctor because everyone called her Doc," answered Xayres.

"Doctor Doc," D mused with a grin.

"Tallin should be right behind me," Doc pointed to the trail.

Jaren watched expectantly. No one noticed Tallin enter the small space and make his way to the doorway. So they watched and they waited. When D turned around, she jumped at the sight of him. He would not look at her. Staring at the ground, hands in his pockets, he acknowledged nothing. Doc followed her gaze, then walked over and put her hand on Jaren's shoulder.

"I know you two had a falling out which accounts for

him being extra sneaky, but he's right over there. Maybe you guys could find it in your hearts to let your feud go. Given the circumstances," Doc said.

Tallin looked up for the first time and looked at Jaren. The expression on his face looked odd like he didn't recognize his brother. Jaren looked him up and down.

He stepped out of the doorway, "I hate to be burst your bubble, but this guy is not my brother," he said.

Jaren sputtered and moved away from him, turning bright red. "No! Don't listen to him! He's not my brother! My brother has hair so red it looks like his head is on fire," he stumbled to get the words out.

Doc stepped between them. "What do you mean?" She looked at Xayres. "How can we tell?"

"We can't," Ra'Ella said. "His family came from One and I am from Four and most of them were born and raised in Five."

"I knew you were a traitor!" Xayres pounced on Jaren. "You bastard."

They saw Xayres swing once before they moved into action. Although Xayres was young and fit, Jaren was bigger in stature and still in good shape. Despite the difference in size, ability, and experience, Jaren could not fend off Xayres in his throws of rage. It took four men to pull Xayres away from Jaren and two to keep him contained. Jaren wiped the blood from his mouth.

"Why do you say that Xayres?" Doc asked.

"He came to us, alone, unannounced. It seemed suspicious. At least my parents thought so," explained Xayres. "But he had the right story and brought the right paperwork and since no one had ever visited us from One, there was no way to verify. They don't have a communication network. Their people risk a lot to communicate with others. So it doesn't happen often," Xayres struggled against the men holding him.

"That's right. We were originally from One. I was sent

out first to Six and they were supposed to arrange his arrival at Five," Tallin smiled.

"He's lying. He's not my brother. He's the impostor," Jaren argued while stuttering.

D thought he looked much stronger than this. But he was fairly weak. Doc nursed Jaren's injuries. His nose was bloody but not broken and his lip was cut.

It took Xayres the better part of an hour to calm down. D took the opportunity to sit down on a nearby rock as her legs were still protesting all this exercise. The sentry sat down next to her.

"Sorry about all that earlier," the sentry said.

"Trust no one. I would have done the same thing," D lamented a little.

"You are more understanding than I would be," he replied.

She looked from Jaren to Tallin and back again, shaking her head. All this commotion and exhaustion made her head hurt.

"I'm Micha," he extended his hand.

She took hold of his elbow and they shook. "Is there a chance you can help us sort this out?" she asked.

"Unfortunately no. I came from Four, remember?" replied Micha. "You look tired."

"Thanks for the assessment," D snapped, then changed her focus. "Doc, let's restrain them both, get with the rest of the group, rest and take this up in the morning." She stood up and heaved a labored sigh that sounded like it weighed as much as she did.

She helped secure the brothers who obviously were not brothers. Then she searched them. Turning out pockets and throwing everything on the ground. Micha joined Ra'Ella and Doc having a hushed conversation. D eyed them, turning on her ear piece. Then she continued searching and examining anything she could on the two men. Xayres strolled in her direction.

"I'm not sure they would hide their 'I am a traitor card' in their pockets," said Xayres.

"I am looking for anything they could use to disguise or hide a tracker. I would hate to get bombed while everyone sleeps. You never know," D said as she finished with Tallin and moved onto Jaren despite his repeated protests.

Then she sifted through all the items. Nothing looked threatening. Grabbing her gun, she set out to destroy everything she confiscated.

"Hey! Some of that stuff might be useful," Xayres said trying to pull her away.

"No! You can never be too careful. Anything may have a hidden transmitter. How many people are in your group? We have to coordinate movements and I can't do that if I don't know how many people I am trying to move," she continued smashing things as she spoke, attempting to shake him off.

She crushed his finger under the butt of her gun. It worked. He yelped and pulled back.

Xayres watched in amazement as he shook off the pain. "How do you multi-task like this?" he asked.

"Comes naturally. Like I'm built for it," she answered without missing a beat, turning her head to listen more carefully to Doc's private conversation. "My brain never shuts up."

"Can I study you? I mean really. You're listening to that conversation, destroying property and planning your next move to get home safely. Can we switch brains?" mused Xayres.

She set down her weapon and sifted through the rubble she created.

"And that's all you can see me doing. I'm my own ninja extraordinaire," she replied dryly, intentionally flicking a piece of shrapnel in his direction.

It pegged him in the knee and stuck there for a moment. He winced again, wiping it away.

"And you make jokes in the middle of it all and are still trying to hurt me in the process," he rubbed his knee. "And how exactly do I get back on your good side."

"Never hold me at gunpoint. After that happens, I write you off. It's a lost cause," she chuckled with a sarcastic smile.

He moved closer, leaning into her ear, "So, just what are they saying over there?"

D gave him a half smile and a wink before standing. Grabbing her weapon, she saw Xayres put some distance between them. She faced him. He nodded toward the conversation and winked at her. She smiled, moving in his direction. Grabbing his collar, she pulled her lips close to his ear.

"I'll take first watch!" she screamed before shoving him away.

TRAITOR

D felt herself drifting into sleep. Sleeping was one of her least favorite activities. Despite multiple attempts to stave it off, she found herself in some dream state, walking through a green space. She saw a young tall man with red hair like it was on fire.

Like watching flashes across a timeline she didn't recognize, her mind shifted to another scene. Now the young man was saying goodbye. He was visibly upset. Everything about the sight told her he was being banished for some reason. Or he simply didn't want to leave. She wasn't sure but his pain rippled through her body causing her to lurch. For an instant, she woke.

Now she was in a room full of children. It was dirty and dark. They were all dressed in rags. Red hair, black hair, brown hair. Something told her this was important, that none of them were the master race. The door at the top of the stairs swung open and two S.S. officers entered the room. She felt the terror and dread of every child. It overwhelmed her. Her stomach wrenched.

The soldiers eyed each one, pacing back and forth through the room. One pointed to a child and the other grabbed the boy. He struggled and screamed but was no match for the soldier. Again, she knew this boy would never be seen again.

Whisked away to somewhere new. It took her a moment to get her bearings. Fields with vegetation she had never seen. The air was cool and she could feel a heavy pack on her back. She struggled to stay upright and balanced. It felt strange to be so awkward. This person tripped over every uneven piece of ground. Everything was blurry. After a moment, D surmised this person was crying.

Slipping away to something...someone else. The red-haired young man looked happy. Feeling his joy, he was almost dancing, a sense he was at peace with himself and his choices. He walked in the direction of the city, which seemed odd.

Trying to hold onto the most recent scene to gather more information, she tightened her eyes. But she failed. Now she saw a darker haired young man. This one looked familiar but she wasn't sure why. He was giving directions. Words phased in and out like they always did. They shook arms and went in separate ways. Despite their separate direction, she felt their lives would always be intertwined.

She pulled away, trying to get into her own head space instead of what felt like someone else's. Her brain refused to find a happy place, forcing her eyes open with a start. She breathed quick, trying to calm down. These moments made her feel like she was losing her mind. Strange dreams had plagued her since the accident. They used to drive them past the point of exhaustion in training. Maybe that had something to do with it this feeling. She shook it off, knowing she may never know.

At least these were better dreams. They weren't as scary or morbid as others she experienced at home. It felt more real. She could hold onto details better than a dream, almost like she wasn't asleep, but dream walking. Her eyes popped open. Realizing she was neglecting her watch, she opened her pack, grabbing the water skin, gulping, she saw the syringe. She had never found use of it before. They warned them of the side effects, but if she was going to get through the next 24 hours, she needed help.

She struggled with the choice for a while, still drifting back and forth. Grumbling to herself, she grabbed the caffeine and injected it as she had been instructed. Pulling out a journal, she began to sketch out what she had seen. As the caffeine took full effect, her hands began to tremble and her already above average hearing was becoming too much for her to handle. She focused her eyes, hoping her vision would drown out the noise.

Micha sat down next to her. "One day, you will have to trust someone you are working with enough not to do it all yourself. If only for the idea of a good night's sleep."

"No such thing. My sleep is never good," D replied. "Do me a favor. Don't tell me how to live and I'll pretend this conversation has nothing to do with getting me off watch for your own objectives. You have no actual interest in me sleeping except to help that guy sneak out of here. You think he may have a better chance out there than back at my bunker. Besides, if he is a traitor, it's better he goes back empty handed, right? It's a win/win. But your thought process is flawed."

"You're not even cognizant enough to know what you're talking about," Micha said.

"I thought we weren't pretending. I think you think he is most likely innocent. But you also think he's hiding something. He has a better chance hiding it out there than here. That's a given. However, if what he's hiding is innocent, then he has the burden of proof, which he does not have. Escape would have the opposite effect. It speaks to his guilt, not innocence. Maybe that's your plan. If you cut him loose and he runs, he's a traitor but if he doesn't, then he's innocent. Right?" explained D dryly.

"How could you possibly know..." Micha found her accuracy troubling and couldn't find words in response so D just continued.

"But escape actually doesn't prove him guilty. Did you

ever study the Salem Witch Trials?" she waited for an answer.

"Salem, I remember hearing something about it. But I never found much interest in your history. So please, enlighten me," answered Micha.

She paused for a moment, considering his answer. Then she began, "In the Salem Witch trials, women and a few men were accused of things they had never done, causing the group to experience mass hysteria. As the allegations increased, so did the hysteria. No one could actually prove anyone wrong or right. But they developed a mob mentality, which is a very scary thing. That's why he would run either way, innocent or not. Because a mob mentality reaction in the wake of these allegations is bound to happen."

"Okay, so what does it mean if he doesn't run?" Micha asked.

"Then by the aforementioned logic, we must assume he is trying to win favor with the whole. Which means he has reason to believe they wouldn't believe him otherwise. And that means he's guilty of something. We can't prove what specifically, but it would mean he is guilty," replied D.

"What? That makes no sense," Micha said.

"Actually, it makes perfect sense. Even if he is innocent, the chances of him running are high, if only to protect himself in his innocent state. On the other hand, if he doesn't run, he is automatically suspicious. By not running, it will appear as if he is trying to garner favor. The natural response is to assume he is innocent, but in actuality, it proves there is a higher probability that he is guilty. If staying lends itself towards innocence or actually garners him favor, this is the first indication that he has no way to prove his innocence, further bolstering the claim he is guilty. There would be a trial but it will be as useful as any witch trial. I understand you want to save you colleague or maybe he is your friend, but to be frank, they were both dead the moment the accusations started to fly. There's no getting past that fact," her tone was flat and unemotional.

She noticed Micha shiver at her cold evaluation and his expression went cold as well. Tallin sighed as if bored. They looked at him. Neither realized he was awake and listening. Jaren just stared at the ground, but she felt something else from him. He was deceptive, like the council. She found it difficult to hide her distaste for him and his insincerity.

"There comes a time in life when one must rely on instincts to accept change. To accept the fallacy of people. I have reached this moment," Tallin said, his voice smooth and unwavering.

D found his honesty refreshing. He knew she was right. She felt it from him.

"And it's this logic and out of the box thinking that makes me want to study her," Xayres walked up on the other side of her and helped himself to a seat.

"Hasn't anyone ever taught you that eavesdropping is rude?" D's loathing seeped into every word.

"You're one to scold someone else for eavesdropping," teased Xayres.

"I'm still not sure her logic tracks," said Micha.

"It does in her mind and to be honest, it would for many people. I am finding she has a way of looking at things that make people uncomfortable. But since she won't leave the watch to just you, perhaps I can be of service as well. You know I'll never let him release that guy," motioning to Jaren, he chomped his dinner as he spoke.

"So no matter what happens here, you think we're as good as dead?" Jaren choked, forcing the words out of his mouth.

"No, she's just trying to scare one of us into tipping his hand. It's an interrogation tactic," Tallin interjected.

"You don't know that for certain. Her logic seems

sound," Jaren retorted.

"Actually I do. Just like I know she knows who the traitor is. She just can't prove it," Tallin winked and nodded his head.

Xayres eyed them both suspiciously. D stood up, refusing to look at Tallin.

"If I had known I would have struggled to get this far out here only to end up dead, I would have stayed back and sacrificed myself," Jaren cleared his throat to sound like he was warding off tears.

"Jaren, you have always been self-serving. You would have made the same choice even if you could see the future. What do you think our futures hold D?" Tallin acted coy.

Trying to focus, D raised her weapon, "Both of you shut up or I'll just end it all now."

"No, you won't. That's not how you work," Tallin argued. "Besides, fake Jaren over here is just trying to make everyone feel bad for him."

"I am not. I'm just being honest with everyone here," Jaren choked, but his eyes betrayed him.

"Well, that's new...being honest," Xayres spat. "Besides, he's not garnering much favor anyway."

"Just because you think I've done something horrible doesn't make it true and even if I am hiding something doesn't mean I can't live with regrets," Jaren tried to sound sad but it was evident it was disingenuous.

D felt the tension rise. She turned but her reactions were late.

Xayres had shot straight for Jaren, grabbing his collar, bringing them nose to nose. "You don't get to regret your choices. You don't get to go there," he couldn't control his tone, screaming uncontrollably.

The tears released, "I'm so sorry Xayres. I am so sorry for all you lost."

Micha tried to pull Xayres off Jaren, but Xayres was

better built and had at least six inches to his advantage. Micha had no leverage. D trained her weapon on him.

"Xayres, you're giving me a reason to shoot you. You have no idea how much trouble I am having controlling this finger," said D. "Release him and move back."

Xayres didn't move. Micha pushed up to his side.

"We all lost people and things Xayres. You are not alone in your grief or anger. But you are no good to us if you can't control yourself. I will let her shoot you," Micha said.

Xayres turned to look at him. D could see the pain all over his face. He wasn't angry, he was hurting. Xayres released Jaren, his arms falling limply at his sides.

"Go!" Micha used a hushed but forceful tone. "GO!"

He shoved Xayres away from them. D kept her weapon trained on Xayres until he was out of sight in the ruins, then she dropped it back to her side.

"And so it begins," she brushed off her pants and grabbed a snack from her bag.

ROOMY

Doc tapped in her code, trying to hustle in the survivors from number Five. They were greeted by a medical team, the Shrinker, warm food and a hot shower. All were required in case they were contaminated or worse, crazy. Doc and Xayres went through the door on the far wall that led directly to the council quarters and only Doc returned to resume her work.

D walked through the quarantine area. What she saw was haphazardly thrown together, but given this was a unique circumstance, it was necessary. Wandering through almost as if she was floating, like a ghost, running through slides without being able to communicate with anyone. She tried to memorize each face, only a few hundred faces from a compound that once held thousands. The thought filled her with despair.

She heard it everywhere she went. People calling all the refugees lucky. Her disdain for the word only surprised her a little. She remembered the last time she heard that word...lucky. The explosion in Wing C rocked the foundation of not only 'the bunker but its peoples. This word was used in conversations with her for weeks, if not months afterward.

Her loss was great that day. And there was that word. Everyone presumed and told her she should feel lucky.

They were all lucky the explosion had been mostly contained and did little damage. The death toll was low and that should make them feel lucky. She was lucky she wasn't in her quarters that day. She was lucky to be alive. But 'lucky' was not how she felt. Luck didn't exist. Her being away from home was probability and circumstance.

Circumstance had taken her to another pod that day. And somehow she knew if she left her bunk, her quarters, her parents, it would not be here when she was done. It looked strange, reliving those days, watching it all happen in convenient flashes in her mind's eye. A cry from a small child ripped her back into the present.

Today, she knew all these refugees felt the same way. Still stuck in a surreal haze, not recovered from the shock. Dealing with the loss. No, none of these people were lucky and she understood it more than most.

She didn't remember submitting her order or how she even arrived in the mess hall. She just remembered the word. It bounced around in her brain, dancing with memories she didn't want to see, mixing with the current situation. There it was again, the despair. Only vaguely aware of her surroundings, she ate the food in front of her because it was routine. There were stares and whispers and blatant pointing of fingers, but no one approached her. No matter what the gossip mill was churning out, she was someone that everyone left alone. She preferred it that way.

Still in a daze, she managed to make her way to her quarters. All she felt was despair and exhaustion. All of them knew she was pushing herself too hard.

"Maybe they'll let me sleep it off for three days," she mumbled.

Every muscle in her body screamed for rest. *Someone else can go out to pick up the traitors and their guards,* she thought. Dropping her pack to her feet and sliding it toward the bed, she slipped out of her camo and dropped onto the mattress. Night clothes were too tedious an option in her current state.

Closing her eyes and breathing deep, she took in the peace and calm her quarters instilled. Unlike many of her counterparts, she didn't waste space or time on unnecessary things. She had a chair and a desk. Others spruced up with color, she loved the original gray. All she needed was her training gear, her coffee machine, and her bed.

Her thoughts shifted to her latest mission, but she couldn't focus on the details. It felt like hours before her mind succumbed to the idea of sleep, but it was only seconds, minutes at best. She felt her body start to drift.

"Didn't need the striptease, but thanks."

The words bounced around in her head and for a moment, she thought she was dreaming. Some of her dreams felt this real. Then she heard Xayres chuckle. Her body filled with anger and it drove her upright, but her eyes were still too blurry to confirm or deny what her mind had already feared. She hated appearing this vulnerable.

"Hey! I have my own room as a perk of my program! And you're uninvited!" she choked, not realizing her mouth was this dry. "I haven't shared a room for almost ten years."

"Well, I guess that perk is a thing of the past." Xayres shrugged as he leaned back, resting his head on his arms. "So I guess you'll have to learn to clean up after yourself."

He eyed her clothes on the floor, agilely sliding his foot under them and tossing them to her bed. She scowled, looking up at him. He had a strange look on his face. He eyed her up and down, taking in her dark skin and her slender toned frame.

"Why did they put you in here?" She hadn't meant to whine, but it just came out, too tired to maintain the control she exercised in public daily. "I don't have the patience for this," D released an exasperated sigh cupping her forehead in her hands.

"Perhaps they decided we're a good match. You know...genetics and all that. Or maybe they have no other option but to bunk everybody with the influx of people. Or perhaps when they offered me my own lavish quarters as a council member, the youngest one ever elected at the age of 21, for your information, I rejected their offer and insisted on being in here with you. Let's see if you can guess," answered Xayres, chuckling and grinning from ear to ear.

"So, now you've aged backward because it feels like you're a little kid right now," D commented.

"Wrong again. I'm 23 but easily excited," he replied. "Seriously, guess how we ended up roommates. I would love your thoughts on the matter."

"Only if you promise to leave once I tell you," D said annoyed.

"Afraid that's not an option at this point," he replied. "But I promise to let you go to sleep if you guess. I'll give you three tries."

She released a frustrated sigh and indulged him. "First, this bunker hasn't done genetic matching for at least two generations. Second, what the hell would make you want to bunk with me?" D grimaced at her own whiny tone again.

Xayres was only shocked momentarily, but it didn't keep his teasing at bay.

"Remember, I asked if I could study you? A request you denied while we were topside. Now you have no choice but to allow me to spend time with you." He paused for a response but was not satisfied with her silence. He hoped she would at least look at him, but her head stayed perched in her hands.

"Besides, I need information on those conversations you've been eavesdropping on," he paused again, waiting for her usual snarky comeback, but she managed to disappoint him again. "So, you guys don't do genetic matching anymore? Hmm...you must have started with a larger population than we did then."

"We're also in a better location. We can afford to go topside for escapists which always brings us different DNA," her reply expressed her annoyance and exhaustion.

He ignored the signs, "So, you're not a product of genetic combining?"

"Nope, I am a product of my environment," she sighed. "Aren't you tired? The way you're verbally running in circles is making me physically dizzy. Your brain is not somewhere I would ever want to be."

"Actually, I'm genetically predisposed not to sleep," he laughed uncontrollably, clapping his knee and rocking back and forth at the force of it.

D seethed at his arrogance. She never wished more for her throwing knives so she could kill him silently.

"I am probably more tired than I realize. All that adrenaline being in new surroundings with strangers and all that. So much to learn about the way you operate and how things are done here. A whole new archive to study. A new section of our history to learn. It's invigorating. Isn't that feeling why you go outside?" his excitement boiled over.

"I go outside so I don't go crazy," she replied, lying back down.

"There's more to you than what's on the surface. You keep it hidden well," Xayres said.

D was beginning to regret not fetching her night clothes. The chill of the bunk permeated her skin. Making exaggerated motions to cover herself with the blanket, she heaved a sigh and flopped back down on her pillow again.

"If you snore, I'll smother you in your sleep," she flipped over so her back faced the other bunk.

"Well, I guess that conversation is over," Xayres mumbled, still smiling.

As she drifted, she walked in an unfamiliar place. It looked like cities she had seen in history class reels, but she never visited a city before so she couldn't be sure.

Moving fast on foot blurred most of the details. Then jostling, meandering through a mix of hallways and wide spaces, like a maze.

With no control over where she traveled, she found herself at the whim of whatever dream she invaded. Now she stepped upward. Stairs. The sterile gray staircase reminded her of the bunker, except these had windows. Windows were on the top floors, but she never had a chance to bask in them like she was in this place. They bathed everything in sunlight, a rare thing to see underground.

Suddenly, she moved faster. Pounding emanated from the concrete steps, but didn't sound like feet. There was an echo. It bounced around her head, so familiar she tried to place it. A melody she heard before.

She flew up into a sitting position, breathing in hard, eyes tearing themselves open. The knocking on the door with the chime tore her away from her dream. Without looking at the clock or bothering to put on any clothes, she stumbled to the door.

As she pressed the button to open it, she found herself whining again, "But I need more rest Doc."

She didn't even look up to see who was actually on the other side of the door. Doc entered, pulling the robe off its hook and offering it to her by extending her arm. D yawned and stretched, waving her hand at Doc's offering.

"So, now you see through doors too? I am beginning to wonder if you actually have superpowers we have yet to discover," teased Doc.

"Eh," D shrugged. "Lucky guess."

"Right," Doc winked.

The sting of the cold air swept over D, so she swiped the robe numbly out of Doc's hand, and put it on without missing a beat, almost appearing to sit down at the same time. Her back was still to the doctor as she used her arms to prop up her head.

"Besides, who else would they send to fetch me?" D continued.

"Actually, I am a little confused. They sent me here to get Xayres, but I don't know why he wouldn't have his own quarters. But then I saw you and..." Doc didn't finish.

D felt her gaze trying to burn a hole in the back of her skull.

"Save your disapproval for someone who needs it," said D.

"Well, given your state of dress or the considerable lack thereof..." Doc started again.

"Pure exhaustion. I don't have the energy or desire for that kind of play. Besides, I hate that guy," D said, pointing in his direction.

"Strong emotions..." Doc tried again

Xayres sat up releasing a loud yawning sigh as he stretched. Doc jumped at the noise then smirked at D. She turned to see them both and snorted in disgust.

"Hate that guy huh?" Doc teased.

"What are you two yammering about? You interrupted perfectly good sleep," Xayres said through yawns.

"Sleeping off a workout?" asked Doc.

D groaned at the question. Xayres stared blankly for a moment, processing the question. Then he looked shocked for a moment which was followed by amusement.

"Doc, nothing happened. I promise. Your confusion is understandable given...everything," he paused to stretch again. "I'm her new roomy. That's all."

D released a sigh, not bothering to respond. Flipping around, she switched on the coffee maker and typed her breakfast order into the module on the wall.

"You're too kind roomy. I love the smell of coffee in the morning but I prefer the taste," Xayres grinned. "I'll have bacon and eggs."

She turned her head as he started to climb out of the covers. His hair was messy and curly and brown. But she had not realized how defined he was or the slight curves in all the right parts of his body. For a moment, she felt herself blushing but her thoughts were cut short with a yawn. She'd never been happier to be more tired. Shifting her focus back to the coffee machine, she tried to compose herself before either of them saw her reaction.

"Order your food from the mess and wait. This is my personal module. You won't touch it if you know what's good for you," D pushed through the yawn.

"I see you two are getting along smashingly," Doc said sarcastically. "So, whatever did you do to gain a roomy?"

"Haha, very funny," answered D. "Reminding me of the invasion of personal space wins you no favors. I was trying to forget he existed. Hoping to make him disappear." D's discomfort was obvious.

Xayres coughed, trying to hold in his chuckling. She felt like he enjoyed torturing her a bit too much. She turned a little to eye him again, hoping he had more clothing on this time. But she found her resolve weakening a little when she saw him again.

"You need not make your presence known." Doc and Xayres noticed her tone was less harsh. She saw the way they both looked at her.

Frustrated with herself more than the situation, she toughened her resolve. "You don't always have to be the center of attention. We both know you're here. Just..." the aggravation made it difficult to express herself, "Be invisible!" she blurted.

"You're in luck. I am here to send him away." Doc said. "We need to debrief him," she grinned at the word, only causing more tension, "and I think they're sending him back out with the retrieval team."

D spun on her heel to face them. "A mission. He gets a mission? He's been here for five minutes. I am the one risking my life."

She sat down in the chair at the desk, frustration

pulsing through her system with every heartbeat. Part of her didn't want to admit she didn't want to go back out yet. Part of her was jealous and part of her, a very small part, or at least that's what she tried to convince herself, wanted him to stay a little longer, without his shirt.

"You said it yourself D, you need more rest. So they're sending out team Alpha." Xayres flexed his arms mockingly, turning around.

"Besides, the council wanted you debriefed in private. That's why I'm here. To assess your ability to go through everything you saw or heard. I'm supposed to review it with you." Doc said.

"Well, this just got interesting," Xayres mused. "Secrets are always good, especially in close quarters. I have ways to shake things loose from any tree." He winked at D.

Doc started, "I don't think that's a good idea..."

Feeling herself start to blush again, D huffed in disgust. A beep broke the momentary silence. The coffee was done.

"Finally!" exclaimed Xayres, walking over with his hand extended.

D poured herself a mug and turned around, shocked Xayres had moved in so close to her. She flinched, almost losing hold of her brew. She felt his fingers graze hers as he tried to grab it out of her hand. Careful not to spill or trip, she maneuvered it away.

"Oh, did the multi-brew fool you?" She fluttered her eyelashes at him. Her voice dripped with fake sweet sincerity. Then her look and tone went flat. "I only have one silo. Req your own!"

Stepping as graceful as a dancer, she slipped away from Xayres, grabbing clean clothes from the cabinet, throwing them over her shoulder, she smiled. Looking at Doc, she contemplated all the events so far and decided it was time for breakfast.

"Doc, tell them I'm not ready. I don't have the patience

for this today," she announced as she jaunted out of the room, sure to take an extra loud sip of coffee as she left.

"So, is this normal?" Xayres asked.

"Actually, she has taken the time to speak to you, even if it wasn't nice. She doesn't really do that," answered Doc.

"Are you just going to do what she said?" Xayres asked.

Doc let out a sigh, shaking her head. "It would appear her lack of caring gives her more benefits than others. Really, we give her leeway because of her past and frankly, she needs it more often than most."

Xayres looked at Doc for a moment. Pursing his lips, the look on his face went stern.

"Her past huh..." more to himself than Doc. "So, do you think me being here is really that big of a problem for her?"

Doc thought about his question for a moment, then smiled, "Actually, given the amount of time she spent blushing this morning and how harsh she was trying to appear, I would venture a guess and say she actually likes you."

FRIENDS

D didn't want to think about it. Doc and Xayres could have their laugh alone. When she walked out into the corridor, she realized she hadn't properly prepared herself to be around people. Sometimes she was too in tune with everyone around her. Finding it overwhelming, she hurried to her closest secret spot and changed her clothes. Her stomach grumbled and her coffee was cold. She sighed knowing full well she needed to head to the mess hall.

"I wish my program came with meal delivery," she mumbled.

She moved gracefully through the hallway, focusing on the movements and making them fluid rather than the energies of those around her. After what felt like only a few moments, she arrived at the Mess. Stepping back to the wall across from the doorway, she stood there, back flat against the wall, staring, watching people. With her lack of sleep and the events of the last few days swimming in her brain, she was unsure of the reactions she would have.

Her heart raced and her breath quickened, hands trembling just enough for her to notice. Releasing a long deep breath, she closed her eyes tight, trying to make the dread go away. All her training and yet she still couldn't walk into the mess hall without fear and apprehension. It was so overwhelming in there. Everywhere she turned, she felt something new, still unable to explain why she couldn't seem to stave off the onslaught.

"Why wouldn't they just take me topside again? Then I wouldn't have to deal with this for another day," she whispered.

She shoved her hand into her pocket. The sketchbook took most of the space. She needed to sketch her dreams, as the Shrinker instructed. The dreams that came shortly after her parent's death. Dreams that haunted her even when awake. Getting them down on paper was the only way to get them out of her head. And she couldn't do that standing here in this space. She needed a quiet corner and as her stomach promptly reminded her, food.

Her body went stiff as she approached the opening, walking through it slowly. She breathed in deep. Stepping forward, she controlled where she looked and turned, focused on the objective of picking up her order and sequestering herself in the far corner. Her usual spot.

She could feel the energy, the emotions pushing in on her as she approached the counter. The girl behind it smiled at her. Feeling relieved and happy was refreshing but she wasn't sure why she suddenly felt this way. For now, it pushed away all the uncomfortable tension from the room.

"Hey D! I hope you managed to get some rest. You look a little tired," the counter girl eyed her robe.

D mustered a small grin, "Thanks, Vick."

Grabbing her tray, she made a beeline for the far, dark corner. Most people knew she wanted to be left alone, so they let her be, which is what she preferred. Pulling out her journal, she flipped through the pages looking for anything to match the images in her dreams last night. Almost like a daily meditation, she scoured them searching for any connection from one dream to the next. She did not find anything, which was normal. She sighed and pulled the pencil from the spine scratching it across a fresh page.

She heard the familiar tread of footsteps coming in her direction, causing her to sweep the book and pencil back into her pocket. No one knew she was like this, even if the Shrinker insisted she had real talent. If someone did see it, she wouldn't be able to explain the images in the book to anyone. It was better this way for everyone, even those close to her.

"What's with the robe? You sleep in the hall?" Erack asked, smiling at her.

She looked up at him as he sat down next to her, juggling the apples he planned to eat for breakfast. Forking her food, she scooped some into her mouth. It was cold. Grimacing, she drank from her cup.

"Cold?" Erack asked. "How long you been sitting here?"

"A while I guess," she replied. "Lost in my own thoughts."

"Typical D." Erack teased. "I wasn't expecting to see you today. Thought you'd be on the recovery mission."

"Me too!" her tone indicated her agitation. "They sent pretty boy instead of me. He's been here what, five minutes and he gets sent on priority missions? Apparently, the new guy is more valuable than I am," she snapped.

"Ah, I see. Stewing in your own misery huh? That's why your breakfast is cold," Erack said.

"Sure, that's why it's cold," she said shrugging and shoveling more food into her mouth.

As she chewed, she looked up at him, which calmed her instantly. His laid-back demeanor generally kept her on an even keel. Maybe that's why she allowed him to get so close. He looked at her, giving her an unsatisfied smile.

"How long would you have to stew if you got bumped off a priority mission?" she asked, mouth still half full.

"D, you go out on priority missions all the time. Not being on one will not be the end of your career," Erack replied.

His avoidance frustrated her. "Seriously, how upset

would you be?" she pushed.

He rolled his eyes. "Honestly, I wouldn't be. I would be catching up on sleep or doing whatever I wanted. It's like a free pass, especially since they haven't released you back to duty or training. It's too soon. You know this," Erack replied.

"I guess I'm not forced to be as regimented as others," answered D.

"Don't we all know it," mused Erack. "Maybe it's less like a free day to you then. But they wouldn't keep you from a mission to spite you. They're just concerned about your well being. You need rest. Everyone can see it," she huffed at him. "Please, your robe is on your shoulder. You weren't even dressed when you left your quarters," he chuckled.

"I had to escape quickly," she explained.

"Why would you need to escape from your own quarters?" Erack asked.

"They're not my own quarters anymore. Apparently, they felt like I needed a roomy," she pushed her tray away and leaned back, arms folded.

Erack's eyes went wide, "Who in this bunker was brave enough...no...stupid enough to take on that duty?" He laughed loud enough to draw attention to their conversation.

"Why is that so funny? I am supposed to have my own room as a perk of my training program," D replied flatly.

Erack sucked in hard, forcing himself to stop laughing, "It's obvious you bought into whatever lies they told you to make you feel better."

Something stung in her chest. Why would he say something like that? There was no reason to be cruel, but to her, his answer felt unnecessarily so. The white noise hit her ears as she processed his reaction. The room was too quiet, tension building in her gut, elevating her anxiety level.

"What's obvious to me is none of them trust me to take care of myself anymore," her tone was a little too loud for the room, drawing more attention. "Who am I kidding? They never really trusted me in the first place."

"You can't know that," Erack said.

"Yes, I can!" she was a little louder, losing control of her tone. "I can just...I don't know...feel it!"

She slammed her hands down on the table. Surprise filled her chest as the sound echoed through the room. How did she scare herself? Shaking off the feeling of being watched, slid her hands back to her lap. Her heart rate was increasing as the moments passed.

"Oh D. Not this again. Haven't we discussed this enough? You're different in a way no one can quite describe. They recognize that and like that about you but it makes them cautious, unsure how to handle those differences," explained Erack.

He was evading again. This tactic made her want to pull her hair out. The room was feeling smaller, pressing up against her. She was finding it more difficult to breathe. Thoughts rushed through her brain faster than she could comprehend them, anxiety pushing up her throat. Out of nowhere she felt sad and curious and annoyed.

"Why..." she croaked. Determined, she pushed the words up her throat louder than she ever intended. "Why do you do that? Avoid answering my questions or not addressing what I actually say? It's so...frustrating."

She reached out and grabbed one of his apples right out of the air, throwing off his rhythm, resulting in a loud thud when one hit the table. The sound reverberated off every wall, illuminating how silent the room had become. Erack noticed instantly but D was lost in her own struggles.

"Look D, they wouldn't send you on priority missions if they didn't trust you. Hell, you just went on a solo mission. Only the most trusted and top-ranked get to do that,"

Erack explained. "And many people have invested a lot of time into your success. Don't throw all their work away."

It confused D. She worked for her own success. Didn't she make it happen? She noticed the room, not even a whisper or the clanking of a dish. Acutely aware of the focus on their conversation, she blanched. Looking up, the emotions of the room hit her like a wall, almost knocking her backward. Rocketing into overwhelm, she lost all control.

"Who's hard work? Who worked so hard?" she barked.

Erack was taken aback and couldn't find a response. She hadn't ever come at him this way before. Certainly, he knew she could be a pain and hard to deal with, but this was something different, definitely not her.

"Are you okay D?" he asked softly.

"Answer the question. Quit evading. Answer the question!" she couldn't control herself any longer.

He backed up, terrified she may lunge at him. Shaking his head, he struggled to manifest words. All the eyes in the room burned into his skin as they waited for him to respond. Glaring at them all, some tried to look otherwise engaged while others could care less if he knew they were watching.

"I'm not trying to be evasive. I just. How is it you have no idea how much people do for you? How much I do for you?" he rose, pacing.

She turned to see Erack, noticing a drop in the pressure she felt closing her in. But he was running his hands roughly through his hair as he stepped back and forth. A breakdown was imminent. She recognized the signs.

She stood up and turned to focus on him. "Erack, what exactly is it that you do for me?"

Stopping only for a moment, he looked at her ferociously. Raising her hands, palms facing him, she stepped back. Although she had witnessed his small breakdowns at different stages, one this size had only happened once before. That time, his parents talked him down.

"Erack, you need to focus on the question. What have you done for me?" she pushed.

He eyed her like prey, "I can't believe you don't know. How can that be possible? Did you know you've never typed in a door code correctly? And who do you think alters the logs when you decide to go AWOL and not tell anyone?" stepping toward her, "Me D!" He poked himself in the chest. "Me! That's right. Me!"

That stinging feeling flooded her chest again. Making the second biggest mistake of the day, she turned and looked at the rest of the room. The wall hit her, this time causing her to stumble a bit at the force of it. Again, she raged out of control.

"So you've been stalking me?" she growled. "You need to stalk me. I'm not a good soldier. It's the only thing I ever wanted to be and I failed." The anguish spread across her face as she turned her back to the crowd and sat back down on the bench, elbows resting on her knees, head in her hands. Erack saw her pain and snapped back to the present. Regret crept up his spine and planted itself at the forefront of his brain.

"D, I'm not stalking you. I'm sorry. Someone needed to protect you. Someone needed to make sure you were okay after...and they told me to...I can't explain.." Erack choked.

"Don't bother. It doesn't matter anyway. It just proves my point," D said, tone sad but still too loud.

Someone in their audience gasped. Erack's rage at himself turned on them.

"What! I know you have better things to do!" Some responded but most stayed frozen watching their drama. "GO! GET OUT OF HERE!" he yelled, springing the room into a new found life of activity.

VOICES

The council was in chambers more often than anyone had ever seen. They had no need of an inquest before and with the debriefing done, the trial now began. With the refugees still sequestered from the main population, the rumor mill was abuzz. The council was cautious about who they could trust. Even Xayres' movements were limited and monitored.

And then the red letters started to arrive. People from all walks of life were being called to testify. By the time the second one was delivered, everyone knew what they meant. Anyone seen with one was automatically talked about and many citizens had taken to following them to the council chamber, hoping to get a glimpse of the proceedings happening inside.

D scoffed at the entire idea. Neither suspect could prove guilt or innocence. She secretly wished they would have saved time and aggravation by just leaving them out there. It would be better to just leave them to their own devices. Although, Tallin did know his way back to the bunker putting a definite chink in her plan.

She hadn't minded the lack of topside missions at first. They kept Xayres busy and out of their quarters. It was much-needed distance so she could get her head clear of all the craziness. They had not been roomies for long but she was fairly certain the current living situation would result in one of them dying. And she was also certain it would not be her.

Unfortunately, this also meant eyes were on her everywhere she went. Not only was she rooming with a refugee council member but she was also the one who went out on the solo mission starting it all. The timing could not be worse as Erack hadn't even attempted to talk to her after the mess hall debacle. She had no other friends and there was no way she was confiding in her roomy. He already knew too much. It made her feel incredibly vulnerable, which she hated and before long, she felt an overwhelming need to go topside.

Then she got the call. The red note she would be required to carry all over the compound on her way to the topmost floors. The thought terrified her. As she made her way back to her quarters, she couldn't help the panic rising in her chest.

She passed the same mom and daughter she always did as they lived in the same corridor. But this time, the girl spoke. D grabbed her by the shoulder.

"What did you say?" asked D.

The girl looked surprised. Swallowing hard, "Nothing," she replied.

The girl trembled. Everyone knew D preferred not to talk to anyone. Her mother pulled her from D's grasp and whisked her away.

"I'm sorry," D cried out but they didn't acknowledge her.

She continued to her quarters. As she walked by people in the corridor, she heard whispers. Not able to make out any of them, she hurried faster. But that only resulted in more voices, coming in faster. She looked at all of them, the people in the hallway. Their lips weren't moving. They weren't even looking at her. Few were even talking to anyone else.

The voices pushed on her brain, filling it and still pressing for more space. She couldn't stop it. She couldn't control it. The cacophony became overwhelming. Everything began to spin. Covering her ears to soften the noise was ineffective. She raced to her room.

Slamming down into the chair as she ran inside, she locked the door. Screaming loudly to silence the noise only served to make it worse. Muffling it wouldn't work. She tried to focus on anything.

The red note was on the desk. She backed away from it like a poisonous snake. This is what started this. She wanted to get rid of it but she couldn't. Even in this state, she didn't want to commit treason. Her thoughts were blotted out by all the voices. Vision blurry from all the tears. And the pain...shooting through her head like a bullet, stabbing her temple like an ice pick. The last thing she remembered was the ceiling spinning above her.

Xayres opened the door with his usual swagger, hoping to get some time to study D, but he didn't see her at the desk or on her bunk. This was odd as lights out was in about thirty minutes and she never missed curfew, at least now that he bunked with her. He walked into the room. Then he felt his foot hit something. Something large and heavy.

Thinking it was a prank, he stated louder than normal, "So now we're going to have to deal with this large thing between us huh? You could've just told me you hated me. It would be..." Xayres looked down.

D was curled up on the floor in a fetal position. Hands over her ears. Tears made her skin gleam. He knelt down and heard her whimpering. He cautiously touched her shoulder. She didn't flinch or pull away or make a snide remark. Picking her up gingerly, he wrapped her in a blanket. As he opened the door again, she released a little scream, as if it pained her more to have it open. Then he worked his way through the hallways to the med bay, careful to keep everyone far enough away not to see what he was carrying.

Xayres raced into the med bay. He knew the entrance Doc used for privacy. Doc rushed them into a room just off her office, the most private bed in the med bay. It was Doc's private sleeping quarters when she had to be on watch. He laid her down on the mattress and allowed Doc to kick him out. Sitting in her office waiting was agony for him. She may be mean to him, but he still cared for her. Doc came out of the room. Xayres stood, expectantly. The expression on his face screamed for answers.

"I've given her a sedative. That seems to have calmed her down," Doc said as she closed the door behind her and walked into the room.

"Is she going to be okay?" he asked.

"Honestly, I don't know. I'm not sure what happened to cause this," Doc said. "Can you tell me what happened?"

"I just found her on the floor that way," Xayres said. "I've been in council chambers all day."

"So you have no idea when it started or what the possible trigger is?" asked Doc.

"I don't know Doc. I wasn't there." he started to panic a little. "I can't tell you because she didn't say anything. I found her on the floor like that," breathing in deep, "Doc, I need to know if she will be alright."

"Again. I wish I had more answers. I don't know." she replied. "And without anyone to give me any details, I have no idea how to prevent it from happening again. I will have the results of her brain scans and blood work in a few hours. I may know more then."

She motioned toward the door, as a silent signal ushering him out of the office. He refused to get up.

"I know this can't be normal, otherwise she would not have been fit for duty. She also hasn't testified yet. We can't have an episode like this tainting her testimony," said Xayres.

Doc sighed and sat in her chair on the other side of the desk. "Look Xayres. I'm really not at liberty to discuss this with you as you are not the patient or their immediate family," she pressed again, motioning to the door.

"Come on Doc. This is me. You obviously know more than you're telling," he insisted. "It's important this doesn't taint her testimony. It could end her career and we both know that would devastate her."

"I won't let this episode out. We'll come up with a cover story," Doc said.

"Have you covered for her before?" Xayres raised an eyebrow.

"I really can't say more than I have," Doc replied.

"I really need to know she's fit for duty and to testify. It won't look good for her otherwise," Xayres said. "Is she going to be okay?"

Doc's eyes squinted at him in scrutiny and annoyance. "Aren't you getting a little too attached to your science project?" Doc asked.

"You'd tell Erack and he doesn't even live with her!" Xayres said. "Stop avoiding the question." he paused, but Doc didn't waver. "You've covered for her before. I can tell by the way you're talking. I need to know what those things are. I need to help protect her. If not from the council than from herself. They're very dubious when it comes to her." Doc still sat with pursed lips. "It took me this long to convince them to even hear her testimony. So if there is something I need to know, then you need to spill it Doc," Xayres pushed. "I won't use it against her, I promise. You know I am good for my word."

Doc leaned back in her chair pensively, causing Xayres to pace. Seeing him this way softened her resolve.

"There's really nothing more I should tell you," said Doc.

"You said there's nothing more you should tell me. That means there is more. I really can't handle you playing games with me right now Doc," Xayres pleaded. "I think she is important, pivotal almost for the survival of this compound and the future of Americans. I need to know if there is anything I will be forced to cut off at the pass if you know what I mean."

Xayres dropped down into the chair after they sat in silence for the better part of an hour. Doc sighed, sitting up straight. She knew him well enough. This resolve should not be tested further. Leaning in closer, they spoke in hushed tones. Doc never took her eyes off the door.

"Whatever I tell you, you must keep it between us. If you want to go playing detective like when you were younger, forget it. This is not the time to have all the answers because it would only serve to create more questions I don't have answers to," she said.

"So you do know more. Just how different is she?" asked Xayres.

"That is far from a simple answer. But before I begin, I have a demand," she paused for his reaction. "You have to allow me to use you for research and that means I get to scan your brain. There was no scan of anything we recovered from the destruct transmission."

Xayres took a moment to think about the idea. "I guess that's not too bad a price. Besides, turn about appears to be fair play. I'm supposed to be studying her. Perhaps I will learn more effective techniques by watching you," he pointed at D.

Somehow he could always spin anything into something positive. Doc found his unending optimism nauseating on occasion.

"And I wouldn't want anyone to know I'm a test subject. That causes too many questions," he chuckled.

Doc went silent, wondering if this was a misstep.

"I have successfully kept it under wraps, just how different she is," Doc said.

"Physiologically or psychologically? I know she has to

see the Shrinker since her parents died. Does that stuff actually work?" he asked.

"Um, I'm the wrong kind of doctor to determine that, but it seems to work. And it's mostly her brain. The way it works and behaves. I won't know if this is normal for her until I can compare her scans. If they look drastically different, then something has changed," explained Doc.

"All of it Doc or the deal is off," Xayres was serious now.

"Her brain, her cerebral cortex, her ability to focus and multi-hyper focus. All these things are because her brain is different. I haven't seen these differences in others her age. But I am beginning to see them in young children and babies suggesting it's a mutation or evolution. My knowledge of the science in those areas is limited at best. That's all I know," replied Doc.

"But what would have caused this new change in her?" asked Xayres.

"My best guess? There are two factors that have changed in her life and either may be the cause. One, she has been pushed beyond exhaustion and that has weakened her resolve and control, lowering her own defenses. Two, she has a roommate now," Doc winked at him. "And although there may be nothing going on between them, she is now never really alone. She has had an extreme amount of exposure to you," she finished.

"So I could be the trigger?" he asked.

"Your guess is as good as mine. I am just looking at everything logically, studying the situation for connections. That's one of the reasons I want to use you as a test subject. To see if there's something I can find...in regards to you and her current situation. So," she rose and tossed a gown at him. "Get changed and we'll get started."

SECRETS

Since her release from the med wing, she felt listless. The pills she was required to continue taking stole her focus and made her feel tired and hazy. She regretted not being more forward with Doc about what she knew. All she remembered was an incident with a little girl and then weird voices and pain, but people who heard voices ended up spending a lot of time with the Shrinker, who D was not so fond of anyway.

Being released from heavy training was a blessing in disguise under the circumstances. But the mundane exercises of basic training with newbies failed to hold her attention. She sat on the bench, trying to remember her stay in the hospital.

Had she volunteered for an experiment? It would not be the first time she had and couldn't remember what happened afterward. But normally they filled in the blanks for her. The things they couldn't fill her in on, she got the feeling she might not want to know. This idea didn't feel right.

Maybe her dreams were the issue. They were growing in frequency and intensity. Now, she saw not only images but heard sounds at the same time. This was new. It had always been one or the other. And now there was also color.

The Shrinker suggested it was all her own doing. That

she was finally becoming comfortable with her subconscious world and started to fill it in with color and sound she preferred. He said it showed remarkable progress in her accepting herself and her past. She always found the Shrinker amusing. This session proved to her he was merely guessing most of the time. No one could explain why this was happening to her.

Perhaps she had overlooked the incident with the girl too quickly. It felt right to assume it had something to do with her medical stay. As she couldn't review this without being watched, she craved being alone where she could process her dreams and her thoughts. With that, she grabbed her workout bag and rushed out of the room. Erack had never seen her this way and it surprised him when she left so quickly.

Using her advanced skill, she found a new hideaway. Every time she thought she knew all of the out-of-the-way places to escape, she found a new one. At least this ensured anyone looking for her would have a hard time actually finding her.

She pulled the little leather journal out of her pocket, feeling its cover helped to calm her. Sniffing the pages reminded her everything smelled a bit damp underground, even the book. Untying the leather strap flipping open the cover to reveal her work inside. Perhaps looking through them would provide her with some clarity.

There were sketches of staircases and hallways and roads. Things she only saw remnants of at ruins. Words from conversations she never had with anyone from voices she didn't know either. She ran her fingers over the smooth lines, smudging them a little leaving her fingertips gray with pencil lead. Wiping it on her pants, she sifted through the sketches, hoping if she touched them, maybe she would find some hidden connection. Discover how they came into her head. These images taunted her, haunted her.

The Shrinker often told her dreams were not literal and to take them that way was a mistake. They were secrets into our hidden thoughts, thoughts we didn't know we had. These sketches, as well as the dreams they came from never, felt like the symbolism of something else. She stared at each page, memorizing every detail again, trying to link any of them together.

Concentrating too hard always made her head hurt. The headaches were becoming more and more frequent despite the medication designed to stave them off. The world swirled a little and she closed her eyes immediately, forcing it to stop. Her ability of mind over matter surprised even her at times.

But again, the strange whispers crept inside her head. There was no escape to the invasion of foreign voices. They infiltrated her dreams and now her thoughts while she was awake. Struggling to stay focused, she knew she had to get control over this. It's the only way they would not kick her out of the service. She was determined not to lose her topside privileges.

The hand on her shoulder made her jump. She covered her mouth to cover up the light shriek exiting her lips. No one knew she was here.

"You okay?" It was Erack.

She released a sigh of relief, "Just trying to get into a good head space."

The interruption and adrenaline from the scare managed to quiet the whispers.

"You looked like you were...well," Erack scrunched up his face trying to find the right words. "I'm not sure how to describe it."

"How long have you been here?" she asked, looking up at him.

He sat down next to her, pulling his knees to his chest. "Not as long as you think."

"Wait!" she snapped. "Were you following me again?"

"D..." he started.

"I can't believe this. You are still trying to shelter and protect me, aren't you?" she asked.

"Can you really blame me?" he responded. "I know

you're not sleeping well, worse than usual. This last mission was very trying and now they're saying you disappeared for a few days due to an illness, but they won't say what it was. It all sounds fishy and scary and I thought...I thought you could use a friend."

"Yeah...illness...right," she replied. "I see they've kept you in the dark as well. Doesn't feel so great, does it?" she quipped.

"Not really. I understand how you can find it frustrating but they obviously don't tell me everything either," said Erack.

"Had you a little worried there huh?" she softened her tone a little.

"Yep. From the sounds of it, you were really sick. Like life and death. I didn't like not being able to visit you or let you know we were there for you," admitted Erack.

"It couldn't have been that bad," she teased. "I survived, didn't I?"

He put his arm around her shoulders. She had somehow become accustomed to his touchiness and it felt natural, so she allowed him to get close.

"We're all just glad you're okay. Can't lose our star trainee," he teased back.

She blushed a little. "I am not the star pupil. You expressed that the other day, remember?"

She shouldered him softly. He retaliated by poking her. As he leaned in, he saw her journal. D never discussed it with anyone. It was her deepest secret.

"What's that?" he asked, pointing at it.

"That is," she hesitated. "Private."

"Well, from a distance, those sketches look really good. Can I see them?" he asked.

"Do you even know what the word private means?" she chided.

"Nope!" he responded, reaching across her nimbly and swiping it off the floor. "Still recovering there ace? Your reflexes appear a little slow," he chuckled.

She seethed, trying to take it back. But she tired so

quickly, she gave up after only a few swipes with her hand. He smiled and laughed, reveling in her discomfort.

"You might as well tell me what this is all about," he joked.

"Fine! It's my dream journal, okay," she retorted viciously. "I see things in my dreams and I record it in there. The Shrinker said it would make the weird dreams and nightmares go away."

"Hmmm..." he said, flipping through a few pages. "And has it worked? Have they gone away?"

"Not really. In fact, they've been more intense lately," answered D.

"Then it would stand to reason the Shrinker is wrong. It would also stand to reason you knew that long before you put most of this down on paper. So, why didn't you stop recording them?" Erack asked.

"I don't know. Helps me calm down after I have one, I guess. It's hard to get the images out of my mind if I don't sketch them. And the words will bounce around my head all day, distracting me from everything. This way, I have it all in one place and I can try and make sense of it. At least, I suppose that's why," she explained.

She saw his level of concentration rise as he turned through the same pages, back and forth, over and over again. Then he touched one of the sketches, awing at it. It made her uneasy. She tried to lighten the mood.

"Sorry, I didn't think my journal had any military significance," she joked.

He ignored her. Then he turned the page back again, stopping this time.

"D, you've never been inside the city, right?" he asked.

"No...why?" answered D, leaning in to see which sketch he was looking at.

"These are sketches of East City. These are locations in East City," he said.

D ripped the journal out of his hand, trying to see what he was talking about.

"What do you mean?" she asked.

"I didn't speak in code D," he took the journal back, pointing at the sketches and turning the pages. "These are places in East City. Or they look like they are from there. It was a long time ago so I'm not absolutely sure, but they look like where I used to live."

D left it alone, attempting to put all her thoughts together before responding. Erack turned a few more pages, studying them more closely. D turned to him, ready to give her analysis. As she opened her mouth, Erack's eyes grew wide. He gasped and dropped the journal.

"What is it Erack?" D put her hand on his shoulder.

He sat there, looking at the book on the ground. Tears welling up in his eyes. She had never seen him cry before.

"These are sketches of what you see in your dreams?" his voice was shaky.

"Yes, they are. That's the whole idea," she answered.

"In your dreams?" he asked again, emphasizing 'your.'

"Yes, in my dreams. What's wrong with them? I don't understand." This was unnerving her.

"You're certain this is what you have seen?" he asked again.

Her patience was wearing thin. She hated being asked questions over and over like someone didn't trust her answers. It was her biggest issue with being briefed or debriefed. She tried to stay calm. She could see he was struggling and she didn't want to make it any worse.

"Erack, I have already said yes to that question three time. I don't know what more I can say to convince you," she tried to sound calm but wasn't sure if she succeeded.

He curled up tighter, hiding his head in his arms, resting his forehead on his knees. She could hear the silent sobbing. Wrapping her arm around his shoulders, she waited.

It felt like hours before he lifted his head to look at her. She sat up expectantly. He looked at the book again, then back at D, as if whatever happened didn't make sense to him.

"D..." His voice timid, barely louder than a whisper. "Why is my mother in your dreams?"

TESTIMONY

The rumor mill circulated wild and crazy stories the longer the council conducted their inquiry. With more stories came increasing levels of unrest. D hadn't seen her home in this much disarray and chaos in years. People were suspicious of one another. Schedules became more regimented and more strictly upheld, causing more disruption. The council feared leaks. People worried the council was taking improper actions and making uninformed decisions. Talk of petitions circulated. Many were even calling for new elections. D felt it was just tough talk during tense times. But now her summons date had arrived and after the accusatory debriefing, she felt no desire to parade in front of them again to give her official testimony.

On a good day, she rarely felt comfortable socializing with others. Now she was being marched across the compound with a scarlet letter in her hands. After leaving her quarters, she became immediately aware of people in the hall eyeing the card. Today, the wall of tension she experienced in public spaces was tighter than she ever felt and it invaded her brain like a wrecking ball, wreaking havoc on her controls. She tried to shake the feeling but as she looked over her shoulder, she found a small group already following her.

She was a little amazed at their forwardness. It wasn't a secret she was on the mission. It should be no surprise she was summoned. Apparently, when Xayres warned her about the experience, he hadn't exaggerated. Walking faster, the group kept pace with her, growing to the uncomfortable size. Maybe they thought they could follow her into the room if there were enough of them. Her speed walk elevated to a trot but it didn't matter how fast she traveled. They were still following and growing.

She rounded the last corner, viewing the council chamber doors with relief. Reaching for the knob, she found it locked. The crowd of people kept coming toward her, getting closer. Panic began to rise in her chest. Tapping on the door vigorously, the only response was the door opened a crack. She raised her red card and a hand grabbed it from her, slamming the door in her face as she attempted to walk through it. The corridor was closing in with the crowd quickly filling in the actual space. She felt trapped, backing up against the door. Feeling it move, she tried to turn around but something grabbed her arm, yanking her into the council room.

They only had one or two big gathering places and the last time she was in this room was her parents' funeral. It felt like a weight pressing on her chest. She wanted to leave, needing to get out of this space. Her discomfort outweighed her drive to keep her commission. Her breathing sped up and she headed back to the door. Her hand on the knob again, she felt the crowd on the other side. Then she felt the hand of the guard on hers. Turning her head to look at the council, she considered her options.

She heard a familiar voice. Xayres was giving his official statement. Wondering if she was early or this was intentional, caused her to finish turning back around. Not sure if she was allowed to be in the room during his statement, she froze, unsure what the next action should be. Slumping down to make herself less visible, she skulked to the back row of chairs in the room and proceeded to take a seat.

"To clarify, you maintain there was false or bad intelligence that was intentionally withheld?" Trey asked.

"Yes, I do," answered Xayres.

"And what brought you to this conclusion?" Trey continued.

"Jaren has been compromised," Xayres started.

"That is not the question. What led you to believe this?" interrupted Trey.

"Because the bunker was attacked. We found the Intel the day before it happened. It said an attack was imminent. Jaren was responsible for disseminating intelligence information to the entire council and instead of giving us both sets of intelligence, he chose which one to follow. When I asked him about it after I found it, he said the contradictory report was not in the best interest of the people. We received that intelligence weeks prior to the attack. The council had the right to weigh all the reports and information. We could have saved more people," explained Xayres.

"So you believe that Jaren was compromised. How could that have happened if your people were not allowed to go topside?"

"I believe it happened when he came from the other bunker,"Xayres said.

"Jaren is not an original citizen of your bunker?" clarified Trey.

"No, he is not an original citizen," parroted Xayres.

"And this led you to suspect Jaren before this incident?" asked a councilwoman.

"Yes. His family's story about a defunct bunker was fishy to start and could never be verified. It was all too convenient. He is too prone to make unilateral decisions. And he even shirked his own responsibility to infiltrate another bunker," Xayres said.

"Can you clarify those last few statements?" Trey asked.

"He left my fiancée to guarantee the bunker's destruction. That was supposed to be his job. He left his post. He disappeared. He ran. So she had no choice but to stay and do the dirty work," his voice rose steadily and before he realized it, his fist was pounding the table.

"Order young man." Trey tapped his gavel a few times. "We expect you to control yourself in here. Outbursts will not be tolerated."

"Sorry, sir. It won't happen again," Xayres replied quietly.

D heard him struggle to clear his throat. When she looked up, she could see he was hurting. She surmised he probably was not a class clown. It was a defense mechanism to hide how soft he had become. He held himself together long enough to enter the private chamber. She felt his pain, understanding it deeply. She wallowed in it all for a moment.

"D, are you ready?" Trey's voice ripped through her consciousness.

"Yes, sir," she stammered a little.

"State your name and rank for the council," commanded Trey.

"D, official enlisted volunteer and first female sniper," she smiled.

"This is an official proceeding. Please maintain your professionalism," one of the council members ordered.

"And you were present when they discovered one of these men is a traitor?" Trey asked.

She noticed both men were sitting, shackled to chairs, one on each side of the council table. Why hadn't she seen this when she walked in? Maybe she was too nervous. Perhaps she was overwhelmed. Not able to dig up an answer, she saw the look on Trey's face and was compelled to answer his questions more quickly.

"You already know the answer to that question," she said.

"Young lady, professionalism," reminded the council member.

"Do you know which one of the defendants is the actual traitor?" asked Trey.

D rolled her eyes. "Well, if any of us knew that, you wouldn't still be asking questions, would you?"

Trey slammed the gavel down on the table. The cracking sound echoed off the walls of the mostly empty room. D flashed for a moment to voices, unfamiliar voices. Where was this memory from? She refocused. Trey had risen, looking large and ominous from his elevated position.

"This is your last warning. Do not make us discipline you for contempt," he stated, sitting back down.

The point was made. D breathed in deep.

"No, I don't know," she replied. "They were already accusing each other when I figured we should take them both into custody for questioning. Personally, I preferred to just leave them out there to fend for themselves, which would have saved us all a lot of time and energy. But something told me none of you would like that answer. And, well, Tallin already knew his way back to the bunker."

"Please just answer the questions we ask," said another council member.

"To clarify, they accused each other?" asked Trey.

"Yes. Tallin said he had never seen Jaren before and Jaren claimed his brother Tallin has red hair," she answered.

"Then what happened?" Trey continued.

"Then Xayres hit Jaren in the nose," D said smirking, seeing it clearly in her mind's eye.

"Why did Xayres hit Jaren in the nose?" asked Trey.

"I'm not Xayres. So I don't really know," D paused. "From what I gather from my limited experience with the two of them, there was a continuing argument about who was at fault for the attack on the bunker. Xayres believed Jaren was a traitor. With someone else accusing Jaren, I imagine it verified Xayres' conclusions," she replied. "But before we read too much into that, I would like to bring your attention to Tallin's strong objections to going on the recovery mission in the first place."

"You think Tallin was reluctant to go on the mission?" asked Trey.

"You were all there. He had some story about a falling out with Jaren and he had no intentions of ever seeing him again. He fought the order until it became an actual edict. You all know this." D was growing more frustrated with the proceedings.

"See, I told you. He is not my brother. He had no intention of ever seeing me because he is a traitor," Jaren shouted from his seat, clanking his metal restraints on the wooden chair.

Trey slammed the gavel again, "Someone please gag him!"

Ra'Ella waved off the guards, rising to talk to Jaren. She leaned in close to his ear. Placing one hand on his, she seemed to have a calming effect. D began to wonder how long they had actually known one another and if there was something between them. Then Ra'Ella carefully placed the gag in his mouth.

"To clarify, you think Tallin is the traitor because he didn't want to see Jaren?" Trey asked.

"I never said that. If anything, Tallin is probably innocent. But either way, you guys will never fully trust either one of them again. So their lives as they knew them are essentially over anyway."

Jaren shook to try and respond, grunting through the gag. Tallin just sat with his eyes focused on the floor. He hadn't lifted his head to address Xayres or her the entire time she had been in the room. They both knew what D said was true.

"That will be all for now. If we have more questions, we will summon you again. Please escort her to the back corridor." Trey waved at her to make her stand on command.

SCIENCE

It was rare for D to report and have no activities scheduled for her day. Usually she was the one who opted to cancel on her activities, but today, she would have to find the reason she had nothing to do. After waiting for what felt like half a day, the corporal informed her Doc was responsible for clearing her schedule. She stomped all the way to Doc's office only to be told she was not to be disturbed. Again, she had to wait which did not improve her mood in the least.

When the door finally opened, Xayres walked out, shocked to see her. She stood to greet Doc.

"We were just coming to find you," Xayres said.

"Why do I feel like I am about to be ambushed?" D asked.

"Not ambushed. Just need to talk with you about something," Doc clarified.

"With him?" she scoffed and pointed at Xayres. "Not likely. He already knows too much as my room mate. He doesn't get to know this stuff."

"Now wait a minute here D. I was the one who made sure you were okay," Xayres stated.

"That has no bearing," Doc began to interrupt but was outmatched by D's reaction.

"I cannot believe you are trying to weasel your way into

this. That is just too much. You are the world's most self-obsessed person!" she shouted as she paced, unable to contain any built up feelings.

"D, you need to calm down," Doc said, walking to her and stepping in her way. "I will not allow him as part of the discussion..."

"Hey! That's not what was discussed..." Xayres interjected.

"Xayres will not be allowed to be part of the discussion if you choose that," Doc's voice overpowered Xayres' as she held D by the shoulders to look her in the eye.

"Sounds like you two already have a plan," D said sardonically.

"We haven't made a plan about your information behind your back. Let's go back to your quarters..." Doc tried to finish.

Xayres interrupted, "Our quarters."

They both eyed him in annoyance. "Let me just grab a file and we will go back to your quarters and go over this information. If you want, we can call Erack and wait if that makes you more comfortable," Doc sighed in relief at managing to finish, turning D toward the door and heading to her office. "You head there and I'll meet you," Doc called over her shoulder. "Do you want me to page Erack?"

"It may not do any good but go ahead," D said as she walked out the door.

She never understood the power Doc had over her, but she always did as Doc told her, without reservation or question. It was as if she had some switch in her brain telling her not to defy those orders. Despite previous attempts to not do as she was told, it always ended up this way. She couldn't help but feel programmed somehow which caused her anxiety.

As she approached her quarters, Erack was juggling an apple outside. For a moment, she couldn't hide her surprise which made him smile. He pulled his snack out of the air and held it tightly as she walked up to him.

"Didn't think I'd come huh? Well, I never miss the chance to learn more about you. Besides, it sounds like this is a big deal and I should probably be here to keep you...level," Erack said, noticing the grimace on her face.

She swung the door open and allowed him to enter first, feeling the need to slam it. When she swung it hard behind her, the loud crack of it crashing into the door frame never came. Only an exclamation of pain and frustration.

"Shit D! What was that for?" Xayres entered holding his eye.

She turned to look at him. "Oh no!" she growled. "You're not going to sneak your way into this conversation. You have to go. Find something else to do."

Erack took his stance behind D. Xayres eyed him with caution as he always made Xayres uncomfortable but he couldn't explain why. He closed the door, taking a step back. Distance in this situation felt like a necessary caution. Standing by the door uncomfortably, he was relieved when he heard the door chime. Sucking in a deep breath, he opened it wide.

"Hey Doc," Erack gave her a two-finger salute.

"He has to go," D said, pointing at Xayres.

"He does live here D. Perhaps we should be a little more accommodating?" she replied.

"How could we be more accommodating?" D asked.

"Just allow him to stay," Doc held up a hand telling Xayres to shut the door. "If he promises not to interrupt or act too interested in our conversation...maybe it will be fine if he is here. Wouldn't you agree?" she looked at D.

D wanted to say no. She needed to protest but somehow, she couldn't. It was as if her brain was arguing against her better ideas. She opened her mouth and despite her best efforts to sat something to the contrary, she replied, "I don't see how that wouldn't work, right?"

Erack eyed her curiously, "Uh, I guess so. If she's okay with it, I guess I am." Erack answered unsure if it was the correct thing to say.

"Then it's settled. Xayres, entertain yourself on your bunk and keep quiet," Doc instructed as she sat down at the table. "I like this addition," she smiled at D.

"He requed it," D threw a hand in Xayres' direction.

"Well, it was a good idea," Doc said, setting her files down on the table and motioning for them both to take a seat.

Erack stole the chair from the desk, sitting on it backwards, crunching into his apple. D fingered the files absently. Xayres bounced onto his bed. Doc breathed in deep, preparing for a long dissertation, but before she could begin, D cut her off.

"Is this a solution for my headaches, because I would really like one. I'm not much interested in anything else," D said.

"Well, to be honest, I don't really have an answer for those yet or a solution. But this may help us figure out a better treatment plan," Doc said. "But before we dive in, is there anything you haven't told me? Anything related to your headaches or your sleep cycle? Any changes I may not be able to detect on a scan?"

"How am I supposed to know what you can and can't detect on a scan?" D asked.

"Good point," Xayres said.

They all looked at him with agitation. He sunk back onto his bunk.

"So nothing that would give you any indication you are different from others?" Doc continued.

"Different. That's funny," Erack chuckled, spraying a bit of apple juice on the files. Doc reflexively pulled them out of the way. "Everybody already knows D is different. Although nobody can really pin down how or why," his fruit crunched loudly in D's ear.

"I may be able to offer a some of an explanation for that," Doc replied.

D looked at the files, noticing the labels. She sifted through them. One labeled Doc, Erack, Xayres and D. There it was, that famous letter. If she had a name, she didn't know it and apparently neither did anyone else. Her parents had never called her by her name, well, at least not one she could remember. Anything prior to the accident was more than hazy. It was practically forgotten, at least for her. The Shrinker said her trauma caused her to block it all out.

"Why is there a file for Xayres here?" D asked.

"I thought I would discuss his results with him afterward, since we're all in one place," answered Doc. "And I suppose if he can actually participate in this conversation, you would be able to participate in his," she appealed again.

"Fine!" she spouted spontaneously. "He can know." She kicked the chair back on two legs, balancing precariously as she folded her arms in discontent.

"Woo hoo!" Xayres shouted. "Finally!"

"May I continue?" Doc asked. "Okay," she opened the one marked D. "Your brain shows unusual activity in this area. Now, many people believe this is the area responsible for extra sensory perceptions," Doc circled a section with her finger. "And you have heightened activity in this area D."

She pulled out a scan from the file marked Doc and set them side by side. "I brought mine so you can compare the activity in the area is elevated. I haven't seen anything like this in anyone your age. I am starting to find these differences, albeit on a lower level, in small children, suggesting it might be normal progression," pausing only to bring Xayres' file to the top if the pile and pulling a scan from it. "That is, until now. As you can see on Xayres' scan, he has elevated activity here as well, but not on as high a scale."

She set the three scans next to one another. D ran her finger over the area Doc had circled with her finger. Then she picked them up in pairs to compare them, holding them up to the light as if it would provide more clarity. She jumped at the sight of Xayres standing across the table.

"So what do you mean by extra sensory exactly." D said in an awed voice.

"It could be many things. The ability to feel or sense others, to hear other's thoughts which I find highly unlikely. And things like predicting the future which is completely laughable," Doc smiled. "Honestly, we really don't know what this area of the brain controls," explained Doc.

"Could this activity cause someone to be able to see into someone else's mind or dreams?" Erack asked.

Doc tilted her head to the left, expressing her curiosity, "I suppose it could, given the range of skills it supposedly possesses. Why do you ask?"

D set the scans on the table, using the move to elbow Erack gently in the side. He looked at her. She glared back.

"There is something you're not telling us," Xayres exclaimed.

"I don't know if it's my place to say," Erack stated glumly, rubbing his wound.

Doc looked at D. "Don't look at me. I have no idea what he's talking about."

Doc's eyebrow raised at the response. "Are you certain?"

D looked at Erack, who shrugged. She scoffed, obviously not the response she wanted to see.

"If there's something more going on here, then we need to know," Xayres said.

"Why is Erack's file here?" D attempted to steer the conversation in another direction.

"D," Doc's tone warned her.

"I will answer your curiosity once you answer mine," she replied.

Doc looked at her, trying to pierce through her outer shell and relented. "Okay. I brought those because I noticed some other differences in his scans. Not in the same area and again, I don't know for certain what it means, but I imagine you have some abilities yourself. I'm just not sure what type," Doc pulled his scan out and pointed to the areas so he could look. "Now D."

"Just wait a moment," D elbowed Erack again.

"Interesting Doc...yeah...I always felt a little different too. But I think it may just make me a technology genius," he joked. D scowled. "You know what. I'm hungry. Maybe we should get dinner and come back to this," he set the scan down on the table and began to stand up.

"Not so fast," Doc stood up to block their exit. "Xayres, can't you use your privilege to order food to your quarters?"

"I'm sure I could Doc, but unlike you, I am not about to lose my credibility with the council. If someone sees me in here with all of you and those files on the desk, there's no telling how long it would be before they trusted me again. My best defense with them is playing like we don't get along at all." he paused, realizing what just came out of his mouth despite his better intentions.

"I don't know what you mean by playing, we don't get along," commented D with a smirk.

Xayres took a deep breath in and tried to start again, "Doc, they see how you coddle her and you do yourself no favors with the council for it." He slapped his hand over his mouth.

"I don't need any favors from the council. I'm..." Doc stopped herself.

They all looked at her. Doc had her hand on her upper chest. D remembered the amulet she played with in the med bay. The chain would cause it to sit just below her hand.

Doc redirected, "D, you said you would share."

"I think they both have something to share," Xayres said.

"How do you figure?" Erack asked.

"Because of your question," Xayres said. "It was a little too specific."

D and Erack looked at one another. "You first." They pointed and said in unison.

"It's not really mine to share," Erack said.

"I wouldn't share something like that without your permission. It's more about you than me," D said.

"Then that means you go first," Erack said.

"So there is something more that we don't know about," Xayres said.

"Yep and you'll be the last to know buddy," Erack replied.

"I understand why you might say that," D lamented. "But I honestly didn't know..."

"You still could have shared it with me," Erack said. "And you're right. I would probably prefer if you kept it to yourself."

"Dear hell!" Doc sat back down. "Just explain what's going on here, right now, or I'm releasing this to the council."

D's eyes went wide. "You wouldn't! They would decommission me for sure," she shook her head at Doc. "Fine!" she relented. "I can hear voices. It may be other people's thoughts. And it started the day I went into the med bay. Not sure how I ended up there. The only thing I remember is hearing the little girl walking in front of me and then realizing she didn't actually say anything. Then there were a ton of voices I couldn't get out of my head. Then my head began to ache. And then I woke up in your private room."

Xayres and Doc couldn't hide their shock, eyes widened at every line. It annoyed D as Xayres jaw dropped further and further. She tapped his chin causing him to close it which was the response she wanted. The room was awkwardly silent for a long time. Xayres moved first, shaking his head.

"While interesting and unexpected, that feels like nothing compared to what I know," Erack was the first to speak.

"You think so huh? It's that good?" Xayres recovered.

"Yeah, it's that good," Erack reassured him.

"And you're going to tell us now," Doc commanded.

"I don't know. I don't want to overshadow D's lies," he winked as D elbowed him in the stomach again. "Okay...okay."

He laughed awkwardly for a moment, then he looked Xayres straight in the eye, as if to stare him down. "D has dreams about my mother. A woman she has never met and I haven't seen since I left the city. She has sketches of her and she knows what my neighborhood looks like," Erack watched in amusement as Xayres' eyes grew to an abnormal size again.

ESCAPE

The clock on the wall told Tallin it was almost time to make their way to the council chamber. Any moment now, breakfast would arrive and they would be herded in to sit and listen. Since neither got to ask questions of their own, it didn't really mimic the justice system they read about in school. But underground, decisions had to be finite and sometimes, they had to make them quickly for the good of the colony.

Like clockwork, two guards came through the door. These were not the regular guards. They were younger and reeked of inexperience. Tallin hoped he didn't see them cower under the greatness that was Jaren. Neither one of them were small men, but Jaren had kept much better shape over the years. But as one approached with the tray of food, he shivered a little and seemed uncertain how close he should get to the bars.

Tallin normally stayed stoic in the brig, just as he did in the council chamber. At this moment, he had been pacing, biding his time. Now he stood observing closely and then he actually spoke, "You should call in back up. He can be a bit of a hassle."

"Quiet!" shouted the guard in front, attempting to sound confident but his voice was shaky.

Tallin felt in the pit of his stomach something wasn't

right with this situation. Someone tampered with the guard schedule. He knew Jaren was a traitor but this told him he wasn't the only one. It appeared the schedule change was his assistance with an escape.

"Seriously guys back up is needed," Tallin repeated.

"I said shut up!" the guard yelled again, slapping the bars with his security stick, forcing Tallin back.

Tallin could see how this situation would go sideways quickly. And almost the moment he thought it, he saw Jaren make his move.

Jaren yanked the guard by the shirt pulling him in close, grabbing his head and bashing it into the bars repeatedly until he went limp. There was enough blood, Tallin guessed he wouldn't live long without attention. Before the other guard could react, Jaren swiped the keys off of the guard's belt, shoving them into the lock.

"HELP!" Tallin screamed. "HELP!"

But no one came. He watched in horror as Jaren unlocked the cell. The door swung open and Jaren rushed out, tackling the other guard to the floor before he could hit the alarm. Wrapping his arm around his throat, the guard struggled for breath. When he stopped struggling, Jaren turned and looked at Tallin.

Tallin expected him to run out the door, but Jaren just knelt in place panting for a moment watching Tallin's every move.

"HELP!" Tallin screamed again but he knew it was pointless.

"Shut up stupid!" Jaren whispered tersely.

After a moment, Jaren stood and moved toward Tallin's cell. He unlocked it and stepped inside, leaving the door wide open. Tallin backed up, trying to keep distance between them. Jaren charged him, wrapping one arm around his waist, hand over Tallin's mouth and slamming Tallin up against the wall. Tallin swallowed hard and his lungs were forced empty. He found it difficult to breathe even as Jaren released him. With no one holding Tallin up, he slid down to the floor.

Jaren looked down, grabbing Tallin by the shirt, pulling him upright. Tallin kept his body limp, making Jaren do all the work. As they met eye to eye, Tallin threw his forehead into Jaren's mouth, causing Jaren to release him, allowing Tallin to dive out from underneath Jaren.

"You may be bigger. But I am craftier," Tallin panted, trying to recover. "Where you rely on brute strength, I rely on brains and skill."

Jaren wiped the blood from his mouth. He was panting too. Both seemed to relax for a moment before Jaren charged Tallin, wrapping his arms around his waist. Lifting Tallin off the floor, slamming Tallin's back into a wall. The force of it caused Jaren to let go, stumbling backward to rev up again.

Tallin was dazed, but he turned around, putting his back to Jaren and waited. Feeling Jaren's arms wrap around him a second time, he piked his legs. As his feet hit the wall, he ran up it, allowing himself to break free from Jaren's grip, grabbing Jaren by the shoulders, he flipped over him. Jaren slammed into the wall, taking the full brunt of the force he created bouncing off the wall.

Tallin wobbled a little out of the door and grabbed the guard's baton. As he got close, he noticed the guard stirring. Slipping in the blood now covering the floor, he struggled to maintain his balance as he took advantage of the free moment to hit Jaren over the head, which only dazed him. Slapping his head again, Jaren fell to the floor. Tallin wiped the blood from his nose only to realize the guard's blood was all over his hands.

Spitting blood from his mouth, "All brawn and a little tiny brain."

He struggled to maintain balance as he moved toward the emergency alarm. Slapping his hand on it, he slid to the floor, still panting. Guessing he'd broken at least one rib, he didn't bother to move.

Back up arrived relatively quickly. The captain surveyed the scene, shock and horror written all over his face. He took the pulse of his men on the floor first. One still had a pulse and was breathing. They sent him to the med bay. Then the captain cautiously approached Jaren, checking his pulse. He proceeded to shackle his wrists and ankles before calling for a medic to nurse the wound on Jaren's head.

Tallin spat more blood on the floor but didn't say a word. The captain eyed him suspiciously. Tallin's response was to place his wrists together and hold them out to make them easier to shackle. Approaching with caution, the captain seemed surprised at Tallin's lack of resistance.

"This wasn't you, was it?" asked the captain.

Tallin only shook his head. They heard Jaren groan, turning their attention to him, watching as he struggled, unable to roll over due to his restraints. Helping Tallin to his feet, the captain sent him with guards to the med bay.

"You," he pointed. "Inform the council proceedings will be delayed. And check on that medic for him."

Jaren mumbled, "Why don't I get to go to the med bay?"

"Because you killed someone. You're not going anywhere," the captain helped him turn over and sit up.

"I have a right to face my accusers," Jaren growled.

"We have a right not to be killed while trying to bring you breakfast," the captain yelled. "If you continue like this, you'll have no rights."

Just as the captain had ensured, Jaren was not in the council room for the last of the official testimony. Tallin sat, like always, watching the floor. He never said a word to defend himself. It was almost as if he wanted them to think he was guilty and had given up.

"Jaren is hiding something. I mean, he tried to escape this morning," Kaya said.

"Yes, but it makes no sense. He doesn't know this compound at all. He would have gotten lost and been recaptured by lunch," Ra'Ella said.

"Except it seems like he had help," said Xayres.

"There are plenty of unanswered questions here. And the more questions we ask, the less sense this entire situation makes. There is a need for this situation to make sense. Tallin has not been very vocal while Jaren has. Does this show us Jaren was working with Tallin?" reasoned Trey.

"Or more likely, it was Tallin trying to escape and Jaren was trying to stop him," answered Kaya.

"That is not what I saw when assessing the scene," the captain said. "Tallin was cooperative and by all accounts, he had to be the one who hit the alarm."

"If Tallin was trying to escape, how did Jaren get out of his cell to try and stop him. It's more likely Jaren thought he could prove his innocence if he thwarted an escape attempt by Tallin and it didn't turn out like he planned. He didn't expect Tallin to be so formidable," Xayres said. "Based on D's logic when we met, he thinks he'll look more innocent no matter how it played out."

The council went silent. None of them completely understood what he meant but none of them were willing to ask questions and reveal they didn't understand.

Trey cut the awkward silence, "Jaren doesn't look very innocent right now."

"I know that. But if we keep analyzing it, something tells me we would talk ourselves into believing he is innocent. Either way, this conversation should not be had in mixed company," Xayres motioned toward Tallin.

"I agree. Captain, please escort Tallin back to the brig," Trey ordered.

When the captain approached Tallin, he could see he wasn't behaving normally. Usually, he lifted his head when they approached. Instead, he continued to stare at the floor. As the captain released the shackles, Tallin slumped over and fell face first into the floor. The thud sounded painful, but Tallin never winced. He didn't move. Kaya gasped. The council stood to get a better view.

"Is he breathing?" asked Trey.

"No sir," the captain whispered.

"Get a medic in here!" Trey shouted the order.

The room erupted into chaos, panic-stricken faces waited anxiously until Doc arrived. She vigorously performed CPR on the stretcher as they ran to the med bay. Like a flash, she had monitors and equipment trying to revive him. After thirty minutes of solid work, she called it.

"Time?" she shouted.

The nurse shuddered, "Surely we can..." he started.

"TIME!" she called out again.

"15:17," the nurse replied.

"Note that please," Doc ordered.

"Why aren't we still trying?" the nurse persisted.

"We don't know how long he's been this way but he was already losing body temperature. If I had to guess, he was probably only alive in the council room for maybe an hour at best," explained Doc. "It's useless to try any harder. Nothing can be done." She put her hand on the nurse's shoulder. "I understand this is hard for you. I'm sorry."

Doc started the autopsy and testing immediately. They drew blood and stomach contents, anything she could think of to give her a cause of death. After spending hours in the lab, Doc called the council to her conference room.

"It's a poison and definitely not one I have seen before. Not natural. A kind of slow release. I am not sure how he got it into his system. Someone in the bunker may have laced his food with it. I didn't see any puncture wounds beyond those we used when treating his injuries and I didn't find any partially digested capsules or similar things in his stomach," Doc told Trey in the autopsy room. "From the moment it hit his system, it began to replicate until he died. Other than that, I have no information. Maybe when the lab work is done, I may have more."

"He walked into the room by his own volition. Is the time release what caused the delay in death?" asked Trey.

"As I said, I am still waiting for lab work. I have no other answers for you at this time," explained Doc.

"Could Jaren have administered the poison?" Kaya asked.

"Honestly, I am not sure. How would Jaren manage to get the poison into his possession? And how did he administer it if he did have it?" Doc replied. "It feels more likely that it was a possible suicide."

"You don't think Jaren did it to look innocent?" asked Xayres.

"We are not here to spin wild theories. We are trying to establish what occurred and how he died," Trey said.

They all shifted uneasily under his gaze.

"I think all we have right now are theories," said Doc. "I am not saying it did happen, but it is possible. Which means we may have another traitor in our midst."

"Another traitor?" questioned Kaya.

"She's right, another traitor. If either Jaren or Tallin did it, they needed someone with access to slip the poison to whoever did it. And someone would have needed access to change the guard rotation," Xayres said.

"But Jaren has assumed we already exonerated him," Trey said. "He already put in his petition to rejoin the council."

"From the brig?" asked Xayres. "And how exactly is he explaining his actions?"

"He is requesting a full psychological evaluation. He claims not to remember any of the events of the morning," answered Kaya. "Is it possible?"

"Jaren did suffer head trauma as a result of being slammed into a concrete pillar," Doc said looking at Xayres.

"And again during the tussle with Tallin. It is plausible he is having memory issues as a result or he could have suffered a psychological break under the stress of the trial. Either one of those things can cause an attack of amnesia."

"So he may never remember what happened?" asked Trey.

"Oh, he remembers. He's a smart guy. He has no idea how advanced the brain studies are here." Xayres said. "Doc, have you scanned his brain to see if it's showing signs of memory loss?"

Doc glared at him for a moment. She felt he revealed too much about their secret conversations. But the idea of brain science was not new to anyone here.

"As he has not been allowed to leave the brig, no, I haven't scanned his brain yet. But if he can come to the med bay, I can. I can't say with certainty he legitimately doesn't remember, but I can see how likely it is."

"Okay, so his petition only has merit if there is evidence of possible memory loss. Can we agree on that?" asked Trey.

"You are not seriously considering allowing him back on the council? He's a traitor and he's all but given us exact evidence of it," replied Xayres. "His petition should never have merit."

"He's right Trey. I don't think his petition should have any merit at all. You can't reinstate a man who was on trial for treason and killed someone, possibly two people," Doc reasoned.

"We can't just release him back in the general population. We need to be able to keep an eye on him," Ra'Ella said.

"But Doc is right. Memory or no memory, we can't consider his petition for reinstatement," Kaya said.

"He can't have a seat on the council if he murdered people," added Xayres.

"If he can't remember it, can we hold him responsible?"

Trey asked.

"We certainly can and we must. Whether we can prove he murdered Tallin or not, he murdered a guard. At the very least, he should be banished. The laws demand it," answered Xayres.

"This is a unique situation. But I agree. He knows his way to the bunker so exiling him puts us all at risk. He is that selfish. We can't just allow him to walk back onto a council. But if he is the traitor and he has help, we can't afford not to investigate and we can't afford to tip our hand. He should be kept under close surveillance," said Ra'Ella.

"I agree. Ra'Ella, look into this quietly. Check the logs and make a list of who has close access," ordered Trey.

"Two or three guards, the captain and the council," Xayres said. "It's a very short list. Which means the traitor is likely in this room right now. Consider our hand tipped."

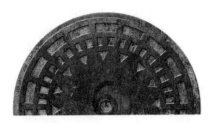

LUNCH

News of Tallin's death swept through the compound like a brush fire on dry grass. The inquest was officially concluded although the details of the outcome still seemed vague. With the change, missions to the surface started again. Erack was lucky enough to be one of the first ones out. They needed to survey the ground to update their maps. His specialized team was trying to calculate where they were located on the continent and in relation to other bunkers.

Erack had quite the knack for numbers and technology. He re-engineered the communication network when he was barely fourteen. Now they didn't have to wait for radio signals to send messages. They could send them through the ground. Everyone knew he was a little genius then which gave him a lot of leeway to do as he pleased.

He liked training. So he became a trainer in his spare time. Everything else was to better their knowledge of the world. Chronically surrounded by maps and other diagrams, he had the run of the communications lab. D had only been there a few times before. She found it all incredibly and unbearably dull.

Erack had been back a little over a week and she knew exactly where he would be. Normally after a survey mission, they spent the next week or two in the lab, day and night, inputting new information. Hoping to convince him to take a break, she trotted down to the third level communications array.

She found them in a mess of maps and scratch paper and log books. Standing there, watching all of them scramble from messy table to messy table. Getting excited at each new piece of information to connect more dots. Smiling at their chatter, she wondered how they could find this so interesting. Erack noticed her in the doorway.

"Hey D!" he smiled.

"Just thought you might want some lunch," she said. "But when I got here, I was trying to figure out what all the excitement was about."

He motioned to her. "Come on over and I'll show you."

Walking to the table, she saw he had a tall stack of papers with handwritten equations on the top of maps. She tried to take it all in, but it was too much. Erack directed her attention to a map covered with glass on the wall.

"So what are you all trying to do here?" asked D.

"Well, we are trying to calculate where other bunkers may be, in case we need to evacuate. That is always the first task," said Officer Essie.

Alex grabbed a wax pencil from the table and joined her at the map. "This map isn't exactly outdated, but it's not completely current. It's from before, well, everything. But it gives us a starting point."

"We know the direction of other bunkers. But we don't have an exact location. However, we can calculate how far away they may be based on the degradation of the underground signal," Essie said.

"The signal travels faster or slower based on the substance it travels through. Faster through water with less degradation. Slower through more compact rock with more degradation," explained Erack.

"So if we know a bunker is out this way," Alex marked the map. "Then based on the terrain we surveyed, the core samples, and the signals, we can estimate approximately where the other bunker is."

"How 'approximate' is the answer?" asked D.

"Well, that we have never tested, but we're guessing the accuracy is within a 20-mile radius or so," said Erack.

"From their communications array. Not necessarily the front door," Essie clarified.

D grinned at her enthusiasm. "I know I don't have those impressive skills. That's a pretty good guess."

They showed her some actual examples and then they all talked for a while, about everything and anything. D's stomach finally grumbled in protest.

"I know you guys are really busy, but I was wondering if you were ordering in lunch. Can I stay if you do?" she asked.

Erack looked her up and down, summing her up. Looking around the room, he said, "Actually, we could probably all use a break. I say we head to the mess."

Everyone cheered. While they loved their work, sometimes it was nice to get away. Alex walked swiftly by Essie. She crinkled her nose.

"And after lunch, maybe we should all bathe. Can we leave the vents open to get some fresh air in here?" asked Essie.

Erack flipped the switch to open them, nodding as he tried to sniff himself without anyone noticing. D grabbed his arm and they all rushed out the door. She hadn't felt this giddy in a long time. Erack and she were getting along and her headaches were becoming more manageable. It felt like everything was finally coming together.

They laughed and joked while they ate. Everyone seemed to be in good spirits despite the recent commotion in the compound. Most attributed it to everything feeling back to normal or as normal as it could be now. The work was a little lighter with more hands available. They were all glad people survived and were able to help them. Many people even thanked D for aiding the rescue. She had gone from popular and despised to popular and appreciated. Either way, her people skills had not appeared to improve.

Erack sat, juggling apples. D loved that he felt so free. Looking around the mess hall, their excitement appeared contagious. Everyone was having a good time, laughing and smiling. D actually felt comfortable enough to socialize. She stood up to walk around the room to take it all in. She returned with another cup of water and some leftovers. The joking and laughing continued. Turning her back to the other side of the table, she was having an in depth discussion with one of the trainees from her class when she felt a twinge of pain in her stomach.

There was a small thudding sound behind her. It sounded like an apple hitting the floor. Then another. She thought, *Erack never drops apples.* She felt the fear and swallowed hard. Turning around, she felt sick to her stomach. Pivoting around just in time to see Erack fall to the floor, he wretched. The smell hit her nose and trying desperately not to follow suit, she sucked in hard.

"Erack!" was all she could muster as the world began to spin.

Someone was kneeling beside her, helping her to sit. She tried to push off the bench and stand. Her legs failed her.

"D don't..." the voice sounded familiar.

"Erack..." she mustered but couldn't say more.

She tried to focus. Her vision cleared enough to see Xayres. He was carrying her but she wasn't sure where she was or where they were headed.

"Where..." she started.

"We're going to the med bay. Don't worry, they took Erack first," Xayres said.

"How..."

"I noticed you were uncharacteristically social. So, I thought maybe you'd been drugged or something. Then I saw you collapse from across the mess," he answered.

"Is Erack okay?" she asked.

"What does one have to do to be the center of your world? Am I going to have to knock that guy off?" joked Xayres.

She tried to slap him on the shoulder but she merely grazed her fingertips across his shirt sleeve.

"Stop it," responded D, trying not to whine.

"I don't know. I think he'll be hungry though. I swear he lost every apple he's eaten for a week," he chuckled. "At least it smelled a little fruity. Doc can answer your questions."

By the time they reached the doors, D had fallen asleep.

"It must have taken a lot out of her," Doc said, motioning to a bed on the other side of the bay.

Xayres could see them working on Erack in the private room. He found it odd that the private room had glass walls. *At least it comes with curtains*, he thought.

"I'll be over in a minute. Don't leave her there alone. She has a tendency to roll off the table," said Doc.

He set her down gently, covering her with a blanket. D was pale. Checking her forehead, she had a slight fever but she was shivering, even under the blanket. Nurses came in and took samples of everything while they waited. Finally, Doc slid to the pair.

"How is he?" Xayres nodded his head in Erack's direction.

"Still not sure," Doc sighed, exasperated.

"Could they have the same virus or something?" asked Xayres.

"Maybe," Doc picked up the report from the counter, scanning it quickly. "But we're not finding signs of anything in her system so far. Almost like this is residual." Surmised Doc.

"So they're super connected?" Xayres motioned to his

head.

"Anything is possible," she said. "We have been working together on control of her special gifts. With medicine and meditation, she's gained some control. But at this point, Erack and you are our most unpredictable variables."

She paused, looking at the three of them. "Could be close proximity to you has amplified their connection. I just don't know."

Within a few hours, Doc was greeted by top council members for a progress report. Erack's involvement and leadership with his surveyors was of utmost importance and they needed him well to continue his work.

"As I suspected," Doc said, walking out of the lab.

Trey, Ra'Ella, Xayres, Kaya and the rest of the council had been waiting in the med bay practically since Erack's arrival. While D appeared to recover rather quickly, he had only gotten worse. And he was showing no signs of improvement.

"It's poison...again," she sighed. "If it's the same poison, I would say we have a confirmed team of traitors in our midst. However, while both strains have similar origins, Erack's strain appears much older and possibly less potent. Neither of which makes any sense," answered Doc.

"Older and less potent than what?" asked D.

They were all so engrossed in the results, no one had noticed her in the doorway. Xayres crossed to the door to cut her off.

"This is top secret information D," Xayres said.

"I have a right to know. I am family," pressed D. "Well, as close as one can get to family."

"We already give you a lot of latitude," Kaya said.

"However, she does have a right to know, I suppose," said Ra'Ella.

"She doesn't have a right to anything," Trey argued.

"Yes, she does. She has a right to know what's happening with him. Besides, Xayres will probably just tell her later anyway," Ra'Ella replied, looking from one to the other.

"I will not. I only tell her what's necessary to keep her in line. This doesn't apply," protested Xayres.

"It's older and more potent than what?" asked D again.

"As persistent as she is, she'll just find a way to get the information anyway," Kaya reasoned.

"But we need to keep the circle on this tight," said Trey.

Doc released an exaggerated growl, expressing her annoyance. She rolled her eyes as the council continued to banter about politics and policies. Walking toward the door, she cleared her throat.

"Tallin was killed by poison and we suspect it wasn't suicide," Doc answered D, silencing the other. "There, I made the decision for everyone. Not everything has to be done by a majority vote."

Trey eyed Doc in disgust. Doc shrugged him off and went about recording her instruments.

"Why?" D pushed.

"We can't tell you that. In fact, we've told you too much already," said Trey.

"The poison in Erack replicates like the poison we found in Tallin, except it does so more slowly. Possibly because there is less in his system. There is a possibility they injected him before he left the city." Doc said.

"A poison that takes 20 years to kill. What would be the point of that?" asked Xayres.

"I have no idea," she answered. "D, you can go in and see him now."

D didn't hesitate. While the conversation was interesting and informative, she wanted to ensure Erack saw her.

"I just can't seem to find the source..." she heard Doc say as she walked into the private room.

"Check out these digs. You must be a top priority. It must be that set of impressive skills," she joked as she walked up to him. "I mean, you're own private roooo..."

She saw Erack and lost her train of thought. He was white as the sheet that covered him. His lips were mildly discolored. Large purple bags hung under his eyes. She brushed his hair off his forehead. It was so hot, she almost pulled her hand away. Not wanting to alarm him too much, she forced a smile.

"Hey," he said, trying desperately to smile.

Erack began to cough. D grabbed the glass of water from the tray. Holding his head up, she helped him drink, her chest aching at the sight of him.

He lifted his hand to her cheek, "Don't worry about me D. You'll be fine and I'm stronger than this thing. I promise."

She actually touched his hand and it forced a genuine smile. Giving him whatever he wanted was all she could think about and she knew this would make him happy. Placing his hand back on his chest, she grabbed a chair from across the room, taking her place at his bedside. He was asleep by the time she sat down.

The door opened behind her. Doc was still talking with Xayres, Trey, and Kaya.

"...I am giving him appears to have slowed the replication process. But it isn't eradicating the poison. I really can't say how long he has," Doc said as they walked into the room, trying to keep Trey and Kaya from following her.

D choked down a tear. No one was going to see her cry, even if it was Erack. Doc put her hand on her shoulder.

"He's asleep now. Why don't you let him get some rest? You could probably use some too," she said.

"No! I am not leaving! Not unless you order me to and even then..." D choked down her tears and emotions.

Doc shook her head, turning to return to the lab to run

more tests and evaluate the results. Every few hours, a nurse came in and injected Erack with some blue-green liquid. D assumed it was the formula slowing the replication. She lost all track of time. Laying her head down gingerly on his shoulder, she let herself drift. If he woke, he would let her know. Before long, she was back walking in dreams.

She looked around. The area looked familiar but she couldn't make anything out clearly. It was so blurry. Why was it so blurry? Suddenly she started coming into focus. A bright light above her stung her eyes. Something pinched in her arm. She flinched. The dizzy feeling felt familiar. Her eyes blinked causing the light to flicker. Trying to move, she realized she was strapped down. This was a feeling she hated.

Voices were in the distance. Straining, she tried to make sense of the conversation. Something touched her head, ran fingers through her hair.

"Just relax sweetie. This is for your own good. You'll hardly notice anything after the procedure," a sweet female voice said above her.

D strained her eyes. This face looked familiar. She'd drawn this face before but couldn't place it. The face disappeared behind her eyelids.

"Can he hear us?" the woman asked.

"No, he should be out cold," said a man.

D tried to open her eyes. They didn't cooperate. All she wanted was to look around the room again.

"Good," said the woman. "I just can't believe I gave birth to that vile thing. My only one out of five. Such an abomination."

"Well, you can take pride in the service he'll be doing," the man said.

"Yes, I just need him to trust me a little longer. So, they'll be able to track that thing?" she asked.

"It's genius really. Relatively undetectable until

activated, not that they have scanners I imagine. Then when activated," the man explained.

"He'll die. No more abomination. How lovely. At least we can put him to good use," the woman sounded almost giddy.

His ears were turning off or her ears were turning off. She strained to hang on. A piercing pain ripped through her thigh and up her leg. She opened her mouth to scream but heard nothing.

"Take it out..." the man faded in and out like someone playing with the volume on the overhead speakers. "kill...faster...remove...faster."

The picture was gone and for a moment, she was nowhere. In a void she couldn't explain. It was cold and wet. Her eyes opened. The scene flashed out of focus. When she could see clearly again, she found herself in the wilderness, outside the city.

There was intense fear. She felt her leg. There was a scar on the thigh. Looking up, she saw her again, Erack's mom. Tears rolled down her cheeks. She told him she loved him and this was the only way for him. Then she forced him away with a small group of kids, pushing them in the direction of the great expanse. The adults walked away. Not one of them turned around and looked back. They looked at where they came from, contemplating whether they should go back in that direction.

"D."

D jumped. Doc was back.

"D, I think based on this last scan, we have managed to almost halt the replication process. But I am not sure how to get the poison out of his system," she explained.

D was still groggy. Some of it didn't make sense. She tried to reconcile what she had seen in her dreams to what Doc was saying.

"How long?" croaked D.

Her mouth was almost unbearably dry. Doc brought her a cup of water.

"You've been here almost two days now," answered Doc.

D gulped the water and handed the glass back to Doc who refilled it and returned it to her.

"I meant how long does he have?" clarified D.

"Erack may have a few days to a few weeks. I can't be sure. Just because we halted the process doesn't mean it won't adapt to the serum and start replicating again. And if that doesn't happen, the poison is still in his body. Again, I am not sure how to clean it out. As long as the poison is there, it is still actively trying to kill him. Not to mention, we still haven't found the source. So even if we could clean it out, it may reinfect him," explained Doc.

"Have you scanned him?" asked D.

"Scan his brain?" Doc looked confused.

"No!" D said, slapping her thigh. "His legs. We need to scan his legs."

"How do you know that?" asked Doc.

"Um..." D pointed to her head.

"So...you need me to scan his legs. Is that the source?" Doc asked.

"I don't know for certain," answered D. "But it's all I've got."

"We haven't developed any technology for that. There hasn't been a need," replied Doc.

"Can't we...use one of the brain things but on his legs?" stammered D.

"I don't know if that would work. It would have to be calibrated differently I think. Why don't you go back to your quarters and rest and I will run some equations and look into our research to see if it will work," Doc brought her to a standing position and placed her hand on her other shoulder.

D saw a slip of paper in her hand. She grabbed it away from Doc, raising one eyebrow.

"To excuse you from exercises and training for a while longer. Go," Doc said, guiding her to the door with a smile.

TINKERING

Doc stared at the machine, cursing her top tech because he was the one sick on the bed. He chuckled at her frustration. Since he couldn't keep his hands from trembling, Doc was forced to do the manual labor while he attempted to walk her through it. But while Doc knew how to use each device at her disposal, when it came to servicing and maintaining them, she was as useful as a baby.

Erack found the entire situation hilarious. He kept laughing so hard it sent him into coughing fits, slowing their progress tremendously. D watched the situation unfold from the other side of the glass. Doc was so engrossed in her current predicament, she didn't notice D laughing at them either.

D knew she was possibly capable of re-calibrating the machine with assistance from Erack. She was also much more likely to need less direction, allowing him to rest. But she was enjoying watching Doc squirm.

Her dreams while medicated turned into horrific nightmares from which she could not wake. And to make matters worse, the higher the dose, the more vivid the dream and the less she remembered when she did manage to wake herself up. So, watching Doc tortuously muddle through not knowing anything about the inner workings of the electronics nor the lingo Erack used, amused her immensely. Erack saw her out of the corner of her eye.

"Hey, you!" he choked. "Get in here and help this woman. I hear this was all your idea anyway."

D walked to the doorway. Doc looked up scowling.

"How long have you been there?" she hissed.

"Long enough to be amused," replied D with a wide grin.

"Knock it off D. We have to see if this will work," chided Erack.

"Okay...for you," she stepped inside. "But I am warning you Doc. If you try to dose me with sleeping meds again, this will be the last time I will ever help you, for the rest of your life."

"The rest of my life?" Doc raised an eyebrow.

"Well, you are significantly older than I am. You're more likely to go first. I'll help cremate you, but you'd be dead by then," D smiled and winked. "But seriously, no more dosing. It makes things worse."

"Are you done complaining yet?" Erack whined. "Anytime now D. It's not like I'm dying here or anything."

D tried to hide her pained expression through mimicking his tone as she walked across the room.

"I'm fond of you too," Erack replied.

"At least you've kept your sense of humor," Doc said. "Or the poison is eating away at your brain."

"My humor may be all I have left in the end," Erack said dramatically.

"Quit being so cheesy," D gently tugged on his ankle.

She grabbed the old scanner from Doc and began fiddling with the insides. It only took her a few moments to complete the task Erack set her to. As she screwed the back plate into place, Doc grimaced and sighed.

"I have been working on all that morning," she said.

"Give yourself a break Doc. You probably already had it mostly done for her," Erack tried to soothe her while D shook her head.

"Not even close," D cut in.

Erack slapped her across the back, but only because he couldn't stand. She scowled at him.

"What was that..." she looked at him.

He raised his eyebrows. She knew he was telling her to shut up and do as she was told. She huffed a little before helping Doc attach the device to the arm over the bed. With a twist of connectors and some buttons pushed on the keyboard, the device was ready for an experimental run.

"So supposedly this should work like scanning the brain. But it should tell us if there is something foreign in his tissue. Not like the poison, but solid foreign objects," Doc said.

"Are there any side effects Doc? I mean, I wouldn't want to get sick or anything," Erack joked.

"Doc, I think you may be right about the poison affecting his brain," D said. "I've never seen him..." D searched desperately for a word to describe it. Then she motioned up and down at him. "Like this."

"D at a loss for words. Now that's impressive, especially when emotional," teased Doc with a smile. "Alright, here goes. D, I need you to move it into one position and then press that button on top."

D did her best to follow instructions. As they took one picture at a time, Doc recorded the location and approximate angle of the scanner in relation to is legs. The process took well over an hour and by the time they finished, D's nerves were beyond frazzled.

The photos actually needed to be developed, which took hours. D paced while Erack napped. She fetched food for both of them. All he could hold down was broth. She asked them to add some spices to give it some flavor, not able to imagine eating the exact same thing for every meal for days. Even their topside ration packs had different flavors.

Doc burst out of the back causing D to spill broth

down the front of Erack. He grimaced. Tearing off his blanket, Doc tried to hike his gown up his legs.

"Hey!" Erack choked, trying to sit up enough to push her hands away. He settled for swatting at them to no avail.

"I need to see if you have a scar," said Doc.

"Okay," D stepped between them, "Being gentle and communicating your intentions might make him feel more comfortable."

"Oh...right. I am just trying to save his life here," Doc said with an exasperated sigh.

Doc stepped back while D helped Erack lay back comfortably. Both pulled up his gown. Doc grabbed her looking glass. It was awkward for all of them. D was conflicted. She couldn't help but think she should have insisted on a male nurse at his bedside, just in case a situation happened.

"Eureka!" Doc yelled. "The scanner worked. I think I found it!"

She left the room as D pulled down Erack's gown and replaced his blanket. Doc came back with a picture.

"Look, right there. Where the scar is. It looks like a device and it's been there a long time. If it hadn't started oozing poison, we may never have known it was there," explained Doc.

"Now what do we do?" asked D.

"We find a way to remove it while doing the least amount of damage. Then the poison will exit his body naturally and we'll be all set," Doc said.

The idea of removing it filled D with dread. She couldn't explain why or how. Grabbing Doc tightly around the wrist, she wrenched her around. Doc looked shocked, trying to break free of her grip but after seeing the look on D's face, Doc ceased struggling immediately.

"Don't remove it! Don't try and remove it!" D was so adamant, she found herself almost yelling.

"Okay D. I'll just go in and take a sample of the poison

to see if I can find or create an antidote," Doc said, prying D's fingers from her wrist.

"Have we scanned for a radio signal?" D looked concerned but appeared lost in a dream.

"A radio signal?" Doc asked. "Why...?" She stopped, squinting as she tried to put the pieces together. "I will."

"I don't know why but it feels important," D said, backing away.

"D, it's okay. Remember, you just need a moment. We've talked about this." Erack tried weakly.

"It's okay D. I'm listening. I'm listening," Doc assured her.

"It's all going to be okay D," Erack repeated.

D looked at them blankly, then ran off. Doc looked at Erack, shaking her head.

"I swear Erack, something tells me the last thing we need is that girl to fall apart." She said.

Erack pursed his lips, "Doc, I hate to be the bearer of bad news, but I am fairly certain she's already walking on that edge."

CHOICES

"I've gone through his logs. He notes a twinge of pain in that leg after he was on his way back home. We figure that's when it was hit by the radio signal, which is how it was activated. At least, Doc is pretty certain on that point," Xayres reported to the council.

"Yes, I am fairly certain the insert was designed to be activated by radio signal. Now, from what we can tell, it has been so long since they inserted it, they may have figured it would never be activated. It would require a specific frequency," explained Doc. "It was designed to activate and kick back a signal on the same frequency."

"There is a chance they didn't notice it was activated then?" Trey asked.

"Oh, I know they noticed. I just imagine that most of the equipment was lightly monitored. And they would have to establish which frequency was pinged to send out a confirmation signal," Xayres said. "Since we have no idea how up to date that technology is, then maybe they were unable to ping him again. But they would have been able to calculate the approximate location of the original signal, according to Erack."

"Can we approximate the location of the original signal?" asked Kaya.

"Maybe, let's look. Based on his logs..." Xayres walked

up to the map and circled an area with a red wax pencil. "According to his notes, it puts them approximately in this area based on direction and pace."

"In his logs, Erack noted he thought he saw soldiers. So did Alex. Neither was sure where the soldiers were from or what they were doing. It looked like they were training. He felt the area had become unsafe and they needed to slip away without anyone following them. Essie then notes a severe change in the weather in the area and they started to hit the trail double time," Doc pointed out.

Xayres looked up at the map again and did some quick measurements. "With that, he was most likely pinged between here and here." He marked the map with two X's in blue, connecting them with a line. "They will have the same issue we will. Pinpointing the exact location will be difficult if not impossible. And that's where it appears we have an advantage."

"Since there is no mention of pain in the rest of the log, we assume he was back in the bunker before they managed to ping the device again," Doc said.

"That's a lot of assumptions," commented Trey.

"We understand that, but that is really all we have to go on. I would love for things to be more certain, but it's just not possible," lamented Xayres.

"Then we need a plan of action," Kaya said. "We need to evacuate and find another bunker and make sure this one gets destroyed."

D listened quietly in the open council meeting. It was more of a briefing for officers and key managers and it wasn't the first time she had been to an all-hands briefing. This was the first time they had called a briefing in the council room as they normally did them in the mess hall. Perhaps they assumed the mess hall was too public.

She decided it should be fine since she already gave her testimony in here and handled it fairly well. However, this room was much too small for a briefing this size and she felt packed inside, unable to move. This made sitting here more difficult than she had assumed, not realizing a place could have such a hold over someone. It held so many memories and it was so crowded with people.

The backlash was overwhelming. Her body started to tremble at the rush of memories again, but she knew this was not the time or place to lose her cool. Erack's life may hang in the balance. She curled her knees to her chest. Not wanting to risk a meltdown, she focused only on the words, not faces, not names. It was a trick that seemed to work for now. One she exercised often. Trying to tune in on someone specific, finding someone in the crowd proved more difficult in sorting through the mental clutter. She changed from focus to shut her brain down altogether. She regretted her choice in coming to this briefing. Why didn't she just wait for Xayres to tell her everything?

Then she heard Kaya and the words bounced around her brain until they settled and registered.

"We can't find another bunker without Erack. Are we going to the city for an antidote?" D rose to her feet suddenly focused.

"This is only a status meeting. We are not taking commentary from the floor," Trey said, banged his gavel on the table.

"But it's on the agenda right? You can't find another bunker without him," D breathed in and out slowly.

She learned the more she lost control, the more readily the voices swamped her brain. In this moment, she started to lose control. For the first time in her life, she could say she knew how everyone felt, literally. This room was too crowded for her to lose it.

"Young lady," Jaren started, then she realized who was speaking, "We are not taking comments from the floor," he sounded less confident.

She grimaced at him. Tallin was murdered and somehow he was involved. But he was very closed off and she wondered how his voice never crept into her head. Maybe it was her extreme hatred of him. Not even D knew the limitations of her abilities.

"At this time, it is not on the agenda because it would be a foolish venture," Kaya said, trying to appease her.

At the comment, the room erupted. Some agreed but many didn't. They thought to let our best chance of finding a new home die without any attempt to save him was cold and wrong. D covered her ears and shrunk back into her seat.

Trey slammed the gavel. As the room quieted, D refocused.

"But we have to try and save him. It's the right thing to do!" pleaded D.

The room erupted again and it took more time to calm it down. He was a soldier, like most of them. How could they ask for his service and then leave him for dead when it looked difficult. Finally, everyone was mostly quiet and seated again.

"It's not a feasible plan. We don't even know exactly where the city is or where we would go in the city for an antidote. Someone would have to lurk around undetected for who knows how long and there's the matter of disguise. It's just not something we think we can risk," Ra'Ella explained.

"But I would volunteer for the mission," D said.

"Which is admirable," Jaren said. "But we can't ask anyone to go on that mission. It's essentially suicide."

"So you're not even going to try and save him?" D asked, aghast.

"D, we are trying to save him," Xayres tried.

The room erupted more fiercely this time. The gavel slammed repeated. Trey's booming voice was not enough to reclaim order. Guards came in and broke up physical altercations and separated out the masses. The mob mentality was in full force.

"Clear the room! Clear the room!" Trey could finally be heard over the cacophony.

Guards shoved and guided people toward the exits.

"Not her!" Trey pointed at D. "She stays."

People tripped over one another, pushing to get through the doors. No one wanted to end up in the brig. Soon, D found herself alone in the room. The silence was eerie and deafening, especially for her.

"D, what are you doing? Are you trying to start riots?" Xayres chastised her.

"No, I am trying to be compassionate about our people. You all know he is the only one with the skills and knowledge to find another bunker," protested D.

"D, we understand he is your friend, but we have bigger issues on our plate," Kaya sympathized. "There's so much more going on here than you can see. We need to focus on the big picture."

"I understand I may not have all the information. But no one is going to survive wandering around looking for a home in the wilderness for the rest of their lives. We may as well put a big sign on everyone's back for the pictures they can take from space. 'Here we are! There are survivors even 100 years later. Come kill us all!'" D said sarcastically.

"Young lady, we understand your loyalty and love for a friend. But we have already put this to the council. To risk it is ill-advised," Ra'Ella replied.

"We don't even know if there is an antidote in the city. We can't ask anyone to take that kind of risk," explained Kaya.

"I already volunteered to take that risk," responded D.

"Anyone who knows Erack would take that risk. Hell, I would take that risk and I can't say we're even that close," Xayres said.

His gaze pierced through her. It made her uncomfortable. So far, she managed not to read any of them by accident and as Xayres made perfectly clear in earlier conversations, he didn't want her in his head. She tried to respect his wishes, despite the fact he appeared to want her in his head at this moment.

"So, you're just going to leave everyone out there to

wander, hoping to run across someone friendly like Xayres' group did?" she motioned at him in frustration.

"Of course not. Erack has given us a general direction. We will head that way and the strong will prevail," Trey said.

"The strong will prevail? The strong will prevail?" D yelled. "You're sentencing all of us to death without a second thought. The strong will prevail!"

The voices broke through like a flood bursting through a dam, slamming her down in her chair at the sheer force of it. Taking her forehead in her hands, Xayres recognized her pain immediately.

"Remand her there," said Xayres, trying to cover up her attack. "You are not to go anywhere D. That is a direct order."

Trey looked at him suspiciously. Xayres raised an eyebrow as he motioned to the guards. They walked D to the door.

"You know she will be the first person to try something," Xayres said.

Trey smiled, "Yeah, I know you're right. I just thought you two were closer than that. You did request her to be your roommate. You've spent a long time behind closed doors with her."

"She may be beautiful, but no one is touching that girl with a ten-foot pole if she has any choice in the matter. She doesn't let anyone in. I get the impression from her that it's out of sheer need to stay out of the brig that I am not dead yet," answered Xayres.

"Okay, with that assessment, we need to start the evacuation of all unnecessary personnel, families first. We have practiced for this. Now let's make it happen," Trey said, slamming his gavel. "Meeting adjourned."

FRICTION

Xayres dismissed the guards at the door of his quarters. They nodded, walking away without hesitation. As long as he was in the room, there was no need for them. He found D sulking on her bunk. The bottle of pills in her hands scared him at first until it shook as she moved.

"You should take those you know," Xayres commented, motioning to her hand.

"I have been. What? Afraid I wouldn't use them now you betrayed me," D said.

"My hell D! What was that, in there?" Xayres asked more out of frustration than needing an actual answer.

"I should ask you the same question. I thought you were Erack's friend too."

She tried to hide the fact that she was crying before he walked into the room, but her voice was weak and the words trembled out. Xayres softened. He'd never seen her this hurt over something he did and he didn't like the feeling of disappointing her. Kneeling at her bedside, he gingerly took the bottle from her hand, placing it on the desk. The extended silence was awkward. He shook his head.

"D, I was trying to be covert. Couldn't you hear all this going on up here?" He motioned to his head as if she could see him even though she wasn't looking at him.

"It doesn't work like that. At least, not yet, if it's ever supposed to," D rolled over and chucked her pillow at him. "But I also recall you telling me if it did work like that, then you didn't want me in there."

He gingerly caught the pillow, tossing it lightly to return it to her bunk, "I'm on your side D. After the meeting, I had every intention of making a plan and getting out of here tonight. But now..." He was pacing viciously across the floor, aggravation flooding back into his system. "Now we'll be lucky to get down the first corridor."

"Speak for yourself. I know people who know their way around," D hissed.

"You won't get out of this room without me though," replied Xayres.

D harrumphed at him, rolling over so her back was to him and the room. "And who's fault is that?"

"Mine," he barked.

She could be overwhelmingly frustrating. He felt bad for the situation and what he did, but she was so impossible most of the time. He couldn't help but be angry.

"But I did it for your own good, whether you believe it or not."

He waited for her comeback, but she just sat there. "You were seconds away from being tossed in the brig. Trey does not like or trust you and he knows you would be the first person to stage your own mission. Besides, this way, they are less likely to increase security since you're not out running around. And believe it or not, that alone makes it a little easier to get out of here and looks to everyone else..."

He stopped explaining. It seemed pointless. Bringing his pacing to a close, he sat down on his bunk, resting his forehead in his hands as she had done so many times. She rolled over to see if he was still there and threw her pillow at him again. He deflected it without even looking up.

"I didn't mean to screw up your plan. I really thought they would send someone. I mean, Erack's mom is on the council," D said.

Xayres looked up at her. She sat across from him, meeting his gaze. He softened again, more out of exhaustion than actual compassion. He smiled and for a moment, he thought she was returning the gesture.

"D..." he started.

"I know. But if we are going to get moving, we have to get Erack ready."

"Get Erack ready..." Xayres shook his head. "What? To come with us?"

"Of course he's coming with us," D rose to get dressed.

"What a minute! Now you're acting crazy again," Xayres also stood. "D, he's not fit to travel. The journey will kill him."

"He won't survive if he doesn't come with us," reasoned D.

"Doc has bought him a decent amount of time. He won't survive if we take him with us," he tried to get her to see reason and logic.

"Then we'll carry him," she grabbed her pack. "He has to come."

"D..." he said, changing tactics. "You cannot leave this room without me and I'm not leaving with you as long as you're in the grips of hysteria," Xayres said.

She threw her pack onto the floor. Placing her hands on her hips, she tapped her toe and looked at him impatiently. He dismissed her with a wave of his hand. Wrapping himself in his blanket, he rolled over into his bunk, feeling the full force of his exhaustion all at once. Her gaze burned into his back.

The chair made a thud as she slammed herself into it. After a moment, the legs of the chair scraped across the cement floor. He turned enough to see her, to maintain his own safety. He had learned she could be unpredictably violent when she didn't get her way. He saw her grab her pack and head for the door.

"Screw this and screw you! I am leaving right now, with or without you!" barked D.

"You won't make it very far. You've been remanded to quarters. Any officer who sees you..." said Xayres.

"I've been skulking around these corridors longer than most patrol officers. And I know most of the forgotten ones too. I spent over a year hiding from everyone," confessed D.

"I bet Erack or Doc could find you," Xayres said.

"Possibly Erack, depending on where I went. But he's not able to look, so I would be in the clear. And that's all I need to know to get out of here without being detected," D replied.

"D, it's about good, strategic planning. Erack's right, you're too impulsive. To fly by the seat of your pants when it comes to executing orders," explained Xayres.

"Ugh...more strategy. I just like to get things done," D grimaced.

"And that is why I remanded you to quarters. To protect you from..." Xayres paused, thinking, "Well...from yourself really."

"So, you're not coming with me?" D asked.

Xayres didn't respond.

"Fine!" she grabbed her pack.

"Well, I guess if you're leaving without me," Xayres motioned mockingly toward the door.

Opening it, she found two guards back on the other side, staring at her. She tossed her pack onto her bunk, folding her arms impatiently.

"I thought you were going to watch me yourself," she spat.

"That doesn't mean I didn't anticipate needing back up," Xayres smirked, shaking the transmitter in his hand. "I know you well D," he sat up again.

"AHHHHHHHH!" she stomped back to the table to sit, arms crossed, sulking again.

"That will be all gentlemen. Just be sure someone

mans the signal," Xayres called as the door closed. "So, are you ready to talk some sense now?"

"Are you prepared not to be a jerk?" she mumbled.

"Obviously, that's a no," he grumbled. "Look, I have all the time in the world until they evacuate us. Erack doesn't."

"Don't you see? That's why we have to take him with us," pleaded D. "What if the Nazis get here before we get back? Then we will never see him again. What if the medicine stops working before we get back?"

"Exactly D. What if the medicine stops working while we're out there? We'll be forced to leave him behind. Can you imagine a death alone taking care of yourself, let alone unable to defend yourself? Don't make him face that. If he's going to go, let it be with his friends and family around," he paused, watching the look on her face change to such a pained expression, he turned away. "And if the Nazis get here first, then everyone here is dead anyway. I've been through that once, remember?" He looked up again. "I'm hearing what you're saying and I'm telling you, it can't happen."

She looked at him, hard. Her brain told her he made a lot of sense. Emotionally, she didn't want Erack to suffer unnecessarily, but she worried if she left without him, she would never see him again.

"This is not the time for your stubborn selfishness. And if you want to save him, truly, sentimentality has no place here."

He watched her as she processed each piece of information. Her expression was rarely so telling but in this moment, she almost wore her heart on her sleeve.

"You need to grow up D. People will die. The best chance of saving him is to leave him here," said Xayres.

Even though she liked his reasoning and it was sound, she hated herself for it. What kind of a friend leaves a friend behind? Somehow she couldn't reconcile the idea of abandoning Erack.

"I guess you have a point. I just..." She couldn't finish for fear she would cry.

"We'll figure out how to save Erack," Xayres prodded at her bag. "I'm going to need you to stay focused if you're going to be any help."

Xayres and D worked their way around, careful to keep anyone from looking too closely. They packed rations, water, and other necessities for their mission, completing each task in silence. D's pack appeared over packed, but neither one knew how long they would be gone.

As Xayres followed D from corridor to corridor, he decided the bunker was riddled with secret passages. On their way to the med bay, D veered off course. By the time he reached the intersection, she was nowhere to be found. He went up one passage, then turned back and checked another. Kicking himself for giving her so much leeway, he found himself lost in the maze now.

Bobbing left and veering right, he tried to focus in on the noises of the people. Or the machines. Or anything that may take him to somewhere he could find D. His pack was getting heavier. The air felt thicker here as if he traveled downward into an abyss of concrete. Somehow, this place was not ventilated like the rest of the compound.

"D, come on. This isn't funny," shouting, not caring who heard him.

Being stuck down here would be worse than getting caught down here. But he felt as if he was all alone and no one came down this way, not even for maintenance. His voice only echoed as the acoustics appeared to close in on him.

"D! I'm serious! D!" he screamed.

The further he walked, the darker it became. Only certain lights worked and most of them flickered. After more walking, he found an area encased in darkness. The smell of burnt concrete and wood penetrated his nose, causing him to struggle forward.

Remembering his lighting scope, he pulled it from his hip belt and clicked it on. The light barely reflected off the walls, scorched black. Pieces of the ceiling were on the floor. The area appeared abandoned and roughly restructured for safety.

A light flickered behind him, causing him to jump and flip around. Ghosts of the past could survive here but nothing else. He shivered as the temperature slowly dropped the further he went. But he continued to work his way through the corridor.

Grabbing his mask, he tried to escape the smell of rot and burn. Why wasn't this area closed by the blast doors? He stepped on glass melted into the floor. The corridor opened to what looked like a room. Metal ceiling joists, rebar, and shards of glass and wood were strewn across the floor. Cracks in the floor caused him to step cautiously. Water was dripping somewhere in the distance, probably condensation from the cool air hitting warmer cement or pipes.

"Is this what she meant? Corridors and areas no one knows about or goes?" Xayres whispered to himself.

As he examined what was left in ruins, he surmised it used to be a lab of some sort. He couldn't tell what they would have studied. Maybe it was a chemical lab and there was some sort of chemical explosion.

He hadn't remembered reading anything about an explosion in the bunker. History was something he loved and he'd made a point to go over the history of the bunker after he first arrived. He had full access to the archives as a council member, but nothing in them suggested something like this.

He reached the edge of the room, charcoal in all directions. Searching for a door, he began working his way down the wall. Passing a blasted out window frame into a room next door, Xayres saw the remnants of the mattress and some charred pieces of paper.

Putting on his gloves on, he heaved himself carefully over the frame. Grabbing the papers off the floor, he shined his light on them. They were burnt, some more than others, but you could still see remnants of the original pages. The edges had stiffened under the weight of something colorful. He took off his glove to touch it.

"Wax?" he said as the confusion set in.

Looking more closely, he found most of the pages on the floor were drawings. Crayon drawings. Children's drawings. For a moment, he studied them. Then placed a few in his side pouch.

"What were children doing in a lab?" he asked himself.

He saw a doorway and proceeded through it into another large room. Across from the doorway was another door. It was closed. Xayres crossed to it.

"Ehhhhh!" he grunted.

The door was locked. A few kicks and the weakened frame gave way, allowing the door open. Inside, it was perfectly preserved. No fire. No blast.

It looked like family quarters. More than one room spanned off the main area. There were bunks in two of them and a double sleeper in the other. He found toys in the corner. Something seemed wrong here. Not able to figure out what, he continued to investigate.

He walked to the bunk rooms. There as some rag dolls on the beds, a teddy bear or two, pillows at the brink of decay and blankets rotting on top. But nothing that seemed out of the ordinary. He went to the master room. The bed seemed in good order. There were some trinkets on the shelves. He spotted a picture in a frame.

Moving in, he choked down the surprise at the photograph. It was D, much younger, but definitely her. He grabbed it and placed it in his pack. Out of the corner of his eye, in the far corner of the room under the shelves, he saw something...odd. He turned and knelt to get a closer look. It was a wrench. Putting his glove back on, he squeezed under the shelf to reach it. Feeling it on his fingertips, it fell over, clanking onto the floor. The sound echoed over and over until it cleared its way out of the room.

Putting his foot on it, it scraped across the floor until he could get a hand on it. Rusty, he turned it over. Some of the rust had chipped away in his attempt to get it out of its hiding place. He sniffed it. Not smelling of rusty metal, he sniffed again. This was familiar but he couldn't place the smell.

Taking it with him, he stood up and looked around the room. On impulse, he walked to the bed, tearing off the blanket. Dust flew everywhere, but he had already put on his mask. The flecks of dust danced in his light. Then he turned it to the bed. Large spots of brownish red were on the mattress and sheet below. He smelled them. Dried blood. That was the familiar smell. When he took his turn in the kitchens as a teen, he smelled it, every day for weeks. He gasped without thinking, choking on the lack of air that responded in his mask.

He backed up, running into the door frame. Turning, he pushed through the door, wiping the cobwebs he was normally so careful to avoid, out of his face. He ran for the door, thinking it was the only way out. He ended up back in the charcoal room. Turning, he shined the light in the direction he came. This was a separate exit but from where? He cautiously walked back through, realizing there was a secret doorway in the master room. Activating it by accident during his panic had taken him back to the beginning, in the lab.

As he worked his way back, he checked the walls for more secret doors. A light flickered. He jumped, dropping the light. Luckily it didn't shatter on impact. He grabbed his light and saw a brown trail on the floor. Stepping back hastily, almost knocking his head on the frame of the door.

Reaching to pick up the light. Shining it on the floor. The trail went up the short corridor to the lab but stopped at the door frame. It looked wiped clean. A hastily done job. He checked the floor in the room and saw no other signs of blood.

"What happened here?" he whispered.

The light flickered ahead of him. His feeling changed from curiosity to dread. Something inside him was urging him to leave this place.

He strode toward the flickering lights, making his way out of the rubble and into the open corridors. Stumbling over himself, he couldn't get away fast enough. He felt something in there he couldn't explain and while it was more than just the cold, it spun his head into a haze. It felt like hours before he emerged someplace familiar.

Walking into the med bay still lost in a haze and forgetting what he was carrying, a bloody wrench didn't scream sanity for him. People eyed him carefully as he made his way to Doc's office. In the private med room to the side of the office, he saw D, helping Erack sit up so he could eat.

"Very funny D," Xayres barked raising his hand.

She turned. Her eyes widened at the sight of him, raising a wrench at her.

"Z," she called him that to annoy him, but it didn't elicit a response. "I'm sorry. I swear it will never happen again."

She backed away with her hands raised. Xayres slowed his pace.

"Hey, don't hurt her okay? I've got my hand on the button here buddy," Erack tried to sound forceful but it came out barely louder than a whisper.

Xayres stopped, suddenly and acutely aware of what he must look like to others. Doc grabbed his arm and pulled him into her office. Forcing him to sit, she removed the wrench from his hand.

"Umm...sooo...what's new with you?" she attempted casual conversation. "And where did this come from?" She asked, raising the wrench.

"I don't know," he replied, barely louder than a whisper, still stunned.

"Okay, so you may be in shock," she said, setting the wrench down and moving around her desk to lift his legs into the recovery position.

"Xayres, where did this come from?" she persisted, putting her hand on the wrench.

"I don't know," he grumbled again.

Doc examined the wrench. Her eyes widened at the sight of blood.

"Did you hit someone with this? Xayres, this is important," she pressed, her voice sterner.

"No...no...it needs to be tested," he turned to face her, grabbing the wrench but her hand was in the way. "It needs to be tested."

She gently loosened his grip on her hand, "Tested for what Xayres?"

He began to come out of his haze. "Tested for what? Tested for what?" he whispered to himself, searching desperately for the answer. "For blood!"

"I can already tell you this is covered in blood, and hair, and possibly brain tissue," Doc replied in a matter of fact tone. "Looking more closely, this is old. So what else can I test for?"

Xayres struggled with his thoughts. "Fingerprints. Blood type. Anything else you can find."

"I will, as soon as you tell me where you got this," she pushed.

"From the burned room," he said.

D stepped into the doorway. Both were so engrossed, neither noticed her. Something flickered in her mind's eye. It was involuntary but she immediately felt as if she was violating someone's personal space and pushed it away.

142

She read his pain and confusion in Xayres' eyes as if he knew things but wasn't sure what he should say. He couldn't put it into words. For a moment, she felt it in the pit of her stomach. She felt bad for him and wanted to end his struggle.

"The burned room?" questioned Doc. "Where is that? Do you mean the burning room?"

In that shared glance, D and Xayres connected in a way she had yet to experience. It was overwhelming and debilitating, almost as if she couldn't control her own thoughts. She jumped into his head and raced through his experience, saw the room and the wrench. She inhaled accidentally releasing a loud whistle. Doc looked at her.

"From the explosion in the lab. He found it in there," D said.

Doc looked at her. Then back at Xayres. He looked relieved. She took another big, deep breath in, closing her eyes, breaking the connection. Now she panicked. She had broken her promise to him. Invading his mind was the one thing he made her promise not to do. Her eyelids fluttered and when they found a resting place, she saw him give her a weak smile.

"The lab...where your parents died D?" Doc asked.

"I think so," answered D, breathlessly.

Doc walked between them, causing D to step back. Neither was aware D had moved in so close to Xayres. Doc took Xayres by the shoulders, bending over so their eyes were level, partially examining him, partially concerned.

"Xayres, how did you get in there? That wing has been sealed for at least a decade," Doc asked, gritting her teeth.

"I don't know," he mumbled.

PREPARED

"I promise. Tonight I won't try and shake you. I need you out there anyway," D said.

Xayres repacked his bag, pulling things out, refolding and organizing. Butterflies fluttered in his gut as he thought about his lack of training and how long they would be topside looking for the city. Forcing himself to be honest, he knew they barely survived the first time. Stumbling upon D was a blessing in disguise. He shuffled things around again. D's back was turned when he pulled out the frame. eyeing it like poison, he buried it back inside before she could turn around.

"I still don't understand where you ended up. And that bloody wrench. Then again, anyone could have known about that maze and hidden it in there. But no one here has been bludgeoned to death, at least not in my lifetime," D carried on the conversation, knowing the silence felt awkward.

"I wouldn't be too sure of that," Xayres mumbled to himself.

"What was that Z? Do you think it could be really old?" asked D.

Xayres grumbled loudly at the nickname. She smiled because his response was instant gratification for her. He changed the subject.

"Look, if we're doing this thing together, you have to quit calling me Z. I hate it," he barked.

She turned, squaring up to him, looking him in the eye. It didn't work this time and she wasn't sure why, but she saw he was more pained than annoyed.

"I don't understand. I thought you wanted us to get along. Isn't a nickname a sign we're friends?" she smirked.

"I just don't like it. Not that nickname. Can you think of something else?" Xayres asked.

"But I like it. It's easy and fun," she persisted, chuckling.

He burst. "It's what Juliette used to call me. She called me Z as she told me to leave so she could blow herself up in the bunker alone."

D looked shocked, frozen in the moment. She stammered but couldn't come up with a response. The silence extended until Xayres pulled the zipper on his bag closed.

"Who's Juliette?" she choked, feeling his sorrow.

"We were supposed to be married. I mean, I wasn't in love with her or anything. But we were very good friends and we had grown fond of one another," answered Xayres softly.

"I'm sorry Xayres. I didn't know." D lamented.

"Of course you didn't know. Because there is no one in your world but you!" he barked back.

"Look, I don't mean to be selfish. I just haven't had a roommate since...well...before my parents died. Obviously, I don't have a family...or friends really. I'm the only person I have ever had to worry about. That doesn't mean I like me this way," she slapped her hand over her mouth.

It was like word vomit, pouring out of her. The intense amounts of honesty she found herself confiding in him. It unnerved her. She kept people at a distance on purpose and he was just there, sucking all her secrets out of her.

Their close proximity caused walls to drop and internal

censoring to disarm itself. Neither could control it. She had revealed more to him than she had ever wanted anyone to know. But it somehow built a kinship between them. No secrets. When she looked at him, she could tell from the look on his face he felt the same.

"Doc said it's because of our brains. You know. Working off one another," Xayres said, hoping the facts would help them feel better.

"Doesn't mean I have to like it," she mumbled from behind her hand.

She heaved her pack onto her back. Xayres sat down to tie his boots, avoiding her gaze. He attempted to keep everything he found earlier to himself. But he found it more difficult the longer they were together. Perhaps it would be better if it came out while they were out there. *She won't kill me if she needs me...right?* he asked himself.

They sneaked out after the call for general quarters lights out. The evacuation hadn't started yet and they knew they would need to be careful. Winding their way through the dimmed 'night time' lighting, Xayres growled when he found she had brought him just outside the med bay again. She winked at him and went inside. When he finally decided to follow, he found her trying to coax Erack out of bed.

"D, I thought we agreed on this?" Xayres groaned.

"What saddens me most about this situation is that you've known her for this long and you thought you actually won the argument," Erack managed to choke out with a chuckle, followed by an uncontrollable coughing fit.

"He's right you know," Doc said through a yawn.

They turned at the sound of her voice. "We were umm..." D started.

"Save it D. I knew you two would make it out here sooner or later," she strode toward them, pulling something off the shelf as she walked. "You're going to need this. It's all the reports on the poison and the device and samples of the anti-toxin that is working, his blood samples and the poison itself. Try to keep it in this ice chest so it doesn't spoil."

D released Erack, crossing the room to accept the chest. It was heavy, but she didn't open it to look inside.

"And there is enough anti-toxin for him to come with us, I assume," stated D.

Doc looked shocked then she shook her head.

"I already told her it's a bad idea and I'm not going with her if she insists on this madness," Xayres said.

"D, you don't want to doom him to die alone. You can't care for him and yourselves out there," reasoned Doc. "Keeping him in this state takes a staff of five going 24 hours a day. You guys can't risk that."

"Your mistake here folks is you think she's going to see reason and go 'okay, you're right,'" Erack stated. "She won't see reason. So I will make it easy for you. D, if you try to take me with you, I won't allow any anti-toxin to go with us. Then I will die and there will be no reason for you to go."

D's jaw dropped, eyes wide. Doc looked amused. Xayres looked confused.

"But why would you..." Xayres asked.

"With her, you have to fight her flame with an amount of water that will extinguish it in one shot," explained Erack. "I don't have the luxury to play around right now."

"You wouldn't do that," D huffed. "You couldn't do that."

"D, I will most likely die one way or the other. This mission has little chance to succeed. And if I'm going to die, I want to be surrounded by people I know. Not stranded in the middle of nowhere. That's my choice and you have no right to take it away," Erack said.

D could not find a solid argument against him, which infuriated her. *He's being so unreasonable*, she thought.

"But you know all the codes and more of the access

points than me. We'll never get out of here without you," D stated triumphantly.

"Yeah, I figured you'd say that. That's why I planned too," Erack coughed and choked. Doc rushed to help him

As if by magic, a young man walked from the family room on the other side of the bay. He was no more than 15 and looked barely old enough to train. D blinked. She knew him from somewhere but couldn't remember. The shock of Erack's declaration was still muddling her brain a little.

When he stepped into the light, she gasped. He looked like his brother, slender, dark-haired and handsome. You almost couldn't tell they weren't biologically related.

"Benji. Why would you send Benji with us?" D asked.

"Who are you?" Xayres asked.

"I'm Erack's brother," Benji said.

"But I thought Erack was an escapist," replied Xayres.

"He was adopted by my parents. They couldn't seem to produce a child on their own. I was their surprise a few years later." Benji smiled, taking Xayres arm to shake it.

"He's not going with you. He's getting you out of the bunker. Then you're on your own," Erack said.

"But...but..." D stood dumbfounded.

"D, we've come up with a compromise," Benji said.

She had to trust Benji. He'd never lied to her and he was willing to risk everything to help them. Knowing he had Erack's best interest at heart soothed her for the moment.

"I don't know if I am interested in a compromise Benji," replied D.

"Well, since I'm the brother and you're just the friend, I get to have the final say. Not even you can argue with that," Benji said.

"I'm not sure..." commented D.

"Trust me D. I would never steer you wrong," Benji said.

This had better be a damned good plan B, she thought.

She leaned against Erack's bed and folded her arms.

"I've got the codes and the skills so I will get you out of here. Since they've already called for an evacuation, I will make sure Erack gets to the rendezvous point. That's my job as his family," Benji explained.

D held back the tears. She couldn't argue with him and there was no way she could go against Erack's wishes. "Okay, if this is the only option, it will work," D said with a smile.

The faces in the room contorted with immense surprise and confusion. She laughed. Doc was the first to recover, whispering tersely to herself as she walked back over to the supply cupboard.

"I requisitioned caffeine shots to help you move quicker and some other things you may find useful," she began pulling things out of the cupboard. "So, you take all this."

She dropped it all into D's pack. Then she knelt down and rummaged through it for a moment, pulling out a stack of rations. Setting the extra rations on the counter, she eyed Xayres, Erack, and Benji talking behind her in hushed tones. D grimaced at her. Doc smiled at her.

"Now that we've settled the important parts," Doc walked over to the intercom. "I need you, for that thing we discussed earlier today. It's time."

Moments later, the door opened and a red-headed young woman walked into the room. She wore a green uniform of some kind and had a pack on her back.

"You won't need these for him," Doc said handing the rations on the counter to the girl who promptly stored them in her pack. "This is Annika. She has helped me with all my research on this poison and she is going with you."

D looked her up and down, sizing up her training.

"In a former life, she was trained in topside survival. So she shouldn't slow you down too much. She can keep an eye on your caffeine use and when you get to the city, she knows what to look for to find the antidote." explained Doc.

D frowned. Erack groaned and rolled back into a comfortable position. His conversation with Benji and Xayres had concluded.

"Annika, this is D and Xayres. Benji here will help you get out of the compound undetected. Then the three of you will head for the city," she paused, waiting for greetings or something. "Well...good luck. You better get headed before anyone else realizes any of you are missing."

Doc stretched and yawned, walking back to the door of her office, switching off the lights in the room as she exited. Taking that as a cue to leave, they filed out into the corridors.

"We only have six hours until dawn," Xayres whispered.

"Let's get on with it then," D said.

"We're waiting for the guard to pass us on his rounds," Benji said.

"Rounds?" Xayres asked.

"Yeah, they started security rounds after D's outburst," Benji and Xayres both glared at her in disapproval. "They should be by in a few minutes, according to Erack."

"You've been spying or he's been teaching?" D asked.

"He's teaching. Has been for a long time. You know, so no one else knows. He said you never know when you need someone to back you up," answered Benji.

"Guess that worked in our favor," Annika mumbled.

She hadn't said a word since the beginning of the mission and she appeared to resent the idea of the mission. D felt she would never trust this woman, no matter what Doc claimed.

They hushed at the sound of boot steps coming down the hall. Benji watched. When the coast was clear, they hurried out the main med bay doors toward their escape.

Benji wound them through the bunker quickly. As they turned the last corner, they came to a dead end. D slid down to her knees, pulling her bag behind her. She started to work on the grate near the floor.

"What the..." Xayres started as Benji pulled him down into the hall and out of sight.

"The fan runs in one-hour intervals. Thirty minutes on. Thirty minutes off. We don't have much time," Benji explained.

"Why this way?" Annika asked.

"It's the least patrolled," answered Benji.

"How do you...never mind," Xayres frowned, shaking his head.

D removed the last screw. Holding her other hand against it to keep it from falling. When she tried to pull it off the wall it didn't budge.

"Xayres, come here," she ordered.

In a moment, they were both trying to wiggle the grate free. The time was ticking too fast. Benji started to panic while Annika seemed passive.

"We have to find another way," Xayres said.

"There isn't time," said D.

Xayres grabbed her wrist just as the grate clattered to the floor. They jumped. Annika screamed at the noise while Benji shook his head.

"There's no way someone didn't hear that," Benji lamented.

"Then we need to hurry," D said, climbing into the opening. "Come on!"

Xayres followed her through and signaled to the others. Benji grabbed the grate as he was the last one through. Just as he placed it in the grooves, more marching echoed off the walls. Benji held up his hands to signal silence. While the patrol was in the hall, they couldn't go any further. He eyed the fan at the end of the shaft with dread. Getting stuck in this tunnel on either side of that fan would not turn out in their favor.

"We don't have time for this," Xayres whispered.

All Benji had to do was turn his head and Xayres knew

now was not the time to speak. They heard murmuring. They listened for another few minutes.

Click. Click. Click. D looked at them in horror. The gears of the fan were warming up.

"RUN!" she yelled, grabbing Xayres by the arm, dragging him with her.

Benji and Annika were not far behind. If they didn't make it, they were dead. Their feet pounded down the tunnel. Anyone under them would have heard it. Or maybe they would mistake it for the fan gearing up. Sounds like these usually indicated a malfunction but no one would believe that if the fan started normally.

"We need to stop the fan from starting on time," Benji yelled.

Most of the time, these tunnels were so loud, people had to wear special equipment on their ears for protection.

At the statement, Xayres dug into his side pocket as he ran. "D!" he yelled, placing something in her hand.

Her feet never missed a beat. Her fingers were agile around the utility tool, sorting through the different ends to find the one she wanted. The clicking sped up. As they closed in on the fan, it became harder to hear one another. She approached the blades, jamming the tool into the frame. Crossing to safety on the other side, she kept working her way down the tunnel. Benji hopped through the blades just as they clicked into motion.

Xayres helped Annika through before crossing himself. As he stepped through, a blade rushed toward his head. He ducked instinctively. The fan stopped short of his forehead, stuck on the utility tool. He opted to abandon his tool and shifted into high gear to catch up with the others.

He found them with D, removing another grate. She was much less careful about noise this time, flinging things at a rapid pace in all directions.

The fan squealed, stuck but fighting it. It sounded like nails running down a chalkboard but at a higher pitch. D resisted the urge to grab her ears as the others were lucky enough to have their hands free. Once that blade freed itself, it was only a matter of time before the fan sucked them back in, cutting them to ribbons.

"Come on D!" Benji persisted.

"Not helping. Let me concentrate," D screamed over the cacophony.

"Now D!" Xayres yelled back.

"I'm trying," she screamed back without looking, trying to keep her focus on the grate.

The squealing turned to pounding as the fan worked at the tool.

"Anytime now D," Annika's anxious tone almost caused her to turn.

She had all the screws out but she couldn't seem to get the grate out of the grooves again.

"What's the problem D?" Xayres asked.

"They've reinforced it from the other side. How in the world did they know?" replied D.

"Because they don't trust you!" Benji shouted near her ear.

This caused her to pause. She hadn't noticed both he and Xayres move in closer. For a moment, they all forgot what they were doing.

"I thought you knew," Benji said.

"Grate now. Explain later!" Xayres pressed.

"We don't have time for this," Annika shouted, pulling them back to the task at hand.

Xayres, Benji, and D slipped their fingers into the grate.

"On three!" said Xayres. "One. Two. Three."

They all yanked and noticed the grate was beginning to give way. Then they repeated the process again and again. On the fourth try, the grate came loose. She tossed it aside, it didn't matter if they found their escape route.

Annika appeared frozen in fear. They called and waved

at her but she refused to move. Xayres picked her up, placing her on the other side of the opening. D followed with Benji and they carried her further down the tube.

The pounding changed to metal cracking metal. Xayres assumed the fan was finally breaking under the strain. He ducked down to crawl through the opening. He heard a thudding sound. Pieces of the fan were breaking away with violent force. Looking up to see how big the piece was, he saw his utility tool.

"Huh, guess you're coming with me anyway," he said.

He heard the whoosh of the fan as it swung into operation. Slipping through the opening, he slid the tool into his pocket again.

They approached the access panel with caution. The electronic locks made it difficult for them to get out without anyone noticing. And if they wanted to get out, they couldn't let anyone notice. Security could lock down the facility the moment they knew it was tampered with and that would end this mission.

Benji pushed passed them, pulling equipment from his bag. He plugged the device into the panel next to the door.

"What are you doing?" asked Xayres.

"We have to get into the main interface to fool it into thinking the door is still closed. If we don't, this door will slam shut and not open again until this place is swarming with security," answered Benji.

"Where'd you get all the fancy equipment?" asked D.

"Where do you think?" Benji chuckled.

"Where would he get the equipment?" Xayres asked.

"I guess that is a question you can ask him at the rendezvous point," replied Benji.

"One day, I have to figure out Doc's secret code to getting you guys to answer questions," Xayres said.

"Got it!" Benji exclaimed triumphantly.

The latch released. For a moment, they all held their breath. No alarm. No flashing lights. Now they knew they were home free.

They pushed their packs through and followed. Benji helped Annika with her things and then hoisted her through the opening.

"See you on the flip side," Benji said, pulling the access door closed.

BETRAYAL

Fall rains barely slowed them down. D was beginning to fear the addictive properties of caffeine. She noticed she needed it more often and in slightly larger doses. But they couldn't risk not using it.

Stumbling upon the soldiers turned out to be a lucky break. They were able to track them back into the direction of the city until it started to rain. This saved them scouting time. Finally, they could see tall buildings on the horizon.

It had only been a few days since they left and at this pace, they would reach the city within a day. Resting seemed like an idea on the back burner, except for Annika, who refused to use caffeine and often found herself behind them. She was the only thing slowing their pace. But she needed to be free and clear. To run tests and to ween them off the caffeine injections required her to be clear minded. If she was addicted too, it would do them all a disservice.

And now Annika insisted they stop and eat. D took the medical chest and checked its contents as she did every time they stopped. Looking at them comforted her somehow. Gave her hope Erack would be okay. Careful not to break the ice pack or the vials, she turned each one, clearly labeled. Then she placed it back in her pack.

"D," Xayres said, startling her. "Can I ask you a question?"

She turned to him, "You just did."

"You know what I mean," he paused.

"Do I?" D teased.

Xayres proceeded with caution. "You don't have to answer if you don't want to. I was just wondering. What did your parents do? You know, for work."

She looked him up and down before answering, knowing if he really wanted the answer, all he had to do was ask one more time and it would come out by accident. "They were scientists. I don't know what kind," she answered.

"How did they die?" he asked.

"Now that's two questions," she joked, but he could tell she was uncomfortable.

"D, how did they die?" he pressed carefully.

She swallowed hard. He saw her uneasiness in the question.

"In an explosion. The whole wing of the bunker took damage. After they managed to extinguish the fires, they dragged out their bodies. I never saw that. I was too young," D teared up for a moment, choking it back down forcefully.

"I know it must be hard to talk about," sympathized Xayres. "My...She..." he couldn't start without the words suffocating him.

"It gets easier. Never easy, but easier," D empathized, putting her hand on his should. "And even though it gets easier, it still hurts."

"How long has it been?" he choked.

She deflected the question. "Aren't we supposed to be resting and eating?"

"In theory," Xayres said.

"But I can't turn my brain off," they said in unison causing awkward silence. They smiled uncomfortably at one another.

"Is it just me or is this thing starting to get a little

weird?" asked D.

"Unfortunately, a little," replied Xayres. "It wasn't exactly what I had in mind when I decided to study you."

D rolled her eyes at him. *This is all his fault, isn't it?* she asked herself. The conversation died for a while as they ate their rations. D finished first and started packing up her supplies.

"So your parents were scientists?" Annika asked.

"What's it to you?" asked D.

"Just making conversation. Xayres seemed really interested. That's all," Annika answered.

"I was just curious. I lost someone close to me too. That's all," Xayres said. "I didn't mean to strike a nerve."

"You didn't," D pointed at Annika, nodded and shoved food in her mouth.

"If you never saw the bodies, then how do you know how they died?" Annika asked.

D swallowed hard, grimacing at Annika, "Because it's what they told me," D said.

"Who?" asked Xayres.

"The council. They told me there was an explosion and about half a dozen scientists died in the lab. My parents were among those people," explained D. "Can we find another topic please?"

"Just a few more questions," Xayres said, looking at her like a puppy dog.

"Fine, but if I choose not to answer, you have to leave it alone," D said, knowing he would eventually get the information he wanted anyway.

"Who else had family that died in the explosion?" he asked.

"I really don't know. Never met any of them," D answered, her mouth full. "All were separate funerals and to be honest, I could barely make it through my parent's funeral. So I didn't attend any of the others."

"Do you regret not being able to say goodbye in a more

personal way?" asked Annika.

I don't think so. It was hard enough as it was and I was really young." replied D. "Seriously, we now need to find another topic."

"Not just yet D," begged Xayres. "Please."

She sighed and rolled her eyes. Knowing he was persistent meant she really didn't have a choice. Part of her hated him for it because he chose the most awkward times to bring up these things. But she wished she could figure out his new fascination with her parent's death. Knowing the root of it would allow her to be more effective in shutting it down.

"Why weren't you there that day?" asked Xayres.

D sighed, "Somebody showed up. I never got to see who. They told me to go hang out with Erack. I figured it was top secret stuff which wasn't unusual. It wasn't uncommon for them to send me away in those instances." She replied.

"Did you hear a voice?" asked Xayres.

"No, why?" answered D.

"Then how did you know someone was there?" Annika asked.

"The door chime," D replied. "Or maybe someone knocked. I don't really remember much before they told me about my parents."

She looked at Xayres but he would not meet her gaze.

"Do you know something?" asked D.

"Did anything else seem odd or off? You know, to you," pressed Xayres.

"Not at the time. But as I've gotten older and thought about it, it does feel like there are missing pieces. Like things didn't really line up. It felt unclear. The Shrinker said the more you analyze something, the more you make out of it and since I felt guilty for surviving, then it was probably just that," explained D. "Why? Do you know something I don't?"

"So you feel guilty for surviving?" interjected Annika.

"Not really. I never really did," D stopped, pensive. "I know that sounds cold, but I was young. I don't know if I truly understood what it meant to survive. And now, well, it's too late to feel guilty. I just wish I knew more."

"Knew more how?" Xayres probed skeptically. "Like details of how they died or what?"

"Just more of the circumstances. The council just told me there was an explosion and my parents were dead. No mention of really anyone else or how it started or if our quarters were involved in the blast. Just unanswered questions," explained D.

"You see, that's the tricky thing," Xayres started. "I make a point to know the history of those around me. You've probably noticed." D grimaced at the idea, showing she understood. He continued, "I've been studying the archives and they don't say anything about an explosion. I don't mean just around the time your parents died. I mean, I've gone back at least fifty years and there is nothing in the archives about an explosion. I would think something like an explosion would warrant more than a tiny note. That's a big, important event. Don't you think?"

"I would think so," Annika answered.

"What does all this have to do with my parent's death?" D asked.

"Because they couldn't have died in an explosion. At least not one that happened in the bunker or it would be in the official history D," Xayres watched her carefully, waiting for a reaction. "If they couldn't have died in an explosion, then how did they die?"

"I don't know. Maybe the explosion was small and it was part of some other accident of some kind," answered D.

"But what accident. There is no mention of a destroyed lab in the histories either. It leads me to only one conclusion," he stepped closer to her, trying to brace her for the information. "I think your parents were murdered and someone on the council was involved somehow and covered it up."

The look on her face went from annoyance to shock. She stood up, looking at Xayres in a vicious way.

"Stop it! You weren't there! How would you know..." She almost shouted.

Xayres looked at her, pain written all over his face. His intention wasn't to hurt her but how could she hold on so tightly to these ideas someone else put in her head. Especially from a group of people she knew didn't trust her.

"It's the wrench. That's where I found the wrench." Xayres stated.

D looked at him ferociously. Roughly packing up her things, she took off toward the city.

Xayres scrambled. "D, it's not safe..." But she was already gone.

He saw her inject herself and knew she wasn't stopping. He hastily finished throwing things in his pack, forgetting Annika, who followed as quickly as she could. By the time they were keeping pace, she was little more than a moving dot ahead of them.

"What was that about?" Annika panted.

"I pushed too hard. She's just sensitive," replied Xayres through each breath.

"Wow! Can she move or what?" struggled Annika.

"Shut up and focus on moving!" Xayres replied, annoyed.

D was not the only one who noticed Annika hadn't kept up her training which caused additional slowing.

The buildings grew in size quickly as they raced through the outskirts. For a moment, Xayres thought D was angry enough to charge into the open streets in broad daylight. Then he saw her veer off in the distance. It took him the better part of an hour to catch her. He found her inside a cave. Her cheeks wet with sweat and her eyes puffy. She tried to hide it from him. But he managed to find her faster than she anticipated. He knelt down next to her.

"I'm sorry to drag all this up D," Xayres tried. "But I was there, in the lab. I saw things."

"No one can get in there. It's been closed up for years. They fixed the structure the best they could and they sealed it up," she shouted.

"D, we are too close to the city," Xayres scolded, panting.

Grabbing his bag, he dug into it. Allowing her a moment to collect herself. He grumbled, pulling things out and setting them on the stone floor. When it was empty, he cursed and kicked it.

"I can't believe I lost it!" He stood up and paced, running his hands through his hair.

"Lost what?" asked D.

Then he remembered the pictures in his pocket. Yanking them out, he turned to show her. She fingered them gingerly.

"Is this what you lost?" she asked, taking them from him.

"No, he lost this."

Annika finally found them. Xayres saw the frame in her hand. Eyes wide, he looked at her suspiciously.

"Why did you go through my things?" he asked.

"Sorry, Xayres. I was just following orders," she turned it so D could see the picture in her hand. "This D. He wanted to show you this."

"Where did...How did..." D's mouth hung open, unable to connect a thought to her lips.

"Because he went prying in places he shouldn't have. And unfortunately, I am supposed to make this entire issue go away. Which would have been much easier if you had just left it all alone," Annika sounded annoyed. "Or if you succumbed to the elements as I was trying to make you do."

D's eyes widened. Before she could move, a black figure appeared behind Annika, knocking her out in front of them. More rushed into the cave, catching them off guard enough to bind their wrists. They taped their mouths and shoved their heads into black hoods.

LAST MESSAGE

Benji ran into the council room, forcing the doors open. He was out of breath from running too hard. Trey harrumphed in surprised as the young man grabbed his knees to recover.

"Glad I caught you," Benji said.

"How is your brother?" Kaya asked.

Benji raised his hand to signal giving him a moment. "The toxin started to replicate again. Doc is trying some new anti-toxins to see if she can slow down its progress. He has been well enough to do some calculations for the evacuation," he replied between breaths.

"So what exactly is your rush sir?" Trey asked.

He held up a piece of paper. From across the room, they could see it had writing.

"Well, don't just stand there. Bring it here," ordered Trey as he snapped.

The young man walked up and handed the slip to him. Trey read it over, handing it to Kaya and then the council member on his left.

"It's a coded message, sir. From Xayres and D," Benji said as he stepped back.

Trey scowled for a moment. Then he pulled out the appropriate key and they began to decipher it.

"Thank you, young man," Kaya said. "You are

dismissed."

"Please, I want to know their progress. We all know why they left and where they're headed. So I can take it back to my brother. Please," begged Benji. "He has a right to know their progress."

"Fine, you may stay for the report. But this is top secret confidential information. We expect you won't discuss it with anyone but your brother," Ra'Ella said.

"Understood," Benji stood silently at attention.

Kaya rose and grabbed a blue wax pencil. "They ran into a Nazi camp in this area here."

She marked it with an X circling it. Then stepped back looking at the map. It still had all the wax markings from the earlier discussion about Erack's tracker.

"Further north and closer than we assumed they would be," she continued.

The man to Trey's left stood up with a green pencil. "They said they were attempting to divert them here. Hopefully, they were successful. If they were, it should buy us another day or two," he said, drawing arrows.

"We need to speed up our evacuation efforts," Ra'Ella said. "Do we want to bring Jaren back into the fold? We could use all the experience we can get. He handled the evacuation of our bunker."

While Trey grumbled and mumbled at the idea, the other council members looked at one another, unsure how to respond. Why would they need to reinstate him? But she was right. He would not share this information unless he was on the council.

"In a limited capacity," replied Kaya reluctantly. "I could not in good conscious allow more than that."

"Yes, in a limited capacity. I would never ask for a full reinstatement after all that's happened," Ra'Ella said.

"It's settled then. We will quicken our evacuation efforts. Prepare for the destruction of the bunker. Someone start transmitting the archives," Trey ordered.

Kaya grabbed Ra'Ella by the arm, pulling her close.

"Ra'Ella, keep Jaren under control. You two seem to have a close relationship. Makes sure he doesn't get us all killed," Kaya whispered.

They dismissed Benji before continuing the discussion. Benji returned to his quarters, grabbing two bags he'd stowed under his bunk and raced through the hallways.

The lights now flashed red with a monotone voice repeating the status change. "Evacuation level three. All hands prepare to evacuate. Prepare for bunker destruction. All unnecessary personnel and families to evacuation points immediately. Follow all orders and instructions given by officers."

For a moment, Benji stared at the papers in his hands. He knew how to copy things decently well, but would these actually fool someone with a lot of experience. Everyone in the communications room thought it was odd he insisted on delivering the last message, but he could find no other way to steal a sheet of official letterhead on which to forge his fake orders.

Looking at the clock, he took a deep breath. They were quickly losing time. He ran to the med bay to evacuate Erack. If he didn't get him out like he promised D he would, she would never forgive him. Now he needed to get him to the rendezvous point. As he approached the med bay, he had it all planned out in his head. He had his orders and they looked legitimate. All he needed was to tell Erack what was happening with D and Xayres and get him ready to go.

What he hadn't told him, even after they talked for an hour, was Xayres asked him to do a very large favor. Xayres needed all the written archives and the written personal logs of all the council members. They would be transmitted and then destroyed. The transmissions could be tampered with and information could be changed. It was a big chore and considered treason and Benji knew he needed Erack's help to get them.

"Xayres asked you to do what?" Erack whispered tersely.

Benji explained again. "And it's restricted, but you have access and I need it. I feel like I'm using the sick kid. Man, I hate that he asked me."

"And why did he ask you?" Erack asked.

Benji bit his lip. Erack recognized how uncomfortable he was with all of this. Xayres was asking him to do a lot and he had never even trained yet.

"He said he couldn't trust anyone else, not even Doc," Benji choked a little. "And she's his cousin. He said there was something fishy going on and it had to do with D's parents. But he knew the bunker would be blown up with all the evidence. So he needed this stuff to make it out so he could figure it out."

"D's parents?" Erack asked confused. "This makes no sense."

"He said if you doubted it, to tell you it involves the wrench. It sounds like he is playing some sort of detective game," Benji smiled.

"The wrench?" For a moment, Erack looked confused. Then the light went on, "The wrench."

"So that means something to you?" asked Benji.

"It sure does. Help me up and get me dressed. I will help but with the elevated alert, it won't be easy and we're going to have to be careful. We'll take what we can," Erack said.

"It will be a lot to carry," Benji replied.

"Not as much as you think," Erack explained. "Now I know the time frame we are looking for, we won't need everything."

Benji sucked in hard, "What about the transmission?"

The shock hit Erack too. They sat and thought for a moment.

"We'll just take the volumes we need to the

communications room if they aren't already there and make sure they get transferred. Then if they disappear, no one will notice in the chaos," Benji said.

"Yep, that's my little brother. The genius in training."

He ruffled Benji's hair for a moment. Then Benji pulled his clothes from the cupboard. Doc walked in, eyeing them apprehensively.

"Now what are you two boys up to?" she asked.

"I've been ordered to prepare him for evacuation," Benji lied and cleared his throat, holding out his paper. "They know it will take him...I mean, us longer to get there. So he needs to leave right away."

She took the paper from his hand, inspecting it closely.

"Well, these all look in order. How can I help?" Doc asked.

"Can you teach me how to administer the medicine? Oh," he gave her a weak half smile, "And help me with his pants."

CAPTURED

She pulled off the black hood and immediately began loosening the rope around her ankles. Forgetting about the tape and gag, she struggled against the knots until her feet slipped out. Her feet felt cold, she noticed they removed her boots. Looking around, she rose and stretched, nursing her wounds carefully. Then she set to work untying Xayres, who appeared unconscious. She hoped he was playing possum. When she managed to remove his hood, she saw a big gash swelling on his forehead.

Gingerly fingering the goose egg, she took the hood and pressed it against the wound to stop the bleeding. Looking around, trying to see through the darkness. The silence allowed the white noise to whip around in her ears. She heard someone else struggling, drawing her attention back to the gag and tape on her own face. Breathing in deep, she gripped the edge with her fingers and ripped it off.

"Ahh!" Her skin stung.

While tending to Xayres, she took in all she could. She heard water dripping or trickling somewhere. The smell was damp and musty. She guessed they were back underground. The cold concrete had some cracks, chips, and divots from wear. There was little more she could surmise in the darkness.

Xayres groaned and grabbed his head but managed to grab her hand instead. For a moment, the touch was awkward. Then she pulled back, leaving him holding the black bag. Shaking his head made him verbally wince.

"Where are we?" he groaned again. "What happened?"

"Taken by surprise, outside the city, possibly because I gave away our position when I yelled at you. Sorry," she said.

"It's not your fault," he coughed. "I'm the one who got us distracted. And that damned Annika. What the hell was that? Following orders? Whose orders? She's the one who kept us from getting out of there," replied Xayres with a weak smile.

She helped him sit up and scoot to the wall. Leaning up against it, he took stock of his injuries.

"So, how did you get that?" she touched his goose egg, causing him to wince again.

"Fought back too hard I guess. Something hit me. Don't really remember much after that," Xayres answered, removing her hand.

They paused, again in awkward silence. He released her hand quickly. She desperately grasped for something to say to break the silence.

"We traveled for approximately an hour on bumpy terrain, I think," she began her report. "I imagine we were outside the city. Then for about ten minutes on concrete, at least, I am assuming it was concrete. Then there was a squeaky door and we got dumped in here," she paused and he nodded for her to continue. "There is water near here, running somehow and I can hear a hum, like electricity. I think we're in the city somewhere."

"Then I guess we achieved our first objective," he mumbled. "Why do I feel so shaky?"

"That's the caffeine withdrawal. I am having a difficult time focusing myself. We need to get help," D said. "But we have to get out of here first."

"That withdrawal will kill you before you get out of here," D heard Annika laugh from across the room. "If they leave you alone, you'll be dead soon enough."

D moved toward her voice carefully as she felt ahead of

her with her hands, they came in contact with metal. Metal bars. Like the brig. Annika's labored breathing came from the other side.

"Yes, they separated us. Apparently, they noticed we weren't getting along," Annika's voice was snakelike. "But I guess, either way, my job is done. Sorry, your mission didn't prove more fruitful."

"Why are you doing this? Whose orders are you following?" asked D.

Annika laughed again. D didn't like her laugh any more than she liked the woman herself. "Now I can't tell you that. You're just as nosy as him and we all know his nosiness got you into this mess in the first place. Frankly, it will be easier for me to be rid of you anyway. No more coddling you," Annika replied.

"Why is everyone always coddling me?" questioned D, more to herself and in aggravation than an actual question.

"Because I was supposed to get more out of you before making you both disappear," Annika's attitude was clear. "It is obvious to me after our conversation you know more than you're telling. Maybe you don't know what you know. But you know," Annika said.

"I can't run in circles like that. I don't know how you haven't exhausted yourself already," D snarled.

"SILENCE!" A voice boomed into the room, bouncing off the walls.

All of them covered their ears, wincing at the pain. The voice vibrated the bars, causing them to hum.

"I guess we're not supposed to talk to one another," D sneered. "I hope they kill you first."

"SILENCE!" the voice reverberated around the room a second time.

D gave a thumbs up signal to show her compliance, working her way to the wall next to Xayres. Sitting down, she tried to recover her senses. The overwhelming pain caused Xayres to throw up a little. Their good fortune was all he had eaten were rations. So it didn't smell too badly.

The humming increased. Something was charging.

Then the lights kicked on. They were so bright, no one could see beyond the light bearing down on them. D blinked hoping her eyes would adjust as they watered uncontrollably. Xayres coughed. Although she could hear him more clearly now, she couldn't see him through the spots in her eyes.

She pinched her eyes closed. Covered her ears in case the booming voice returned, curling up into a ball. Xayres laid the side of his head on his knees. And they waited in the cold, dank room to be executed.

Hearing the hinges again, she tried to focus on the noise. Not sure if she was looking in the right direction because of the echoes. She yelped at the pain. Hearing steps echo, she braced herself for more brutality. Someone yanked her upward to her feet. Then they tugged at her, turning her slowly, pulling on her clothes. It took a few minutes before she realized they were cutting them off. Then they threw her back toward the floor.

The cold sting of the ground permeated throughout her body. Her skin covered in goosebumps, she began to shiver. Suddenly, she was acutely aware she was naked in the same room as Xayres and maybe he was naked too. The thought made her blush, warming her face for a moment. She hoped they would turn off the lights because no one had seen her naked. She hadn't even looked at herself naked.

The door opened again. She tried to cover herself but had no idea how effective she was. Then she heard the water, not trickling, but a hard spray. Xayres yelped and cursed. A spray hit her, causing her head to slam back into the wall. It was ice cold. They continued to spray her off, half drowning her. Then the water turned off and she heard the door close again. *What form of torture is this?* she thought.

After listening for a moment, she realized she heard the water trickling in the drain pipe in the middle of the room. But before she could try and find it, the door opened again and she was pelted with fabric.

Blinking her eyes, attempting to get them to focus, she felt the fabric. It was coarse and scratchy, but if she could find a way to wrap it around herself, she felt she had a chance. She found what she thought were armholes, a hole for her head and a hood. So she maneuvered it on and curled back into a ball, still shivering from the water.

Memorizing the direction of the sounds in her head, she began to formulate an escape plan. Then the door opened and someone pulled her arm to help her stand. Trying to fight them off, her resistance was met with a fist to her gut, knocking the wind out of her, followed by a slap in the face.

"Don't fight D. They'll just put you through more torture if you do. Save yourself from all that extra pain," Xayres said weakly.

"SILENCE!" the voice boomed, causing her to recoil from the sound.

She heard Xayres whimper at the noise. The injury to his head made that voice even louder and more painful. Assuming his pain and torture would continue if she continued, she stopped fighting and allowed them to drag her out of the room.

After pulling her for a small distance, she heard door hinges creak open. They dropped her into a chair and someone shackled her to it. Her eyes didn't have time to adjust during the walk. They just watered with the changing saturation of light. Bright lights stung her eyes in this room too.

"Where am I?" she grumbled.

After receiving no answer, she sat looking at her feet, trying to bring her dirty toenails into focus. Her throat was too dry for words to flow smoothly. The white noise creeping in slowly. She tried to focus on just one voice. The one that sounded the most important.

Whispers rang through her ears as she squeezed her eyes closed. She breathed deep, slowing her heart rate. Knowing that focus would give her a better chance to control her skills, she could possibly save herself. At the very least, she wanted an answer to her question.

She heard creaking and footsteps. Someone was giving orders. But it was like her ears were spinning around the room. The volume of the voices raised and lowered sporadically, making them difficult to decipher.

Realizing she was alone in the room, she surmised she was successfully hearing a conversation in another room. But what other room? Where was it located? Was it close to her? Then with some random words, she discovered they were watching her from an observation room.

"Turn off the lights," she gurgled.

"Silence!" the same voice boomed and echoed in this room as the other one, telling her this was the same person.

Why was he the only one speaking? Drilling her toes into the floor, causing mild pain helped her focus more clearly. Now she could see blurry figures and hear noises. Trying to tune it all in like an antenna on a television, she dug her toes into the concrete floor harder, feeling one snap.

Her toe cracked again. Biting her bottom lip to keep from crying out, the pain served to clarify her skills. Now there was less swirling noise and the images were coming in more clearly. *If I break another, it may bring more focus*, she thought. But she had to bite down so hard to hide her whimpers, it didn't take long before she was tasting blood.

The combination appeared to do the trick. For a moment, she saw a clear flash and then there was another and another. It was disorienting, like watching a strobe light fly past her eyes. But the voices were strong. And images were more clearly defined. What she saw confused her. Her brain rejected it over and over. Finally, the blood and the pain was too much. She released and before she could stop herself, the words flooded through her lips.

"Tallin has fire red hair?" she choked out loudly.

Then silence. Not so much in the room but in her head followed by an overwhelming feeling of panic. *Did she see us despite the lights?* not her thoughts. *How can she know who may be here?* still not her thoughts. Now they were invading, pushing through and she couldn't stop them.

"What did you say?" the voice asked.

"Tallin has fire red hair," she croaked.

The room went dark. She looked up letting her eyes adjust. No windows. No cracks under doors. Nothing to allow her to take in her surroundings. She now felt cold, which added to the quelling pain. Musty concrete and smells of moss filled her nose. All had a taste of metal from her bleeding lip.

She heard the door open, but no light came into the room. Unable to establish where the sound came from, she decided to ignore it. She felt a presence behind her. Her ears couldn't tune into their thoughts or even their breathing.

Suddenly, she felt woozy. Stomach acid slowly climbed up her throat. Horrified by the reaction, she swallowed down hard. The burning rose again. Why was she woozy? This must be a reaction to her forcing her gifts to the surface. This was the first time she had effectively managed them at all.

The spinning began. Slamming her feet into the ground, trying to root herself, she knew she was not physically spinning. Then the pain in her head caused her to forget the burning in her throat. This felt familiar like she had seen it before.

Pulsing pain radiated across her forehead and around down her neck and her spine, dissipating in the shuddering pain in her foot. She gripped the chair with her hands. It was cold. Longing to lay on the floor, she tried to rock the chair. Someone caught it and held it still. How long had they been there? The brightness and the darkness and the lack of noise were exacerbating every little detail she tried to focus on, making it overwhelming.

Feeling hands on the top of her head, she tried to speak. Her mouth filled with acid and she immediately snapped it shut to keep it from escaping. Not able to clasp her hands over her lips, a little dribbled out the corners, her lips stinging from the flow.

A pressure was lifted off her shoulders and her forehead. When she opened her eyes again, she saw a dim light. When she turned her ears, the sound of water had returned. She heard the person behind her breathing. The smells changed, less musty and more like wet grass and flowers.

She was able to crane her head and see the concrete walls. Suddenly she was reminded of being underground. But something told her she wasn't. Something clanked to the ground next to her chair. Turning her head, she saw a strange helmet by her feet.

Breath grazed over her ear. Bracing herself for a loud sound, she scrunched as best she could to get away.

"How did you know what color my hair is?" the voice was even in tone and almost pleasant in the level of volume.

She turned her head as far as she could, just enough to see him out of the corner of her eye. But when she opened her mouth, all the acids spewed out instead of words. The spinning slowed and her stomach calmed down immediately following the release.

"Ugh," the voice muttered something incoherently.

"Sorry," she whimpered, trying to wipe her mouth on the scratchy covering.

"You're bleeding," said the man.

He carefully stepped around the contents of her stomach and motioned for someone to come in and help. D saw the mirror behind his shoulder.

"What did you do?" he asked.

She took the opportunity to run her tongue over her lips, realizing she had cut right through them. He grabbed a rag from his pocket and held it to her wound. Swerving away from his grip because she couldn't swipe at him.

He laughed. She scowled, the motion causing her stomach to lurch. Trying to suck in air, she coughed uncontrollably. Backing up, watching her closely, he didn't want to get hit by anything she may emit. Spitting blood on the floor, missing his boot by inches, he raised an eyebrow at her.

"Water," she scratched through her vocal cords.

The door swung open. A woman rushed inside toward her mess on the floor, cleaning it with vigor. Swinging open again, D recognized the medical symbol on his bag. He was here to help her.

"Water," she hissed.

Pulling a metal flask from the med bag, he knelt to the other side of her. Dumbfounded because she wouldn't take it when he presented it, Tallin pointed to her shackles. Nodding, the medic placed one hand under her chin to tilt her head and slowly dripped water into her mouth. Every time she swallowed too fast, she found herself gurgling and choking.

"So little girl. Tell me. How do you know who I am?" the man asked, glowering at her.

As her head cleared with the liquid, so did her eyes. His red hair looked ablaze glowing in the light. She wondered how it came to be that color.

"She really needs stitches for this cut. Probably only one or two," the medic told him.

"I'll be fine," she hissed, throat still burning. "What is that thing?" She eyed the helmet on the floor.

"I've no time for your questions. Now you tell me what I want to know and maybe, you'll save your companions," said the red-head.

"Don't care about them," she spat.

"Should we test that idea?" he snapped his fingers.

Again, the creaking door echoed across the room. She wondered how they kept this place a secret with all the squealing hinges. They kicked Xayres in front of her, fully bound and in the black hood.

"You need him alive and I know it," D replied.

"D now is not the time to taunt our captors," Xayres shouted hoarsely.

"He's not an enemy. He's Jaren's brother," she smirked and tried to fold her arms, but only tugged on shackles.

"This guy isn't going to hurt us. He'll help us because his colony needs us more than we need him."

"You sound very assured at that fact," the man said. "What makes you so confident?" He leaned into her.

"If you wanted us dead, you've had plenty of chances to kill us," she started, staring him down. "But you're curious. How did we get here? Where did we come from? Why did we come? Those answers are important to you to protect yourselves."

"Then you're spies," said the man.

"If you truly thought that, we'd be dead already. You recognize we're here because we need something," D's volume slowly rose. "So if I'm a spy and I tell you, then you'll kill me anyway. There no way to prove I'm not a spy, except what is actually in my pack," she paused to catch her breath and clear blood from her mouth again. "But quite frankly, I am running out of time. So I don't care what happens to anyone else as long as I finish my mission."

She stood, shackles unlocked, swinging them at the red-haired man and the medic. Her blow landed on the medic's forehead. He fell backward, hitting his head on the floor, heaving all the air out of his lungs. Pivoting on her good foot, she swung in the other direction.

"How..." the man said while ducking under the swinging shackles.

"Never underestimate..." He heard her start but missed the rest as the shackles slammed against his ear. "A determined soldier. I. Am. Not. Someone. You. Mess. With!"

He heard the shackles swinging around again. His hands covered the injury reflexively. She moved clumsily to avoid a counter attack. He backed away, holding up both hands in surrender.

"Untie him!" she ordered.

"Now, just because I resigned doesn't mean you give orders," he chuckled. "Look around you. You're in a foreign place and for all you know, you're in the heart of my stronghold. There is no out for you. Not even for the two of you together."

"Jaren was right. You're a cold-hearted ass. At least you're true to form," responded D.

"My brother is the cold-hearted one. He would sell out our own mother to save his hiney," he said.

"Now is no time to argue. Guys, let's work together," pleaded Xayres. "We can work together now and kill each other later."

"Work together?" the man asked.

"Yes. She needs your help as much as you need hers." Xayres said.

"Shut up Xayres!" D shouted.

"You knocked out my medic. You owe me and I say he gets to finish," the man said, careful to keep his distance.

She attempted to step. Looking down, her hands were covered in blood. The price she paid for her freedom. The red-head saw and blanched. Dropping to her knees, the metal shackles clanked on the ground. Voices echoed and the ceiling spun.

UNDERGROUND

The haze lifted. D was relieved she didn't pass out because she was able to partly listen and take in her surroundings would help her get out of this place. But she still had a difficult time processing all the outside stimuli. Two voices, familiar voices, were in the room with her.

The table was cold and a light breeze blew through the room. Her burlap sack was replaced by a soft thin gown. It smelled unprocessed, fresh. *How did these people get fresh air underground?* she asked herself.

Fresh air. She missed fresh air. Taking in heaps of it, she reminisced about her training on the surface. Breathing in felt irregular. A weight pressed on her nose. She tried to shake it off, but it stayed in place. Like the helmet they managed to get her head in and out of, this felt restrictive.

Pushing herself upward, every muscle ached in protest. She groaned, drawing attention to herself. While Xayres appeared on her left, the red-head appeared on her right. This had to be some sort of trick. *They're good at this*, she mused to herself.

"I see you're...well...moving. I would say awake but you never actually slept," Xayres said.

He appeared twitchy, shaky, like he was unwell. D did her best to look him up and down, to establish he was

Xayres. The voice was correct and the stature, but his posture too relaxed, shoulders hunched. Placing his hand on the small of her back, helping to support and steady her, "Careful."

She snorted.

"Caffeine withdrawal and massive blood loss is nothing to scoff at," said the red-head.

"Wouldn't have lost so much blood if you would've just let me go as I asked," she mumbled.

"You're right. She's a feisty one," the red-head said, looking at Xayres. "I imagine your recovery will be much slower than hers due to sheer force of will."

"Why would I lie Tallin? The last thing I want is for anyone else to be caught unawares of her level of pain in the ass-ness," Xayres chuckled.

"Nice," she groaned, glaring at him.

"D, Tallin," he turned her head in the other direction. "Tallin, D."

"Tallin is dead," she tried to keep herself from slouching. "But you do fit the description."

"Yeah, Xayres told me," the red-haired Tallin said.

"Dear hell, how long have I been in here?" she uttered in exasperation.

"Eh, like a day or so," Xayres said. "I'm still recovering from the caffeine withdrawal. Doc didn't tell us too much combined with an abrupt halt of use could actually kill us."

"Seeing as how she sent someone to kill us anyway..." D replied, her tone laced with sadness. "They taught us the possible side effects in training. I knew the risks."

"And you didn't share them with me? You let me take that stuff knowing it might kill me?" Xayres pressed.

"Oh shut up!" exclaimed D.

She grabbed her forehead. The pain had all but subsided. Every pulse was like a shock to her system. All this talk of death and side effects and this stranger was making her uneasy. Trying to pull it all together was too difficult right now.

"I'm not sure this Doc person is the one who gave the order," Tallin said.

"And how would you know that?" D asked.

"The same way you figured out who I am," Tallin smiled at her.

"What?" her response was breathy.

"Well, we've had some time to talk," Xayres coyly replied. "He gave me a tour and tons of information about him and the inner city resistance. So, I told him about, you know, the thing," Xayres motioned around her head.

"How in the world..." she slapped Xayres' hand away. "You trust too easily," she scolded.

"You should be nicer," he scolded back. "He took the samples and their guy says this is a common poison used by the Nazis, but is much older than anything they have seen. Right now, he's trying to come up with an antidote from the other versions they have. He was excited about the possibilities of a vaccine."

"Or he's modifying it to make it contagious," D said.

"Wow! Caked in cynicism too. This one is a real firecracker, isn't she?" Tallin awed.

"You're hair is a firecracker," she retorted.

"I see why you like her Xayres. She never backs down," Tallin laughed heartily.

"Just get out. Both of you," she commanded.

They shrugged at one another. The second Xayres removed his hand from her back, she slumped backward. Unable to stabilize herself, she rolled back down clumsily.

Aren't they just two peas in a pod, she thought.

"No, we just have a mutual understanding," Tallin threw over his shoulder. "And he's still recovering from caffeine withdrawal," he turned around. "Causes bad judgment. Your wrists should give you proof of that."

"When can we get that antidote and head back? We are running out of time," she asked wearily, lifting her arms to look at her wrists.

Much to her dismay, Tallin just waved her off. Turning around, he helped Xayres to the door.

"You're right. She never stops..." she heard Tallin start again.

She slapped her hands down at her sides.

"He was right. You should be careful."

Turning her head, she saw a man. Assuming he was the doctor, she turned back to stare at the ceiling.

"Don't you guys have any blankets around here?" she whined at him, recoiling at the sound of her own voice.

"You're actually under three of them. You feel cold because of the withdrawal and the blood loss," he answered.

"Okay. How long can I expect to be cold?" she asked.

"Depends on your body chemistry. You're actually recovering more quickly than I thought you would. And much more quickly than your counterpart. I'm surprised Xayres is walking around," he replied, walking out of the room.

She was stuck in the medical facility for at least two days, but if she was honest with herself, she lost count. The stay had swayed her opinion of being in enemy hands. Why would they get her healthy just to send her to a slave camp and kill her. No Nazi would waste resources on her. It would be tantamount to sacrilege. Biding her time, using her pain to her advantage, she secretly honed her new extra sensory abilities. No matter where she was or who these people were, she needed to become good at harnessing her powers to help her bunker.

Tallin sat in a chair next to her bed, asking her questions and having her relay information. She was careful what she released as this was a trade. Her only reason for agreeing was so she could ask whatever she wanted and he had to answer her.

"It's my turn to ask questions today Tallin, if that is

your real name," she eyed him suspiciously and he could not tell if the look was fake or genuine.

"Fine, what do you want to know?" Tallin grumbled.

"I want to know how you came to be here," she said.

He raised an eyebrow at her, just as Xayres had done so many times. The two of them had become so close while she was stuck in this bed. The two of them together annoyed her but he appeared to keep Xayres in a good mood so she usually just suffered through the emotion. But now Tallin was starting to remind her of Xayres and that had to stop.

"Just tell me," she insisted, trying to prop herself up.

"Can't you read it?" he asked motioning to D's head.

"I'm not that talented yet," she replied.

"Fine, then I'll tell you the old fashioned way," Tallin sighed. "It all started when I was 14."

"Wow, with the way you say that, you must be ancient," she mused.

"Do you want to know or not?" Tallin barked.

These were difficult memories for him to dig up and he didn't do this for just anyone.

"When I was 14, my older brother Jaren was supposed to leave the bunker and travel to a new one, as a fail safe for communication. He didn't want to go. So he petitioned to have me sent instead. The council refused. But I was starting to show signs of being different, up here," he pointed to his forehead, "And people noticed. I scared them because they didn't understand. Since the bunker Jaren was supposed to travel to was yours with Doc and all her brain studies and technology, my father negotiated with the council to change their mind and send me.

I was devastated and didn't want to go. It was unfair and I felt like my brother had acted like a coward allowing all of this to happen. He is a coward. He'd sell out his own brother to maintain his comfort. So, they packed my bag, gave me some coordinates and dropped me off topside. The first week was rough. We didn't have topside training, me especially. They'd been prepping my brother and the timeline didn't change just because I wasn't ready. I had to figure most of it out for myself.

When I arrived at the coordinates, no one was there. I figure I had gotten there too late and my brother had finally gotten his wish. He always wanted me exiled. Never trusted me. He said I was too different to fit in and didn't deserve to be there."

"That's sounds...vaguely familiar," D said.

"Anyway," Tallin sounded annoyed, glaring at her for the interruption. "I didn't really know what to do. So I just stayed near the ruins for a while. I had no interest in keeping track of time. Then, one day, someone arrived, but it wasn't your bunker. He was an escapist. He'd managed to escape from a slave camp with about a dozen others, most of which were dead already.

They tried to stay with the resistance but they were too easily tracked, causing the destruction of the base on the other side of the city. They exiled him for it. Now he was stuck wandering the wilderness. We spent a lot of time talking, knowing once we went our separate ways, we would probably not have anyone to talk to for a long time."

"What was his name?" D asked.

"Who's name?" Tallin asked confused.

"The guy that showed up. What was his name?" she asked again.

"Raynjure. He wanted somewhere to hide and I wanted somewhere to go. I liked it topside anyway. Much better than a stuffy bunker. So, we exchanged information. If he ever got picked up, he'd pretend to be me and I would go into the city and stay with the resistance. Seemed like a fair trade to me. So we did it," he finished talking, leaning back in the chair casually.

"And you never knew if he got picked up by a bunker?" D asked.

"Not until you came along, knowing what my hair color was," replied Tallin.

"You can thank your brother for that. He said Raynjure was a traitor. I guess it would look that way if I look at it from his perspective," commented D.

"If there is a traitor from our bunker, I guarantee it's my brother. He's weak and gullible. And he values his life over all others in every situation," Tallin said.

"How can you be so sure?" pressed D.

Tallin wouldn't answer. He'd just called his brother a traitor and he believed he was too. They sat in silence for a long time while they contemplated the weight of his statement.

"How did Raynjure die?" Tallin asked timidly.

"He was poisoned and if what you say is true, Jaren killed him and made it look like suicide to make himself look more innocent," D said softly, seeing the pain in his eyes as she told him.

"And he said I was the one who couldn't be trusted," muttered Tallin.

"I guess I don't need more proof I can trust you then," replied D. "Because I knew Jaren was the traitor all along. All I wanted to know is who was helping him."

"So those skills are more developed than you allow anyone to see," Tallin reasoned.

"I didn't know it was a skill. My preference is to acknowledge I am more in tune. Makes me feel...less different," D lamented.

INTERRUPTED

When D finally got word she was being released, she marched straight for the research doctor's office, after getting lost for a few hours trying to find her own way around the compound.

"Hey doctor. I'm just here for an update," she smiled sweetly.

"You realize this is not the only thing I am working on right?" he asked.

"But it should be," her grin faded to a grimace.

He watched her for a moment and realized this was not an argument he needed. And she wasn't much for compromising.

"Okay, here is what I know so far. This is a much earlier strain than the ones we have previously encountered. I'm surprised it's not more degraded but that works out in our favor. I have made some variants of the antigen and have begun testing their effectiveness on the blood samples. Here," He moved her over to another table, "I will check these in the next hour or so and figure out which direction to go. We are close. I would say two maybe three days."

"No. Faster," D said sternly.

He glared at her.

"So hopefully two maybe three days but not more than

five?" D clarified.

"I would say that's an accurate rehashing of what I just said. But I cannot guarantee anything and I still think we need to test it further to possibly develop a vaccine. We could give it to everyone," the doctor replied.

"We don't have time for you to test a vaccine," Xayres said from the doorway.

The doctor sighed. Now it was two against one.

"You don't have to be here for me to test it. But I can't guarantee I'll have enough to test if you leave with the antigen. Once it's replicated, it starts to disintegrate with every replication," explained the doctor.

"So you want the original antigen and to give us a weaker strain. I'm not sure I can accept that. Unless you can guarantee the effectiveness of the weaker antigen. But according to you, you can't guarantee anything. So I vote no on that plan," D stated.

"But just think of all the people we can save with this. I think I am looking at the original strain. They designed this to exterminate people. I'm surprised they didn't try to make it contagious," the doctor tried to get her to see reason. "Nothing says the second round of replicated antigen will be less effective. It takes many more replications for it to become benign. Your friend could still survive pending the damage was not too great."

"How long will it take you to get to the second round of replication. And why are you replicating replications? Why can't you just use a smaller sample of the original to replicate it. Then the original sample will last longer and the antigen will be more effective as a vaccine," Xayres reasoned.

"You obviously have not..." the doctor instinctively started into his own tirade, but stopped to consider what he said.

"There, I may have a point. With that, we need enough antigen for our man in two days. We don't have any more time than that. See to it that you make it happen," Xayres commanded before disappearing out of the doorway.

Leaving the med bay without saying goodbye, she barely noticed Xayres trailing behind her. Tallin had asked her to train with him to develop more abilities. She didn't see the harm in it and started training before they released her from the hospital wing. Pulling out her map, she followed Tallin's directions to his quarters.

Xayres had taken to following her around a lot lately. If he were truthful, it was probably jealousy more than protection that drove him to this. Tallin hadn't asked him to train. But he told himself some of the training sessions seemed dangerous and D was too eager. In fact, she was so eager to improve her control, she would have followed a Nazi claiming they could help her.

She approached Tallin's quarters, knocking on the door. Xayres watched closely as Tallin guided her inside. He slipped in while they were occupied, closing the door without being noticed. D had already changed into a nightdress and Tallin had set up a bed in the main area of his quarters.

"What in the world..." Xayres asked out loud.

Both were shocked. D turned and scowled for a moment, followed by a strange empathy Xayres couldn't understand.

"Why are you...How did you..." D started but found herself shy in this awkward situation.

"Are you two...well, you know? Tallin, I thought you were married?" Xayres said.

"He is," Tallin's wife came from the cooking unit. She had a vial of a green colored liquid.

"Hey D, you need to come over here. This stuff is sick and crazy," Xayres said.

His command knocked D's shyness right out of her. She walked toward him, taking him by the arm, pulling him closer to the door.

"We're training. He's teaching me how to hone this thing," she said motioning to her head. "Then we can use what I can do to find everyone new place to live," D explained.

"Not to worry Xayres. It's perfectly safe," Tallin said.

"And how would you know?" Xayres asked.

"Because this is what I do," Tallin's wife replied. "Tallin took very well to this and it has helped to hone his abilities. So, we assumed D would benefit from it as well."

"And you are?" Xayres asked, looking her up and down.

"You can call me Lee. That's what all my friends call me anyway. I was born without a name," she introduced herself, holding her arm out to shake his.

"And what makes you qualified?" Xayres continued his interrogation.

"Both of my parents were Nazi scientists. They tossed me away for my eye and skin color. Dominant genes be damned," she replied. "They didn't bother naming me because you don't get a name until you are determined to be the master race. People simply can't be bothered. The resistance discovered me and my superior intellect has assisted them on many occasions."

"You're a Nazi?" Xayres could hardly fathom let alone ask.

"No, I am a resistance fighter. I hate what my parents did and what other parents do. They are not parents," replied Lee, finding it difficult to control her tone.

Lee started to shake, so upset at the idea. Tallin rushed to calm her down. He ran his hands through her hair, holding her upright.

"She has an amazing ability to focus and problem solve. She is a great scientist and her skills would have been lost to being murdered by some wild animal or dying because it was too cold if it wasn't for the resistance," Tallin insisted.

Xayres raised an eyebrow at them, uncertain what to

believe at this point. Secret training, Nazi's on the inside on purpose, the city resistance with no ties to the bunkers. It all sounded troubling.

"We are training. You can stay if you want to see," D said as Tallin glowered, shaking his head, implying he wanted him to say no.

"Yep, I'm staying right here. I want to see this training." Xayres said, folding his arms, smirking at Tallin's disapproval.

"That's fine but you must keep your distance," Lee said.

"I'll do whatever it takes to protect her. That's my new mission," Xayres said nodding proudly.

"And who exactly gave you this new mission?" D scoffed.

"I did and as your superior, either you agree to allow it or you are coming with me right now," his eyes narrowed as he assessed their reactions. "Tallin wouldn't dare try to step between an officer and their commander as I am sure his resistance force here wouldn't want to think their own commander could fall into a pattern of mutinous behavior."

D only glared at him but they both knew she would comply.

Xayres gently touched her elbow, "Besides, I kinda promised Erack I'd keep a close eye on you. Keep you from doing anything stupid. And honestly, that kid is so smart, he could find a way to kill me for breaking that promise," he whispered into her ear.

She unnecessarily jerked her arm out of his grip. Then she walked back to the table, looking at Tallin.

"Fine!" Tallin replied indignantly. "Sit over there." He motioned to a seat across the room.

"Have you ever had a dose of this stuff D?" Xayres asked, moving to his seat.

"No, this is the first time. They recommended it to help with the deep sleep cognition or something like that," D replied.

"I assure you it's safe," Lee tried.

"I'll be the judge of that. If you know all you claim to, you would know everyone's body and brain chemistry is different. Even if there are similar traits," Xayres preached.

"I do understand that. But her chemistry is very similar to Tallin and yourself," answered Lee.

"So you've scanned her then?" Xayres continued the inquiry.

"Nothing can be proven one hundred percent. But we have done all we can to minimize the risks," Tallin said.

"Knock it off Xayres. I have agreed to do this. That's all that matters," D said.

"Okay," Xayres sat down and stayed quiet as they prepared her.

First, they gave her a sleeping shot. Lee said they needed to wait at least 20 minutes to administer the green booster liquid. This would ensure she would enter R.E.M. sleep. Xayres watched and waited patiently, even pushing them to wait a little longer before giving it to her.

For about ten minutes, she seemed fine. But then she started to groan and moan a little.

"This was perfectly normal. Tallin had a similar reaction. She'll be fine," Lee said.

Xayres felt differently. For some reason, he was a little unhinged. Uncomfortable. He rose and started to pace, startling Lee. One of her assistants entered the room with some paperwork. As Lee began to read it, D let out a blood-curdling scream.

NIGHTMARES

D was already nervous about the new level of training. Xayres sneaking in just made it worse. Now every time she tried to relax, she couldn't. She never wanted a sleeping shot more than right now. She expected it to take as long as it usually did to kick in, but in moments, the world started to spin behind her eyelids. Her stomach lurched. *Not again*, she thought.

When her world ceased to spin, she found herself in a bunker, staring at the control room. There was movement everywhere but she wasn't in the middle of it. It was as if she wasn't inside the control room, but on the outside looking in from somewhere high. Panic coursed through her. The eyes would not move. Who was she seeing the world through today? She scoured the faces to see who was in the control room. To verify what she could take away.

Lights flashed but no alarm sounded. The color signified a black alert, a silent evacuation. She was almost certain she saw Trey. No other council members appeared present. It seemed odd Doc was not transmitting her medical information from the control room. Ra'Ella had been placed in charge of communications when they realized Erack had been tracked. She had experienced evacuation twice and they thought she could handle it better. But the thought of her filled D with dread.

The images began to blur. She was shifting. Trying to hold onto the images, the world spun more fiercely this time, defying her every intention. The more she fought the shift, the harder it became. Then her head pushed against her, radiating pain down her spine. So intense, before she could control it, she released a blood-curdling scream.

She breathed in deep, attempting to relax, allowing the shift to happen almost seamlessly. Her nose told her she was topside in some wilderness. Who was this now? Was she a Nazi? Was she an escapist? The head responded to a name too distorted for her ears to make out.

Tripping awkwardly, this person weren't trained in topside procedures. Anyone trained would be able to watch all angles, including the ground. Looking back, she saw it, through their eyes. A dead child, one from the bunker, shot there, left to bleed out and be ravaged by wild animals. From the looks of it, the animals may have already started.

D recognized the girl or at least the person who tripped over her did. They must've run into a Nazi search party. The images began to blur again. Not because she was losing the image, but this person was crying. Fear overwhelmed her and she found it difficult to keep herself stable. Her body trembled.

She heard the weak voice again. The head turned. Someone else was on the ground, trying weakly to turn over.

"It's okay Benji," the voice whispered.

D shot up, breathing in sharply, wide awake and alert.

"Erack!" she screamed.

The drugs hadn't worn off. Her body felt woozy and tired but her brain was working. She tried to grab for her journal but found her reactions stunted. Opening her mouth, trying to speak, everything was in agonizing slow motion. No voice came out. Panic rising as her body refused to respond. Her brain was awake but her body clearly was not. She forgot about training, fishing in her brain for what experiment she signed up for.

Shuffling steps seemed to come from far away. Trying to turn in their direction, to open her eyes. She needed to see. She needed to slow down her breathing. She was failing...

"Hey D. They told me you would be out for a few more hours. What's up?" she recognized Xayres' voice.

She tried to make words but all she could do is croak.

"Just relax. You don't want to hurt yourself. Allow your body to finish resting and we'll talk soon," Xayres helped her lie down. Her breathing slowed. Stroking her hair, she drifted back into a restful state.

Now she saw a red-haired young man, crying in the wilderness. Assuming it was Tallin, she wondered how she managed to penetrate his defenses if he was so trained. Then she shifted again, slowly this time. Now she saw kids, young ones, scared, cold and alone. Her heart ached for them, tossed into the wilderness without a thought for their survival.

Then, there was only one again. This was a moment she couldn't understand. Parents never sent out one single child for recovery. Most were aware they survived better together.

Without warning, the pain returned. She tried to breath through it but her mind shifted erratically from scene to scene. She couldn't grasp anything she was watching or stay long enough to clarify it. Some in the bunker. Some in the wilderness. Places she didn't recognize. It was such a jumble, she could feel her head pounding. Her heart rate shot up over and over with every passing scene. The world spun out of her control. Lungs tightening. She slashed at her neck expecting to find hands cutting her circulation but found nothing.

She tried to scream. Opening her mouth but emitting no sound. Then she was restrained. Something had her arms. Attempting to shake loose, she whipped her body from side to side. Or at least she tried. Every action she took was met with no actual physical action. Paralyzed.

Every inch of her kicked up in fight or flight. She tried to force her legs to kick but they wouldn't. Signaling her arms, her eyes, her neck, her hands, her mouth. Nothing. No sound. No movement. No hope. She was going to die, paralyzed and alone. Defenseless.

What felt like anguished minutes of torture came to a swift end as her eyes flipped open. She saw Xayres, holding down her arm. Wheezing, flailing and screaming, the volume amped up in a millisecond. She was acutely aware she was out of control but unable to achieve the control she needed.

"D calm down. It's just a dream. Calm down!" Tallin tried to top her screaming while holding down her other arm.

Lee and three of her assistants held D's legs and midsection to keep her from throwing herself off the table.

"D, stop screaming," Xayres looked her deep in the eyes

Then he chanced releasing one arm to tap her on the chin. The subliminal message worked. She closed her mouth and the screaming stopped. Afterward, the struggle began to subside. She started to feel aching in her limbs and back, certain of bruising. When she stopped thrashing long enough to control her breathing, everyone released her. Her body hurt from head to toe.

"What the hell was that Tallin? I thought you said this was safe! How dare you..." Xayres had Tallin by the collar up against the wall.

Lee dared to interrupt, "She had an adverse reaction to waking up early. It fired the wrong transmitters in her brain," she placed her hand on Xayres shoulder.

Xayres reacted by launching her backward. Lee stumbled before her butt plopped onto the floor. Tallin scowled.

"She will be fine," Tallin choked. "The training and evaluation led us to believe she was more green."

Tallin forced Xayres' hand off his shirt, pushing him away. Rushing to Lee's side, he helped her to her feet.

Xayres spun around, "Before you guarantee someone is safe, you better make damn sure you know the history."

He rushed to D, cradling her head gently, running his hand through her hair.

"It's okay D," he whispered. "It will be okay."

While D's ears and eyes were working, nothing else was responding. Her head was pounding. His actions sent an awkward sensation through her and pushed itself throughout the room. It was clear he cared for her a great deal more than he ever expressed.

"We'll leave you be. I'm sorry Xayres," Lee said, pulling Tallin from toward the door.

"Do us a favor and let us know when you're done...with whatever," Tallin's anger and disdain seeping into every word, but allowing Lee to drag him.

D sat up. Her eyes still blurry and head still dizzy, throbbing at her temples. Xayres fetched her water from Tallin's stash. Her throat hurt as she swallowed every last drop, wincing.

"Clothes..." she garbled.

"You want me to get them," stammered Xayres. "Or help you?"

This was the most vulnerable D had ever felt. This dream was nothing like the others. It hurt. Thinking about it pushed the panic back into her chest.

Xayres heard her start to wheeze again. He placed his hands on her shoulders.

"It's okay D," he whispered again.

She had never been this close to anyone except Erack and maybe her parents but she couldn't really remember much about them. She felt naked even though she was fully covered. He seemed much too close. And yet somehow, she didn't feel the normal violation of her personal space.

Trying to push the awkwardness away, she slipped out of his hands. Her feet padded the floor and stepped toward the full mirror across the room. He looked hurt for a moment but recovered quickly.

"Sorry if I made you uncomfortable. It wasn't my intention," he couldn't meet her gaze in the mirror.

"It's...it's alright," she swallowed hard, wincing again. "Can you grab my clothes from the other room please," she continued weakly.

He stepped into the other room but must have come back too quickly because she was naked and examining all the bruising in the mirror. Scurrying over, trying not to look up, he tried to hand her the clothes. She was too exhausted. So he helped her into them.

"I just wanted to make sure you were okay," he said as he wrapped his hands around her waist to fasten her pants.

He looked up, seeing the two of them in the mirror caused him to pause. Just as she looked up and their eyes met. His arms whipped back so hard he almost knocked himself over. Stepping back quickly, she instinctively covered herself even though she was fully clothed already.

For a moment, they stood staring silently until D couldn't handle the level of discomfort.

"There's no need for this to feel or get weird," she cleared her throat.

"Let's just call this what it is," Xayres nodded, looking unsure as to what it actually was.

"A moment of strange interaction between close friends," D helped, rationalizing. "Can we change the subject now?"

"Sure," he said unsteadily.

Again the awkward silence penetrated the room. He danced a little. She stepped back, stretching her arms to mask her unconscious reaction. Xayres clapped his hands, looking up and smiling.

"So, tell me about your dreams," he hopped up to sit on the table.

D's eyes widened and she started, "I thought..."

"Not your hopes and dreams. The dreams you had so we can break them down and learn something...if anything," he chuckled, shaking his head.

INTERROGATION

Tallin sat on the other side of the glass, watching intently. His foot tapped impatiently as he watched one of his men administer the dose of serum to Annika on the other side. Sitting in the dark cooled his system. Still upset over the incident in his quarters, hoping this interrogation would take his mind off the events of the last few hours. No one here would challenge him, at least not the way Xayres did earlier; it was unacceptable. Hoping for some release from watching the scene unfolding on the other side of the glass was falling short of his expectations.

Frustration tickled up his neck the longer he watched. Watching was not the answer for him today. He needed to be in the room. To hear her breath. To feel her reactions as they came over her. Natural. Unaltered by serum. So he waited and watched until the serum started to wear off. He knew she must be a Nazi because her level of resistance training was high. But she had also been sent to the bunkers. Life there is not easy and could account for some of her resilience.

His fingers fidgeted, his toe tapping impatiently on the floor. Growing tired of waiting, he looked around the room again. Running his hand roughly through his hair, feeling himself lose the control he admired so much, the room closed in on him. Being in this space was becoming unbearable. Watching was making him more tense and agitated. He made the swift decision to step in because this job just needed to be done.

Recalling the man back to the room, bringing them into this tight and tense space, Tallin straightened up his posture and held his body as still as possible.

"You guys can call it a night. I'll keep an eye on her and if there's signs she may break, I'll just pick up where you left off," he ordered.

Neither man questioned the command. This was not an unusual request. Tallin often took over interrogations that proved to be difficult. And this one was proving to be more so than usual. He could sense his mens' frustration. Watching them leave, he felt the room start to close in on him again. Why did this smaller space feel so constricting today?

He stepped out the door, locking it behind him, checking the hallway to ensure no one saw him. Then he stepped to the heavy metal doors and breathed in, regaining his composure. Twisting the cold knob in his hand, a blast of light filled the room. Annika's head turned. He saw her squint, feeling her shock at the light and the burst of cool air.

"Ahh - now they send in the bigger man. You must be the man in charge," she sneered, struggling against her restraints. "Wow! Look at that hair. No camouflaging that feature. No wonder you hide in here," she chuckled, launching spittle in his direction.

He stood, looking at her straight-faced for a moment before releasing the door. It swung shut, sucking the light out of the room. The door slammed against its metal frame, echoing around the room. Annika jumped at each noise, unsure what came next. Tallin felt her fear, smiling at her level of surprise. She was on edge already.

"I see you've been trained to be a certain degree of difficult," Tallin's voice slithered around the room. "I'm not sure whether to be annoyed or amused."

"You pick. Not my business," Annika said.

She heard him walk but the footfalls echoed around the room. Illuminating the room from one corner was a sliver of light, allowing her to see his outline when her eyes adjusted. The light went out. He felt her heartbeat increase, stress rising into her chest. Smiling at himself, he whistled an eerie tune. Already tense, the melody caused her abdomen to tighten, unable to catch her breath. A long high-pitched creaking reverberated off the walls. Her confusion rose.

He hadn't exited because she saw no flash of light from the hallway. When there was more light in here, she hadn't seen any doors or boxes. Maybe there was a secret compartment she had failed to assess. Annika fought the mild panic rising in her throat. She heard the hinges groaned again followed by a slight click. Then more steps in the dark.

"I thought you were supposed to be nice. Play like we're going to be friends. You help me then I help you. Isn't that how this goes?" she sneered, trying to hide her discomfort.

No training prepared her for this. No reports of these tactics made it back through intelligence lines. The unknown shook her deep to her core, working against her. Suddenly, warm breath wafted across her ear. She froze, breathing in hard at the shock. The proximity allowed him to smell her surprise, propelling him forward, feeding his craving.

"Oh, but I have every intention of you helping me," his voice laced with an unfamiliar tone. "But there is no need for me to help you."

She shivered at his words, dead calm and cold. The hair on the back of her neck stood at attention. His tone changed the energy in the room. He took a deep breath in, running something sharp and cold up the side of her neck, chilling her ear and slicing through her hair. Then she heard him step back, making a production of sniffing her hair loudly, feeling her uncertainty, feeding off it.

The small sliver of light flashed back on, momentarily blinding her, throwing off all her senses. This time her eyes adjusted more quickly. The serum had completely worn off by this point, resulting in better reflexes. His new position was in her line of sight. She struggled with her restraints for a moment, allowing panic to cloud her judgment.

A smile crept across his face, strangely crooked and stretching closer to his ears than could be normal. He made a swift, jerking movement, meeting her nose to nose. She breathed in hard again while his eyes went wide. She noticed he lit up at her surprise and fear. Lighting up in an uncomfortable way. Almost twinkling. The sharp cold object was now running across her cheek. Then the pain ripped through her jaw.

"Ahh," she winced, just above a whisper.

He hadn't cut deep, but enough she felt it in all the right places. Instinctively, her face jerked sideways, away from the blade. Tallin grabbed her, just under the chin, applying just enough pressure to her jugular with his hand to cause her to panic a little more. Turning her face, moving his head slightly, he allowed the light to illuminate her injury. She saw his eyes take it all in, watching the wound drip blood onto his thumb.

She saw him out of the corner of her eye, enthralled by the pain he inflicted. Something told her to control her reactions. Returning to her training, she counted her breaths as she watched him. He jerked his hand away, licking the blood off his thumb and frowning.

"Now, why did you have to do that? I was enjoying all you were experiencing so much," he shook his head at her. "If you're going to insist on ruining my fun, then I may just have to come up with another game for us to play."

"Exactly what game are we playing now?" she managed to regain most of her control and kept her voice and physical reactions level and even.

"I liked it better before you took away all that adrenaline," Tallin replied. "Torture, as you call it, is a series of learned techniques. I'm sure you're aware," he moved to get a better look at the blood trickling down her cheek. "It requires someone to take on a lot of study in numerous areas," he paused, tilting his head at her. She still garnered no reaction. "Something I am sure you are also aware," he started to circle her slowly. "Psychology, weaponry, communication and, well, something I really enjoyed, anatomy and physiology. How far can one push a body to comply? What are the most vulnerable places on a person's body? We're really so much more alike than you may ever want to admit."

She continued counting her breaths as she listened and watched, determined not to allow the speech to shake her. Knowing she could not continue to give him what he wanted.

"See, by this time, most Nazis get a little nervous. I love that feeling. Someone else's dread is so much more fun to feel. Makes me ravenous for other things," he continued to move around her slowly, getting more upset when her gaze didn't attempt to follow.

He pulled in close again, not quite nose to nose. There was no shock this time. No sharp intake of breath. No fulfillment of his need to feel her fear. She stared into his eyes, now cold and hard, while he examined her closely. His hands leaped to his hair as he backed away, tugging at it in some fit of frustration. A smile flashed across her face, causing him to stop and freeze for a moment.

"You can't win!" his voice raised an octave, exiting more like a whine than a scream. She jumped, almost audibly, head turning and delivering scattered looks around the room.

"Oh, I know what we can play," looking at her like a cat looks at yarn after taking a dose of catnip. "This is a brand new game just for you," he laughed maniacally.

A cold chill swept through the room. The light flashed off. Frantically looking around the room, she strained her ears to hear his footfalls. Only white noise swirled up against her ears. Her gut pinched a little, fear rising from deep within her again. No! No! She mustn't give in. This is what he wants. She was safe as long as she didn't give him what he wants. Holding her breath, trying to push the feeling in her stomach down.

"Untrue," he whispered tersely in her ear.

The breath released with an small audible shriek. Her body shook. Feeling the color drain from her face, her brain scrambled. How had she not heard him approach? How was he so quiet now? A clicking sound echoed around the room. Annika couldn't triangulate where it came from. Breathing faster, throat tightening. Her training was failing her as her hands began to tremble. Her pulse pounding in her ears. Now virtually deaf, struggling against her restraints, throwing her face in the direction of every echo.

"Yes dear," he was in her other ear, or was he?

She didn't know. Could he force his thoughts into her mind? She now knew he can feel her emotions. So disorienting in the dark. Her palms begin to feel clammy up against the arm rests. Trembling uncontrollably. She felt his tongue lick her wound. Stinging deep, she winced again.

Hearing a light clank of chains. Was he bringing out more? Was his intent to strangle her into submission? Another clanking sound. And another. Her panic took over, no longer in control of her reaction, her stomach ached from holding it so tensely. She convulsed and felt something warm run down her leg. Jerking her leg at the pain. Was she bleeding? How did he move in and away so quickly? She could no longer think clearly.

The light flashed on. She pushed back, causing the chair to squeal across the floor. His eyes dazzled her, filling her with terror as they twinkled with delight in her fear and panic. Walking in her direction, she closed her eyes. She shuddered inside, not knowing his next move. Slashing her across the top of her hand, she yanked it into her chest, protecting it with the other. She paused. Something felt different. Her brain took in the new scene. No shackles. Her face betrayed her and with it, the smile on Tallin's face transformed into something grotesque, inhuman. She looked up at him. His grin so big she could see his back molars glint in the shadows.

"New game," he whispered jovially.

The light clicked off. Pitch black filled the room. Annika dropped off the chair, crawling in a direction she hoped was away from him, bumping into a wall. Tallin's laugh echoing in all directions. Cold fingers wrapped around her ankle, pulling her back. How could he find her in the darkness?

"No need to be so quiet in here dear. For no one will ever know how weak you were," cringing at his warm breath wafting across her neck. "In here, no one can hear you scream."

ARCHIVES

Nothing made Xayres feel better than digging into the archives. After losing his bunker and ending up in so many new places, he found comfort in learning the histories of others. It helped him identify with the people around him. He found the information in all the volumes fascinating and helpful. Attempting to learn all he could about their common enemy and the resistance, he spent his spare moments there.

He skimmed through the pages, glossing over information of no tactical use, sipping a hot drink they called cider. Nothing appeared of value in this volume so far and he found himself teetering on bored to sleep. Then, he saw the next title and sat straight up, reading carefully.

Destruction of Bunker Four in Network Six

Unsure how they would know which bunkers would be in which network, Xayres concluded they were being monitored by someone. But if there was a centralized head out there, why didn't any of them know about it? Why hadn't the head come to their aid when the Germans were on their doorstep? Was the resistance here actually supposed to be leading the charge?

Pieces of the bunker survived as officers were able to deactivate many of the charges. The bunker was caught that unaware. A handful of soldiers died in the blast, estimation of 20. The radio equipment could not be salvaged but other technology was brought back for inspection.

Over 100 survivors were captured. We are unable to establish if these were the only survivors from the bunker. After being detained for questioning, the adults were determined to be too defiant making them of little use. The children they could not assimilate were cycled in for slavery and testing. Public executions and gladiatorial games were held for the following:

Xayres turned the page, scribbling notes in his log, skeptically thinking they must have been incorrect about the survivors. They would only know what the Nazis assumed unless they had a better surveillance network than the Germans did. The following page was a list of names, most likely incomplete as it was the list of captives the Nazis announced. The end of the list held the names of the children they managed to identify.

He scanned the list, almost writing it off. As he reached the bottom for the third time, he spit up his drink, sitting straight up. The book fell off his lap, flipping to another page, making a loud thump on the concrete. For a moment, he looked lost. Then, he picked up the book, flipped to the correct page and bolted toward the door.

He knew time was running out and he had to find D They must get on their way immediately. He wasn't sure they had enough time to return to the bunker before it was too late. No longer worried about Erack's survival, he charged around the compound looking desperately for D.

Xayres' search was made more difficult by D wandering to find Tallin. Although she had put a halt to training, she had learned a lot about him as she recovered and found he was full of useful tactics and interesting information. The resistance was a long standing movement in old tunnels. Apparently, the Germans just took out everything on the surface and built on top of it. She was eager to continue a conversation she had started with him, but she was unsure where to find him.

After D finally gave up on finding Tallin, she headed toward the medical facility to discuss the medicine for Erack with the doctor. She had spent a large amount of time pestering the local doctor because she needed the antidote.

"D, I wish you could respect the privacy of my patients," he said exasperated.

He was not pleased to see her at all. But many years of being the outcast had taught her how to make people dislike her quickly. She assumed the more he disliked her presence, the faster he would work on the solution.

"If you could hurry this antidote along then I would leave here and you'd probably never see me again," D smiled.

She skipped over to his side, startling him. A flask slipped between his fingers. Catching it gingerly, she handed it back.

"If you could refrain..." he huffed.

"I just need an update on your progress. If you saw fit to seek me out before lunch mess, none of this would be necessary. But since I have to run you down everyday..." D sounded annoyed.

"I don't have the time to..." he sighed deeply.

"You do now doctor," Xayres had finally found her. "Is that antidote ready to go now?"

"I told you two days was not enough time. I can't make the chemistry go any faster, nor the physics. Those are things I have no control over," the doctor argued.

"Just tell us the truth," D said. "You still want to hold on to the original solution so you can test it for a vaccine."

"Is that really what's happening here? Do you have the

solution?" Xayres pressed into the room, making an already small space even smaller.

He hoped proximity and pressure would force the doctor to give up the precious liquid. Setting the book down on the desk, he moved in closer.

"We need honest answers here," said Xayres.

"Are we running out of time?" D hadn't thought much about how much time had passed.

"We can discuss that in a minute," Xayres said. "Right now we need to discuss this."

He put his hand on the doctor's shoulder, hoping it would foster a different answer.

"I have to do what is best for everyone, not just one man. I have an obligation to do everything I can to make sure this vaccine gets made," the doctor replied.

"So, it is ready. You just don't want to give it to us," D shouted.

Xayres turned to her and signaled for her to calm down and be quiet. They didn't need to draw attention to the lab, although he was certain she'd already done that. She stepped back, desperately trying to contain herself.

"Doctor, she's a loose cannon. You really don't want her to go off in here. If you're work is important to you," Xayres said. "Right now we are all calm here. But that could change in a second. We need the antidote and we need it now."

"Just tell me why it's so important. You said two days and that was almost five days ago. You've been flexible until this point. What's changed?" the doctor pressed back.

D looked him over. Then she remembered the book he set on the desk. Changing her focus helped her calm down. She put her hand on the book.

"Is this the change Xayres?" she asked.

"Yes, I found information in there. It says the Nazis are inside Bunker Six and they were inside Bunker Five. No one is safe as long as they don't know. We have to get back there to tell them," Xayres explained. "If we don't, the Nazis have access to our entire communication network and they can take down the rest of the system. They'll exterminate us all."

"You can go without the antidote and bring your friend back here," the doctor reasoned.

"He won't make it back here in time for it to do any good," D said, holding back tears at the idea of Erack dying. "You're giving us that antidote one way or the other."

Xayres held up a hand, signaling her to back off.

The doctor looked shaken but responded calmly, "I told you, I have a responsibility to the many."

"The many won't be served if I allow her to destroy everything in here," Xayres said. "I may not be able to help her much longer."

"Then your friend will die," the doctor said. "What would be the point of that."

"The point would be that no one benefits from your work with the vaccine. Take him from me and I'll take everything you're working for from you," D gritted her teeth as she spoke.

"That would be...careless...brutal...heartless," the doctor struggled for words. "You would lose so much."

"I've already lost my whole world," she lamented. "Nothing is as it appears to be here or there. Nothing," she moved to the table. "So I have nothing left to lose."

"Except Erack," the voice sounded familiar.

"Tallin..." Xayres said.

"Save it Xayres! I would hate to tell your people you have mutinous tenancies. Perhaps they would rethink your leadership role," he sneered.

"But Tallin," D said.

"I know D. I know," he waved her off. "Show us this evidence that makes this an emergency Xayres."

Xayres looked surprised. D just stared at the floor.

"I'm not one to hold a grudge. Not anymore. Everybody

has their triggers and I happened to hit yours," Tallin shrugged as he moved to the desk, waving a hand for Xayres and D to join him.

"Right here," Xayres flipped the book open to the list. "This right here."

D looked at the page. She sucked in hard. Xayres leaned into Tallin's ear, explaining her reaction.

"I'll pull together some men and we'll go with you. You know the wilderness. We know the Nazis," Tallin said, looking at Xayres.

"We accept any help we can get. But we won't get her out of here if..." Xayres nodded at D.

Tallin nodded, closing the book.

"Doctor, get them the antidote...now! That's an order!" Tallin snapped.

"But sir..." the doctor attempted to protest.

"No, that's an order! Now, get it ready now," Tallin commanded.

D shook her head, "I guess we know who's been helping Jaren then."

AMBUSH

Flashing lights blinked all around them. They were surrounded. It only took a few repeats to decipher the Morse Code. Tallin returned from scouting, guessing there was a small encampment about two miles south. So far, as much as they could tell, they had gone undetected by the Germans. Since they left the city, the small group managed to scout a lot of information about how the Nazis did their dirty work. It was clear this was not the first time they had set up this type of search.

They surmised the SS sent out small search parties to cover more ground. But they only searched under the cover of night now. However, this strategy was working to the bunker's advantage, slowing down the search and breaking them into smaller forces. Since they slept during the day, it was also easier for those escaping to detect and possibly avoid the camps.

Decoding the messages, they decided this was the main camp. Turning it on its head would buy the bunker and themselves even more time for evacuation and possibly make the Germans think twice about pursuing other survivors.

D sat half listening to the report from Tallin. It was nice to be surrounded by people who didn't judge her for being different, making her again question whether she wanted to go back to living underground. While they made great time getting back, part of her wished she stayed in the city. But Erack was more important than her freedom.

She moved into position as one of the the observers. Counting six men currently in camp, she signaled the team. It was too dark for hand signals. So they too relied on light to communicate, assuming the Nazis would ignore the extra chatter as messages between teams. Trying to zoom in on the voices in her head was exhausting, like sifting through a ruin or junkyard to find something beautiful.

Her attention veered. The thought of returning to the bunker unnerved her. Someone ordered Annika to kill her and apparently her parents were killed. How deep did the cover up go? Why lie to her at all? Do they think she knows more than she thinks she does? She couldn't remember much before she was told about the accident. Trying to remember, she noticed nothing new.

She heard steps. Heavier foot falls than her men. A twig snapped, echoing off the trees around her. A heavy weight fell in her stomach. Searching for a response in the lights. Realizing her lack of focus may just have gotten them all killed. She froze. Lifting her weapon to the ready. Remembering her training. Scouring the darkness as best she could.

"Gotcha!" she heard the voice, possibly near her or in her head.

Determining the difference was still difficult. She turned her head. Something glinted in the corner of her eye, veering to one side. Feeling it before she saw it, the knife dug into her thigh. She screamed before she could stop herself. Assuming this was not the intended target, she shot rounds in the direction of the arm. No confirmation of a hit.

Arms wrapped around her from behind, lifting her off her feet. Slamming her into the ground. Loud buzzing filled her ears on impact. More boots trampling in her direction. She spat and swore, knowing now this may be an ambush. Her lack of focus dropped them right into it. Where were her men?

Recovering quickly, she yanked the knife out of her thigh. Jamming it into her assailant. Not sure where it landed. She heard a yelp. The arms released her. Pushing her forward to create distance.

"Doesn't feel nice, does it?" she growled in German.

Rolling around to face her attacker. All he did was smile at her. His blond hair glowed in the moonlight. The foot falls of heavy boots usually indicated SS soldiers. Her men traveled more lightly on their feet. She knew they were outnumbered.

"How many comrades?" she asked tersely.

He only chuckled, lunging at her. She shot off more rounds. Pushing him back. He stumbled, losing his balance. She remembered their uniforms. Standing on one leg, she shot him once in the leg. Then in the arm. He screamed.

Twirling around. She tried to position herself for another attack. Turning on her ear piece, she found them. Firing rounds in their direction. German curse words broke the silence. Her shots found some marks. The sounds of breaking grass told her some had taken cover.

Listening for her own men, she realized she left them too far away to come to her rescue. And it seemed the Nazis moved faster, recovered faster. Perhaps there was some truth to some of those genetically altered soldier claims. Maybe they were still preparing for more war.

Something rustled behind her. Training and instinct took over. Rolling into a safer position, wincing in pain. Her original attacker was attempting to scoot away. She heard the shot, seeing the impact before realizing it came from her weapon. Her eyes blurred ass she viciously wiped away tears, jerking her focus back. *Yes, this is your first kill. Yes, you are in the middle of a mission. You have been trained for these moments. Keep moving. Deal with it later.* She swallowed it down hard. *Be like ice,* she told herself.

Refusing to close her eyes, now she concentrated on the threat. She pushed all the thoughts out of her mind. For a moment, she thought she saw the outline of Tallin and Xayres. Three men intercepted them. They needed her. But she wouldn't get to them in time.

Something slammed into her shoulder. She swore at herself for being taken by surprise again. A hand flipped her around. Something cracked against her skull. Unable to establish what hit her, the buzzing in her ears fortified. The world spun. Stumbling backward. This may be her first and last time in combat.

The new injury exacerbated the original one in her leg. She fumbled with her weapon. Desperately trying to recover. To save herself. The world tilted. She lost focus. Hands shaking, head aching. She resolved this was the end.

She saw him move in front of her. One last attempt. She crab walked backward. Her slow reflexes outmatched. He grabbed her hair and wrenched her upward. She saw the knife. Closing her eyes hoping for a swift end, an honorable death, or one that stalled their forces, maybe this was saving someone else. Her lungs filled deep with air. Waiting.

Feeling something warm and sticky spray across her face, her hair fell back to her shoulders. The spray tasted heavy with alkaline. Her eyes popped open and her hands moved immediate to her throat expecting to find a large gash. She fell to her knees. The German made weird gurgling noises. She focused just in time to see him. A stranger stepped out of the way. An expression of surprise frozen on the Nazi's face. He fell face first into the grass.

The stranger was covered in camouflage leaves and grass. He wore a helmet and had long hair and an unkept beard. While he smiled at her, she saw his teeth were yellow in the moonlight. Before she could speak, he saluted, rolled back into the underbrush and disappeared.

Xayres cried out. Grabbing her weapon, she tried to run. The gash in her leg screamed for attention. Dropping down, she found her med kit. Bandaging herself as well as she knew how, she rushed to assist the other men.

She saw Tallin first. He looked left for dead, but he wasn't as bad as he looked. Two other men were with him. They were breathing and not too bloody. Must have knocked them out and figured they were dead. Pulling the water skin off her belt, she nursed them with its contents. Then she set to bandaging them up, following others instructions. All she could hope for was they had a reprieve from attack...at least for a moment.

Tallin was the last to get attention. Somehow she knew he would want her to save his men first. As she assisted with his wounds, he scanned the men he had left.

"Seven. There are only seven of us left," he croaked. "We walked right into that, didn't we?"

D looked at him skeptically. She only counted five. Then the number rang in her head and guilt filled her gut.

"Wait!" he counted again. "Where's Xayres? I know I heard him," he asked.

"They must've taken him. I don't know why," D replied.

Tallin sighed, "I do. They're trying to suck us in. Finish us off," he paused. "Xayres is smart enough to leave a trail for us to follow."

"They probably assume that too," D frowned.

Within the hour, most of them were ready to move someplace more concealed. Only one of them was too injured to move on their own. They made sure he was well hidden and had enough supplies to get back to health and make it to the city.

D worried it took them too long. Xayres may be dead by now. But Tallin was confident they would keep him alive long enough to ensnare them.

"Trust what your gut is telling you. Yours is more refined than anyone's so far," Tallin told her over and over in training and now in the field.

Now the words bounced around in her head. If she had just listened to that in the beginning, they probably wouldn't be in this mess. So much of this was new to her. Her extra sensory abilities. Running into the Nazis. Killing people.

Watching people be killed. She remembered the gurgling noises. The spray of blood on her face. Her hand found itself touching where the spray hit her, now dried. No one even said anything. Maybe they hadn't noticed. Maybe they thought it came from her wounds. Or they had noticed and it was a normal thing for them to see. Perhaps they didn't want to upset her. Tallin knocked her in the shoulder.

"Pay attention D. Where are you right now?" he hissed in her ear.

"Trying to trust my gut or hear my head. I don't know," she whispered back.

"Right now, we need your tracking skills. This is unfamiliar terrain for us. Do you have any idea where we are?" he asked.

"I have a pretty good idea. I'd have a better idea with the sun up," replied D.

"Then..." Tallin raised his eyebrows at her.

She told him they were about half a day's run from the bunker from here, but the exact direction was a guess. He pressed her to track Xayres, which she found increasingly difficult. Having this much trouble with focus was not normal for her but she couldn't stop the gurgling sounds from bouncing around in her head. Every time it pushed its way in, she questioned her choice not to say anything about her mystery man. But if she did, they may think she was breaking from reality, a result from killing someone. At this point, she wasn't sure.

Xayres was dragged across the rugged ground, leaving scraps along the way. Following him was relatively easy. D figured they allowed him to leave the trail. Which was less tracking and more about finding pieces of his pants.

She watched as the men followed Tallin. They trusted her because he trusted her. Now if only she could trust herself.

The Nazis weren't careful to conceal themselves, as if they dared people to find them. With some observation, they counted six men they could see. None of them could tell where there were more. The area was too infiltrated. Confirmation all the signals were pointed in this direction made this the base camp.

D tried to focus on Xayres and his whereabouts. Thomas volunteered to go in closer. If there were more soldiers in this camp, they needed to know.

Grabbing Thomas before he left, "They're hiding, Waiting for us. At least a dozen, but there may be more," D was frantic.

She pointed to the tall grass on the other side of the camp. Although she couldn't pinpoint them exactly, she knew they couldn't move in any closer than that outer circle. Tallin smiled at her progress. D knew achieving focus on anything kept the details of her private encounter out of her mind.

"We need a better plan," Thomas said. "We can't just run in there. They'll pick us off one by one."

"Not if it's a surprise," Tallin said.

"I think we have clearly established they have the upper hand here and it would not be a surprise," reasoned Peyton.

"Then what would you suggest? We have people we've left behind, possibly more of our team is out there without assistance, left for dead. And we're here. Xayres wouldn't want to waste our time like this. He would be the first to say we leave him behind," D said.

"Is that your gut speaking or your emotional state?" Tallin asked.

"Both I imagine. I'm still finding it difficult to establish the difference," D whispered.

Her toe began to ache, crouched in this position. Her thigh protested her movements. She desperately wanted caffeine, but Tallin insisted it dulled her senses. Hands shaking, she sat down.

"We may as well watch for a while to come up with a better plan," Thomas suggested.

"And nurse our wounds," Peyton added, pointing at the makeshift bandage on D's leg.

Tallin pulled out his med kit, threading a needle. Removing the bandage, Thomas looked at her sympathetically.

"This will sting. Bite on this," Thomas handed her a dirty towel.

She pushed herself away, disgusted.

"Trust me. It looks bad, but you're going to need it," Peyton said.

Her expression soured as she put it in her mouth. Thomas pulled a vial out of his med kit, popped off the cork with his thumb and poured it over the wound. The shock drilled up her leg. It was cold, but mostly, it stung, piercing her thigh again. Biting down hard, eyes wide, she nodded her head as they smiled back. Tallin moved in, drying it as best he could. He stitched up what he could find. Tying it off, he pulled out a clean bandage and covered the wound.

"Why didn't you say something? No wonder you can't focus," Tallin scolded.

She grunted, the gag still in her mouth, the pain riveting through her. They handed her a water skin. Thomas yanked out the gag, slamming her teeth together. She growled again.

Closing her eyes, she used some of the water to clean

her face. All she saw behind her eyelids was the man in camouflage and the gurgling German. Shaking her head vigorously, hoping to erase images permanently. She needed to focus on the present. The light hit her face as the sun peaked over the horizon. It burned her eyes a little.

"I'll take first watch. Until this pain dulls a little, I won't be able to rest," D grabbed her weapon and propped herself up against a tree.

"We'll wait until the sun is at high noon. Maybe some of them will come back to camp for sleep. In the mean time, let's all try and get some rest," Tallin responded.

RESCUE

D sat watching them talk, her mind somewhere else entirely. Rations crunched in her mouth, masking most of the outside noise. Feeling drowsy, she lamented they didn't use caffeine. She traveled better on caffeine. Sleeping was her greatest enemy. Remembering the withdrawal from it was one thing she never wanted to go through again. She prided herself of keeping control and during that time, she was anything but in control.

They all assumed Xayres was in the tent on the south side of the camp. It seemed the only logical place to hide him. That's all she remembered from the conversation. She knew she wanted to help rescue Xayres, but she couldn't focus on the strategy discussion.

"Hey D?" Tallin snapped his fingers at her. "Do we need to go over this again?"

"Go over what?" she asked.

"D, we've been planning this for at least an hour. Haven't you heard anything we've said?" replied Tallin.

"I'm not sure..." she stammered. "I know...I'm hopeless right now."

She was losing more time than she realized and she blamed not being able to rest.

"Was this how we got ambushed?" Thomas motioned at D. "Because she can't keep her head on straight? Damn it

Tallin! Who have you put your trust in now?"

"This is normal. In the beginning of training. She's not dangerous. This situation is," Tallin defended.

"Some super human you brought with us. She can't even focus," Peyton lamented. "She's less effective than you are," he pointed to Tallin.

"Less effective than Tallin?" D appeared confused.

"His skills are nowhere near as refined as yours...or so he claims," explained Thomas.

"But it's sure not looking like he has much claim," inserted Peyton.

D placed her finger on her lips, "SHHHHHHHH!"

They looked at her then one another, clearly unable to understand.

"Someone is coming," she whispered.

"Shit! Did they hear us?" Tallin asked.

She slapped her hand over his mouth. Then placed the finger over her lips again. Creeping a few steps, she grabbed her weapon, turning just in time. Someone grabbed the barrel and pointed it upward. For a moment, she wanted to pull the trigger but every instinct told her not to do so. She looked up.

"Jax. Liam," Tallin crawled over to their position. "We thought they got you guys."

"No, we've been scouting the other side. They have guys positioned around the perimeter," Jax said.

"Not as many as they had when we started," Liam chuckled.

Jax jabbed Liam in the side with his elbow. "It's almost like they're waiting for us to actually enter their camp. Why would we be going in?" Jax asked.

"They've got Xayres," Peyton answered.

"Oh," said Liam.

"And at this point, we need to get close enough to put him out of his misery at the very least," Jax concluded.

"Why do you propose we kill him?" D asked, clearly

agitated by the idea. "I said leave him behind. Not kill him."

"Trust me D. If we can't rescue him, he'd prefer we kill him," Tallin told her.

"We know what they do to captives. He'd want it that way. You must trust us on this," Liam said.

"None of us like that choice either. But we have to do what's best for him and us," Peyton weighed in.

"There are things worse than death and the Nazis know everything that applies," Jax added quietly.

"But I gotta give them credit. They have set up a first class wrangler trap. If we go in there together or separate, we're dead. We give away our position here, we're dead," Liam said.

"I'm not so sure it would work out that way," D replied.

"What do you mean?" asked Tallin.

"I think we should stay together, at least for now. We have sharp shooters. We'll have them take some shots and if we eliminate enough of them, the guys on the perimeter will have to come out to protect the camp," she started.

"Then we give away our position with the first shot and we're dead." Liam corrected.

"Not if we're already mobile. We watch where they are moving from and we move. It will flush them out. By the time they reach our old position, we'll be gone without a trace," continued D.

"It may only work two times, maybe three at the most," Jax said.

"With the guys already taken from the perimeter, this would eliminate most of the guys in camp, evening the odds more," Peyton posed.

"And they probably have orders to stay in the perimeter unless there are men being taken out in camp, which tells me they underestimate us," Tallin said.

"That does give us better odds," Jax said.

"Then we split up. Half into the camp. The sharp shooters on the perimeter to provide cover fire if needed.

They will think we are still trying to move them around. Because they think we're stupid," D finished.

"And we could actually take them by surprise." Thomas said.

"Rescuing Xayres," D smiled.

"Hopefully, if he is still alive," interjected Liam.

D frowned at him, "Even if we have to kill him anyway."

"It's worth the risk." Tallin said. "We'll give it a try. I don't see a better option. Get ready to move." He motioned to everyone to start packing and cleaning up. "Jax. Liam" He waved at them. "We need your Intel on the perimeter position." Turning to D, motioning to his head. "D, do this thing again and try to focus this time."

They moved into position. Thomas and Jax watched. Taking aim, they took out two guards in clear sight. Then they prepped to move quickly. The kills drew out the Germans from the far side of the camp. Now they had to stay to keep guard. Seeing the grass sway against the wind signaled where back up was coming from. Leaving the smallest trace possible, they moved to a new position.

As everything was going to plan, D's stomach filled with butterflies. She had never been on a mission this critical and she wasn't sure if she could kill someone again. Tallin tapped her on the shoulder. It was time to split off from the group. Liam went with them.

They worked their way through the cleared area to the tent, careful not to be seen. Tallin stayed as a look out. D couldn't help but think this was happening too easily. They had fooled them, gotten here and hardly experienced any resistance. Much too easy.

As she climbed under the fabric of the tent wall, it hit her. A trap within a trap. A back up plan. It was so obvious. *How did I miss it?* she kicked herself for repeating the mistake, coming to grips with her surroundings just in time to roll away from someone in the tent.

Grabbing the knife from her boot, she buried it in their

foot, pulling it out as the attacker jumped and screamed. He fell against a tent pole, trying to regain his balance almost taking the entire structure down with him. Thomas saw the commotion in his scope but couldn't determine who was who.

Close combat was not the German's strong suit. She had a clear advantage. As the soldier finished teetering, D flipped back, locking his legs in her grip. He stumbled backward again. He hit the ground with a loud thud next to her. She rolled to her knees taking the full force of her motion to slam the blade into the side of his neck. Lots of blood but no gurgling. Her training had taken over before she realized what she'd done. He stopped moving.

Someone was tied in the chair, gagged and bleeding. It wasn't Xayres. She approached with caution. Gasping at who she saw, she quickly worked on the bindings. She heard someone coming. The German's blood was flowing under the wall of the tent.

"Shit!" she whispered. "Benji, can you run?"

"I don't know," exhaustion seeping into every word.

"You're going to have to. Do you understand what I am saying to you?" she asked.

"I think so," he replied still sounding dazed.

"Have you seen Xayres?" she asked.

"No, is he here?" Benji replied.

"Don't worry about that. Where is Erack?" she asked.

"At the rendezvous. They caught me when I was out getting water. Guess they thought someone would come for me," he groaned as the ropes released, lurching forward. D caught him. "I'm sorry D. He's been there alone for a while."

"It's okay Benji. It's okay. Don't worry about that now," soothed D.

She helped him steady himself on all fours, praying he could steady himself later on two feet.

"I'll give you a direction to run and you just go," ordered D. "Don't stop Benji. Not until you find someone named Jax or Thomas."

"I understand," he choked.

They crawled under the back of the tent. The voices were coming at them from the opening in the front. She heard a shot and a thud. Cover fire.

"Crawl to that bush over there then run toward that tree. Point to the tree Benji," she ordered brusquely. "Don't stop running Benji."

He pointed and began to crawl. She couldn't decide if it would be better to go back or take the punishment in here. Either way, only one of them had time to get to the brush. Someone had to stall the others.

The momentary break in movement allowed her to feel the pain in her leg. She had been hard on it and it looked like one of the stitches popped open. She had to find Xayres. Moving to the side of the tent, she saw two soldiers step over a body to go inside. Tallin joined her at the side of the tent.

They spoke in code. She told him the person in the tent was not Xayres. Then she tried to get him to understand Benji. When he couldn't understand, she shook him off. They needed to find Xayres.

She signaled to Jax and Thomas the prisoner was not Xayres but was heading in their direction. Switching gears, she focused on hearing Xayres distinct brain chatter. This left Tallin to fend for himself and her. One of the soldiers came around the corner. Tallin ran toward him, wrapping his arms around his waist, taking him to the ground.

"Where is my man?" he garbled in rudimentary German.

Tallin didn't expect an answer. His hands were wrapped around his wind pipe and his knees were on his chest. The soldier struggled for a few minutes, looking Tallin in the eye.

Thwerp. Thud. They both turned to see another officer fall to the ground.

"D. You get it?" Tallin asked, fighting the soldier.

"I think so," answered D pointing to the outer rim of the camp.

Tallin cracked the soldier's head into the hard ground. D hoped he just knocked him unconscious. He signaled to the snipers to clear the camp in the direction she pointed.

"Just another day at work," Tallin said as he rose to take the lead.

They made their way carefully around the camp. Any resistance was quickly cut down by their snipers. Part of D knew reinforcements were on their way from others camps. They needed to hurry. After a moment of cutting through the tall grass, they found Xayres stretched between two tree trunks.

"See, if we can't save him..." he started but she waved him off.

"Careful, may be traps," Tallin proceeded with caution.

Now she understood what they already knew. These people were brutal and this was war. War has different rules. But she could also see becoming as bad as her enemies would make her no better than they were. That was a fine line they couldn't cross.

As they crept in, she was more terrified to find he was wide awake. The pain hadn't knocked him out or they found a way to keep him coherent. The weight in her stomach came back.

Once they were close enough, she pulled her knife. His eyes went wide as it closed in near his head, cutting off his gag. She gave him some water.

"Thought you were going to kill me," Xayres said, panting.

"Did you notice them booby trapping any of your ties," Tallin asked.

"Not that I noticed," Xayres replied.

"Well then," D said.

Wasting no time, she cut one of his legs loose. Nothing

happened. Without warning, she cut the other and he slammed into the ground. Even the short distance hurt with his injuries. Tallin took out a towel to nurse his wounds. D cut his arms free.

"We don't have time," she stated, motioning in the direction of other camps, "Reinforcements. This is our only shot for a clean break they can't follow."

She signaled to the group to meet at the end of camp behind the tent.

"You ready to move," D smiled, positioning herself under his arm. He was coming right now whether he liked it or not.

Following Benji's directions, they made their way to Erack in the ruins near the Nazi base camp. No one could have known they would be this close by now. Erack had been administering his medicines but he was out of food. And dangerously low on water.

They set Xayres and Benji next to him. Smiling at one another, Xayres winked.

"No one said you had to try to make your pain match mine. There are better ways to get her attention," Erack's voice was garbled as he attempted to wink back at Xayres.

Both chuckled causing them both to cough uncontrollably. D shook her head at them.

Xayres stopped laughing first, "I couldn't even dream of putting up with her that way. What a nightmare."

His face contorted in a way none of them had seen. Then he coughed after laughing too hard at himself.

"Well you two are delirious and clearly in no shape to travel," D snickered.

She didn't like the laugh they were having at her expense.

"Neither is Benji," Tallin said.

"We'll have to leave them here. It's too risky to try and take them with us," Jax said.

"From these ruins, we're only a few hours away from

the south access," Erack coughed. "Well over a day to the front door. We've managed to evacuate a lot of people to the east and south."

In the commotion, D found herself wondering why they needed to meet out here. She looked at the cold kit.

"Oh!" she dropped to her knees. "I brought you something.

She smiled at Erack, pulling the case off her shoulder, carefully putting it on the ground. Opening it, she sucked in quickly, in relief. The vials were in tact. Her hands shook as she started pulling out the doctor's hand written instructions.

"Oh yeah. We brought you a gift," Xayres mumbled.

Peyton knelt down next to D, putting his hand on hers. She jerked a little at the touch.

"How about I do this? I'm a field medic," Peyton said, holding out his hand.

He smiled to reassure her. She handed over the vials. Peyton handed the instructions to Thomas while he prepared the dose.

"It says he needs three doses over the next 24 hours," Thomas relayed.

Peyton checked the vials, establishing each one was a dose. He verified he had enough to give Erack until they returned to the city. Then he pulled out one vial, he prepared to administer it to Erack.

"Then it's settled," Liam said. "Peyton should stay here with them. We'll go to the bunker to make sure it gets blown up. That shouldn't take us a full 24 hours."

"That seems like a quick deadline," D said.

"Did you see how close the Nazis are to the bunker?" Tallin asked incredulously.

"Any longer than that and we'll all be in a worker camp," Jax said. "If you guys aren't back in 24 hours, we'll head back to the city."

"You're not coming?" Thomas asked.

"They're going to need more than just one hand if we have to head back without you. Besides, Peyton's bed side manner leaves a lot to be desired," Jax chuckled.

"Hey, my bed side manner gets the job done okay." Peyton retorted.

"This sounds like a job for a stronger, more sensitive soul," Liam flexed as he talked. "So I guess I'll stay. You two should be together anyway. In case you blow yourselves up or something."

He winked at Thomas. Jax smiled.

"Would you all get serious here. We're in the middle of a war," Tallin barked.

"Thank you Liam," Jax said, as Liam helped her to her feet.

"Good, now that's settled. Let's eat some dinner and hydrate. We move out in an hour," Tallin said.

MISTAKES

Jaren sat facing the council, rubbing his wrists. Having no shackles took some adjustment.

"Because you have disabled a communications array before, we are asking you to make sure that happens here," Kaya said. "This does not mean you have full privileges and rights of a council member."

"You will be able to give orders in the communications array but that will be the extent of your authority," Ra'Ella explained.

"I understand. I wouldn't trust my mental state either," Jaren replied.

"Ra'Ella will accompany you to the communications room. You are not to leave her side," ordered Trey.

Ra'Ella nodded as she rose. Jaren walked with her to the doors, leaving the council behind. Doc was down the hall from the council doors when she noticed them exit together. Thinking it was odd they would be working together, mainly because they came from the same bunker, she opted to ditch her earlier tasks and follow them.

As they wound their way through the corridors into the opposite side of the compound, Doc crept close behind, carefully rounding corners, dipping in and out of doorways, evasively maneuvering despite the strange looks she received. The last hallway was secluded, mostly due to where it went. Not many people needed to come down this way. As she rounded the bend, she was surprised to see them stopped and whispering tersely. Cautiously moving closer, in and out of doorways, they appeared too distracted by their conversation to notice her.

"Look Jaren, you just keep doing as you're told and maybe you'll get out of this alive," Ra'Ella ordered, careful to keep her tone stern but low.

"But you have given me no proof they are still alive," replied Jaren.

"How can I get proof down here? There is no way to safely do that. You have to take my word for it," Ra'Ella insisted.

"The word of a Nazi. At this point, not likely," Jaren replied.

"You took my word for it when your neck was on the line," she scolded. "Jaren, you'll do anything to save your own skin. You've already proven it. So, I'll take you there and you'll do as you're told."

Ra'Ella spread a wicked smile across her face. Doc accidentally kicked a corner, causing her to let out a light whimper before she could stop herself. Hearing the echo, she dove agilely into the nearest opening, closing and locking the door. Ra'Ella grabbed Jaren's wrist.

"Shh!" she put her finger to her lips.

Ra'Ella walked back up the corridor, checking every space. All doors appeared to be closed and locked but she wasn't about to take any chances. They needed to keep moving. This conversation was too public.

Doc held her breath and waited until she heard two pairs of foot falls continue up the hall. She knew she was waiting longer than needed but she didn't want Ra'Ella to trick her either. Her suspicions now confirmed, she continued toward the communications room.

Arriving in the doorway, she found Jaren mostly alone. He had ordered everyone else out except the officers in training, of which there were two. Jaren fiddled nervously with the console, but Doc couldn't tell which one. She sneaked into the back of the room hoping no one would notice until she managed to find something to use as a weapon.

Jaren walked to the front of the room with a slip of paper in his hand, placing it in front of one of the young officers.

"Send this message immediately," ordered Jaren.

"It's already encrypted sir. How am I supposed to know what to send?" he asked.

"You send it just like this," Jaren ordered.

"Via groundwaves, right sir," the other clarified.

"No, by radio," Jaren insisted.

"Orders during the alert are for groundwaves only sir," the first replied.

"And won't that enable the Nazis to pinpoint our signal?" asked the second.

"They would have to pick up the signal first! Why am I explaining this to you? Why are you questioning my orders?" Jaren huffed. "I am not to be trifled with in this way."

"Don't send that message," Doc shouted.

Jaren flipped around, shock written all over his face. The officers froze, uncertain which orders to follow.

"Do not send that message or I will have you both tried for treason," Doc persisted, making her way to the front of the room.

"Doc, you don't..." Jaren started.

She pushed him in the chest. "Don't you dare! Don't you dare! You're about to kill us all just like you killed Tallin. Underhanded and sneaky. You're a traitor! A traitor!" she screamed, unable to control her voice. "Destroy the communications equipment! Destroy it now!"

The volume jolted the officers out of their state of shock and confusion. They went swiftly into action.

"Don't follow her orders! She's the traitor!" Jaren bellowed.

"Don't you even..." Doc started.

But instead of finishing, she took a chair and started bashing the electronics herself. Jaren approached her, trying to throw his arms around her waist to pull her away. She slammed him in the head with the chair, knocking him off his feet, disorienting him. Then she stopped. Walking to the other side of the room, she opened the panel and turned the dial. The broadcast message changed as well as the color of the flashers.

"Upgraded to black evacuation alert. All hands, evacuate immediately. This is a black evacuation alert. All hands, evacuate immediately," the mechanical voice repeated.

Pressing more buttons and slamming the door shut, she locked it and swallowed the small key.

"How do you..." Jaren tried to overcome the cacophony of smashing equipment and recorded messages.

The message changed again. "This is a black evacuation alert. All hands, evacuate immediately. Destruction sequence set for minimum 48 hours. No override. All hands, evacuate immediately," it repeated.

"Officers, you want to get blown up. You heard the order. Evacuate!" Doc said dismissing them with her hands.

The officers didn't hesitate, running directly for the door. Blood dribbled down Jaren's nose as he looked up at her from the floor.

"You don't know what you've done!" he screamed.

"It doesn't matter what she promised you! It's not worth it!" Doc yelled back. "You betrayed us all!"

"She has my sister!" he choked past tears.

"Don't be stupid!" she yelled back.

He managed to make it to his feet. Now he was moving in. She backed away, struggling to find something to defend herself after breaking the chair. Her hand found a heavy tool sitting on one of the consoles. Swinging it wildly in front of Jaren, she smashed the control panel. Jaren released an anguished scream, slamming her into the wall.

Doc slumped to the floor in a daze. The room spun and her ears rung. Legs seemed unable to respond. Jaren desperately fumbled through the broken door and turned the dial. In his frustration, he began to sob uncontrollably.

"You're probably right. She's dead. I know she's dead. I just..." he covered his eyes.

Doc was sore but her legs began to respond. She stumbled slowly in his direction.

"We all live in desperate times. I'm sure..." she started but found herself without words.

Jaren moved his hands away to see Doc. His sincerity showed on his face. She moved a little closer, trying to comfort him. As he held out a hand to help steady her, his eyes went wide. He couldn't seem to speak and Doc couldn't turn fast enough. He jumped up, trying not to knock her over, charging whatever was behind her. Doc heard a shot. Her skin paled. As she managed to turn and survey the scene, she saw Jaren, wrestling on Ra'Ella in the back of the room. Another shot rang out. Jaren stumbled backward. As he fell, he locked eyes with Doc.

"Please forgive me." he exhaled. "I know..." but the life drained from his eyes too quickly.

Doc saw the barrel of the gun in his hands. Instinctively, Ra'Ella raised her hand and motioned to pull the trigger, shocked there was no response. She hadn't noticed it was gone.

It stunned her long enough for Doc to make a move. She dove at Jaren's body, trying for the gun. Ra'Ella pushed her at the last moment. Landing hard on the floor, Doc turned to see Ra'Ella swipe blood away from a head wound. She appeared clumsy on her feet. Doc tried again but Ra'Ella got there first, pulling the gun from Jaren's grasp and cracking it across Doc's forehead.

EVACUATION

Doc's eyes burst open. The headache was intense. Trying to move her hand to her head proved illusive and she couldn't understand why, until she felt the binding around her wrists. Eyes coming into focus, she saw the metal duct around her. *How did I get here?* she thought.

"It's about time you woke up. Lugging you around is definitely not my first choice," Ra'Ella snickered.

Doc hadn't noticed her on the other side of the duct yet. Hearing her voice reminded her of nails running down a chalk board.

"Where?" Doc whispered.

"The main control room. The last place to stop the self destruct sequence," Ra'Ella smirked.

"Why?" Doc scratched out, still trying to rub her head.

"Well, at first, I was going to say we were evacuating together. Then I remembered, I sit on the council. My last duty is to destroy this bunker and they may not believe I wasn't running from my responsibility. Besides, I tried that in the last bunker and it didn't work out well in my favor. So, instead of using you as cover, I decided you would help me shut off the self destruct sequence," Ra'Ella laughed.

"I won't help you," Doc spat at her.

"Oh, I think you will. See, if I don't manage to stop the sequence, all those people down there will die," Ra'Ella feigned compassion.

"And thousands more will be saved if I don't help you. So, no, not happening," Doc said.

"Oh, you're still thinking of your precious Erack and your precious D and Xayres will save you all," Ra'Ella mocked her. "Well, there's little chance of that. I mean, you sent one of my field medics with them in the first place. Annika can be very cute and all, but she's twice as deadly as she is sweet."

Doc knocked her head backward in disappointment. She forgot where Annika came from. The pain ripped through the front of her head and a groan escaped her lips.

"Best be careful now. You may have a concussion and that can be a very serious brain injury," Ra'Ella mocked and scolded.

Doc seethed, "I will never help you. I'll die first."

"That can be arranged. I imagine you'll find a time when you're eager to save your own skin just like Jaren," replied Ra'Ella coolly.

"I imagine you are more prone to want to save yours," commented Doc. "Not all of us are as weak as Jaren."

"Oh, so you know me and my desire to preserve my life? I have been this deep for years. If I can't be welcomed back into the ranks, it would be a welcome release from this hell," Ra'Ella motioned all around her. "I don't understand how you all live down here and think it's okay."

"There are enough of us that one day, we will stand together and rid ourselves of your kind," Doc scowled, tone laced in her disgust.

"You think there's more of you? Dearie, you're the last hold out. The last bunker. We have been systematically removing your kind from the planet for over 100 years. Dividing yourselves was a genius plan until you realize it made you weak. Provided no back up," scoffed Ra'Ella, followed by cackling.

Doc tried to swallow the idea they were the last

Americans, the last hold outs. She couldn't process it let alone believe it. And she refused to believe the Nazis were that close to winning.

"Love the look on your face. That's right, swallow your pride," Ra'Ella coughed.

Shaking her head, Doc realized the temperature in the bunker was higher than normal. The air was thick and more humid. Watching Ra'Ella closely, she realized they may be getting less oxygen. Underground they had some training in this but she had grown up in a city with ample oxygen sources.

"Why is it so hot in here," Ra'Ella blurted.

"Well, the destruct sequence is starting to shut down all the vital systems to allow more access for escape. Most of the ventilation fans have been permanently shut down. So..." Doc tried to explain.

"I wasn't actually asking you," Ra'Ella interrupted fanning herself.

"It's only going to get worse, the longer we stay. It's a fail safe in case people don't know the evacuation level. The environment will tell them," said Doc.

"Shut up!" shouted Ra'Ella without realizing. "I need to think."

"The system is no longer filtering in fresh oxygen. It's only a matter of time before there is nothing safe to breath. That's what's jamming up your thinking processes," Doc said.

"Now you're trying to trick me again. If that's the case, why are all those people still down there?" Ra'Ella motioned to the other side of the grate.

Doc saw people scrambling around the room.

"That room has it's own oxygen system. And they will be feeling the effects shortly as well. Their oxygen probably shut off in the last hour," Doc said. "But they are committed to our cause."

Doc yanked her hands from under her legs and kicked

the grate open. It flew down to the floor. All movement in the room stopped. Ra'Ella turned, screeching at the top of her lungs. She was met with Doc's two fists, knocking her backward, out the same way as the grate.

"Don't just stand there. Shoot her!" Doc screamed.

No one was sure what to make of the scene. Doc looked like she was bound. Ra'Ella had multiple injuries as if she was attacked. A closer look at Doc showed she had multiple injuries too. Trey's voice boomed across the room.

"What is this?" he trotted past the group of shocked onlookers.

Surveying the scene, he took swift action.

"Get her down from there, but leave her bound. Bind this one. We don't have time for this. You both just gave your lives for the cause," Trey ordered.

Ra'Ella moaned as they dragged her to the back of the room and bound her hands. Doc didn't fight it.

"I suppose that's all I can ask for. That she doesn't live," commented Doc.

As Ra'Ella came to, she protested, "Seriously, she is the one who aided an unsanctioned mission. She's the one you know is hiding information from you and you don't trust me?"

Trey looked from one to the other.

"Untie Doc. She may be a pain in the ass and she may ignore orders but she's not a traitor. Her attitude and responses show she is dedicated to the cause. Part of that is dying to protect the greater good which you clearly are not ready to do Ra'Ella," Trey said. "Gag her," he pointed at Ra'Ella. "I cannot stand hearing her voice during this time of crisis."

"You'll regret this. I have friends here," Ra'Ella fought until they successfully lodged the gag between her lips.

Doc looked relieved as the medic nursed her wounds, "She's probably telling the truth you know, about having friends. We don't know who is on her side and who isn't."

"We don't have time for this Doc. I am trying to get this bunker evacuated and blown up right now," Trey lamented.

"Which will be made all the harder if there are more Nazi plants running around, in this room for example. Are any of these people plants? You don't know. You need to thin out the ranks and let everyone but the necessary personnel you know you can trust, go," Doc advised.

"How many friends could she possibly have? There's no evidence to support she isn't alone. I can't imagine anyone else being on her side," Trey replied.

"That's a very cavalier attitude. You are taking this very lightly. I am not sure I understand why," said Doc, eyeing him up and down suspiciously.

"Perhaps all the answers will come to you in time Doc. We're all dedicated to our cause in here," Trey said.

ARRIVAL

Digging into her pack, D pulled out her extra med kit, water skin and rations. She told them there should be replacements in the bunker. They always had more than they needed. Jax and Thomas followed suit, tossing their rations on the ground near Erack, but Tallin refused.

"Take care of my boys or I'll track you down," D faked smiling sweetly.

"I wouldn't test her on that," Erack said.

"Take care of my boys..." Xayres mimicked.

"Shut up! She's talking about you too," Benji sounded stronger, bumping Xayres in the shoulder, causing them all to groan at the pain it caused.

"No more than 24 hours. By then, the bunker will be gone and the Nazis will flood this place. Understood?" Tallin ordered, "Let's go."

D led the way as the time passed swiftly. Tallin kept pushing the pace. These were moments she felt he should allow caffeine. If they continued at this pace, they would be too winded and tired to help anyone in the bunker, let alone themselves.

When they reached the south side of the bunker, they saw all the hatches open. Tallin scanned the scene, suspicious. D approached the first hatch. Not hearing the ventilation fan, she carefully stuck her head through the hole, despite Tallin's attempts to object. No one was in the corridor but she recognized it. She'd used it before. Signaling to the team, they joined her around the opening.

"These things would have been very well hidden," commented Jax.

"That was the point, wasn't it?" D replied. "In we go."

D dropped her pack off her back and slid through. Tallin passed her pack through the hole and then his own, following it through. The rest of the them did the same.

When they reached the main hall, she saw the black alert. Confused and dazed by a silent evacuation, she looked for signs of infiltration. Items were scattered everywhere.

"The black level evac took them by surprise," D murmured. "Like they thought the Germans were already here. I guess they know about the traitors now."

As they slowly made their way through the hall, all signs were the same. People looted the mess and the stores rooms. The weapons cache had been cavalierly left ajar. D worried about this state of evacuation. Unorganized, untrained people were left to fend for themselves against experienced killing machines.

"This isn't right," she murmured again.

"Then we need to get to command. Which way..." Tallin began.

D pointed and was already moving before he got the question out. He looked at the others.

"Gather up what you can and get back to the others. Take everything of value you can carry. Then get back to the city. Do not wait! Understood?" Tallin ordered.

They responded with a salute and a unison, "Yes sir!"

Tallin wasted no time catching up to D.

"All hands, evacuate immediately. Destruction sequence set for three hours thirty minutes. No override. All hands, evacuate immediately." the mechanical voice was quiet, but echoed in the emptiness of the space.

"Looks like we got here just in time," Tallin said.

"I hope so," D said, turning a corner.

They arrived at the council chamber. Jumping over the long table at the front of the room, she slid off and right to the double doors behind it. She turned the handles, aggravated by their lack of movement.

"Arrrrr!" she growled. "Locked!"

Tallin watched her back away, hands on her head. She sat for a moment, breathing. Then she began to look around the room. Every wall looked almost the same. Grates and lights in the center.

"What is it?" Tallin asked.

"There's a grate leading to the ventilation in the control room. But I have to remember which one," she replied.

"From training?" he asked.

"Yeah, but apparently I was not as good as I thought I was. Erack's right, I forget this stuff all the time," she huffed.

"We can't worry about that now. You need to focus and figure it out," Tallin encouraged her.

Her forehead crinkled and her eyes squinted. She tried desperately to remember which one it might be.

"Damn it! They made it this way to keep people from figuring it out," D said.

"So only one of them leads to the control room?" asked Tallin.

"Yeah," her response barely loud enough to be heard.

"But the others lead somewhere else?" clarified Tallin.

"Yeah," D replied absent-absentmindedly.

"All hands, evacuate immediately. Destruction sequence set for three hours. No override. All hands, evacuate immediately," the voice chimed.

"Ahhhh, shut up!" D screeched.

"Focus D. Focus," Tallin said, "Where is somewhere else?"

"Don't know. They never told us that," she replied

uncertainly.

"What did they tell you D?" Tallin asked.

"Well, only one of the grates could be used as an emergency exit and it was on the south wall," she spun around slowly, trying to get her bearings.

"D, which direction are you facing?" Tallin asked, trying to jog her memory.

"East, I think," she answered tentatively.

"So..." Tallin prodded.

She stood for another moment. Then she grabbed a bench and started yanking it across the floor to a wall. Tallin hustled over to assist. Rummaging through her pack, she produced her driver. Hopping up on the bench, she touched the grate and lifted her driver. The grate wiggled against her hand. She looked up, noticing it was loose. She jumped back, watching it fall away from the wall.

"That can't be good," D lamented.

"You're sure this is the right grate?" he paused.

"I think it falling was the answer to that question," replied D as she made a makeshift ladder to climb into the vent.

Tallin followed suit and within minutes, they were scooting through the shaft in the wall. Within a few minutes, they could see the opening. It was close. There were pieces of an argument echoing in from the other side.

Pop! Pop! Pop! Gun shots. Both froze, trying not to breath. Tallin signaled for them to wait. D was anxious. After what felt like forever to her, Tallin proceeded forward with caution. The noise was subsiding.

As they approached the hole, she saw Trey on the floor. The angle of the opening didn't allow for much more of a view. They couldn't see the front of the room.

"Give us the code," a male voice shouted.

Then someone walked up to Trey as he struggled to breathe.

"I'll put you out of your misery if you just give it to me," the man said brandishing his weapon.

"I've got nothing left to lose. You have no power here," Trey coughed out as blood started to dribble down his cheek.

Tallin and D pulled back a little to keep themselves hidden. The man looked up. It was Micha. D gasped. Tallin clamped his hand down over her mouth.

"I didn't know..." she shook her head. Tallin released her. "I knew about Ra'Ella after Xayres, but I didn't put it together."

Tallin put his finger to his lips. She nodded. Trey gurgled. D's stomach wrenched. Watching the scene unfold. Micha growled and walked back out of view.

"You shot the one that has the codes stupid," Ra'Ella was out of view.

"Nah, this one knows the codes too," Micha said.

D was concerned they had a hostage she couldn't see. Tallin placed a silencer on his weapon, grabbing hers and doing the same. They inched carefully to the edge. It looked like a large scuffle occurred here. Tallin lowered himself down, careful not to be seen. After handing down his pack, it was her turn.

"How long do we have to try with this one then?" Micha asked.

"Out technicians should be here any time now. Our people have had more than enough time to bring them here," Ra'Ella replied.

Micha was not alone. At the bottom of the ramp was another soldier. They talked with Ra'Ella although she never turned around, Tallin signaled and D followed. Tallin took his shots, moving to catch the other. Trying to keep the approach as silent as possible.

As D pulled back from her catch, she saw Doc in the front of the room. She pulled back behind the console. Someone unfriendly was on their way in. Just as she thought it, two other people came through the hole in the wall. She turned and saw Tallin had laid himself down near Trey, covering himself in blood for camouflage.

"Pretty smart Sarge," one said.

"Your kill skills are top notch. Thought you'd be rusty by now. Ya know, with all this time undercover," the other commented.

"Maybe I'm weaker than I expected. My interrogation skills are not what they used to be obviously. And, not my kills. They're Micha's," Ra'Ella huffed, despising their false flattery.

The two men headed toward the front of the room. When they were closer, she kicked herself for not being able to hide the body.

"Well, pity he went down in the fight then huh?" the first one replied.

"What do you mean..." Ra'Ella turned.

Her complexion blanched. She gasped.

"Micha..." She ran, dropping to her knees at his side, checking for a pulse.

D thought she saw tears. Ra'Ella sniffled for a moment, then she stood, turning toward the front of the room.

"We have to get this thing turned off. That's your expertise right?" Ra'Ella said.

"Yes sir. That's why we're here," said the first soldier.

"Then get it done!" she barked. "Get to work!"

Ra'Ella took a stride toward the front of the room. D saw Doc was bleeding, almost free of her bonds. Tallin took his moment, shooting one of the other soldiers. His body thumped to the floor. Ra'Ella turned, weapon drawn but still no sign of the sniper.

She backed up the ramp, turning around only to check on Doc. Ra'Ella gasped. Doc now stood face to face with her. The moment forced Ra'Ella to pause. Doc grabbed her by the top of her head, slamming it into the console next to them.

D popped up, taking a shot at the other officer. Hitting

him in the shoulder. He drew his weapon. The man turning in her direction, Tallin stood up. One shot to the head. The officer was down. D watched him fall.

Holding her breath, she allowed the tear to roll down her face. Why was she upset by this death? It made no sense. She saw Tallin in slow motion even though he was racing up the ramp.

Weapon ready, he yelled at Doc. Doc didn't respond. D rushed to her, grabbing her shoulder. Doc flung herself around. Taking D by the collar, D allowed it. Then Doc released and stepped back.

"It's okay Doc. It's me" D forced out.

"D?" Doc was confused.

Tallin stepped closer, "So this is the clever Doc?" he asked.

For a moment, Doc could only blink. D looked dismayed. Without warning, D backhanded Doc across the face, causing her to fall.

"That's for trying to have me killed!" D spat at her as she fell.

"D!" Tallin yelled, "What the hell?"

Tallin hopped over Ra'Ella to help Doc up. He looked at Ra'Ella.

"Wish you hadn't managed to break that chair. Kinda wanted to shoot her," Tallin lamented.

"I didn't order you killed. Ra'Ella did. Annika was from bunker Four remember? Because I sure forgot about it," Doc replied, spitting out blood from her mouth.

Tallin was tending to Doc's wounds as D considered the possibility. Ra'Ella groaned, starting to move. D straddled her, restraining her hands behind her.

"Pity, now we do have to manage her in a civil manner. Should have hit her harder. Then we wouldn't have to worry," Doc said.

"What do you mean 'now you have to.' Shouldn't that be a constant?" D asked, finding herself surprised by Doc's response.

"I could just shoot her now. No one would know," Tallin replied.

Tallin finished bandaging Doc. D stood up, pulling Ra'Ella to her feet.

"I suppose it wouldn't hurt anything," Doc said.

"Wouldn't hurt anything. I guess as long as it serves your purposes, then no matter," D said.

"This is war. The rules are different," reasoned Tallin. "The only certainty here is not one of them would hesitate to shoot us. Look at Trey?"

D looked down the room. All the bodies. All the death. This was war. She didn't like it.

"And I'm pretty certain Annika was ordered by her commander Sarge over here," Tallin gestured to Ra'Ella.

"But we have to be better than this," D said, waving her arm toward the rest of the room.

"We are better than them D. We don't seek them out to use them as slave labor or to be experimented on. We don't believe an eye color or skin color makes you a better person," Doc retorted.

"Being a better person doesn't mean we sit back while they exterminate us," Tallin added.

Ra'Ella moaned again. Tallin finished restraining her in a hog tie, careful not to come too close to D. He knew she was hot around the collar. They needed to talk her down before it got out of hand.

"All hands, evacuate immediately. Destruction sequence set for two hours and thirty minutes. No override. All hands, evacuate immediately," the mechanical voice chimed.

"Maybe you guys are right, but I will never allow myself to be so cavalier about it. Killing someone should not be decided arbitrarily unless in self defense," D scolded, looking at Ra'Ella. "Regardless of their personal views on the matter."

She felt something in the pit of her stomach. It was all about to come flooding through. But instead of her stomach pushing back, her eyes went blurry for a second. Only long enough for her to choke the reaction back down. This was unusual for her. She was losing her emotional control.

"That may be true in most circumstances, but in the midst of survival...other rules apply to these ethical situations," Tallin's frustration was evident in every word.

"We should all give careful consideration to the lines we cross. We wouldn't want to become worse than our enemy. I'm not saying we shouldn't fight fire with fire. All of us should be cautious about how we use the fire and how we put it out," D's words resonated through both of them, resulting in heavy silence.

"Oh yes. You're so much more noble than us," Ra'Ella remarked snidely.

None of them had noticed she was fully conscious.

"Exactly what a lesser race would say to justify such weak behavior," she continued.

D cracked her on the back of her head with the handle of her gun. Ra'Ella's head slammed into the floor. One of her teeth rolled out of her mouth. Tallin and Doc's mouths dropped open. Ra'Ella groaned, trying to touch her wound. D shrugged her shoulders.

"I didn't kill her," D said.

"Mercy is weakness," Ra'Ella cursed, spitting blood from her mouth.

"Mercy is the sign of a highly evolved mind," Doc retorted. "Arrogance is weakness."

Doc pulled a needle out of her med kit and shoved it into Ra'Ella's arm. She fell unconscious. Tallin and Doc relented, dropping Ra'Ella harshly to the floor. Replacing the grate back on the wall and moving the makeshift ladder from beneath it should keep any unwelcome visitors stalled long enough. D followed, weapon at the ready. If she was the only one not carrying Ra'Ella, it would keep any of them from shooting her. But D found her emotions on the issue conflicting with her logic.

They wound their way through the corridors, Ra'Ella in a makeshift shoulder cot. Part of D hoped she woke up and fell off, causing herself a terminal injury. She was certain they all felt this way, but none of them voiced it. Trying to be more ethical, she turned her attention to their direction.

"They should have a time finding the right controls anyway. Then they have to guess the pass code," Doc said. "No chance they could shut it down now.

As they entered the main hall, they put Ra'Ella down and began filling their packs with whatever was left, Some rations and canned foods. Some water skins with water. A few arms. It looked like either Jax and Thomas had lugged back too much or there were still people looting during evacuation. Tallin assured them the Nazis would have nothing to do with these things.

"All hands, evacuate immediately. Destruction sequence set for one hour and 45 minutes. No override. All hands, evacuate immediately," the voice chimed.

The clunking of heavy foot falls echoed from down the passageway. All three of them froze, scanning the area for places to hide. They didn't mean to go in different directions.

D saw Doc and Tallin on the other side of the room. The boot thumps reverberated. They saw them. At least a dozen Nazi soldiers came marching through, no doubt headed to command. When they saw Ra'Ella on the floor, they didn't even stop. The one in front made a signal and the last man in line shot her in the head.

Slapping her hands over her mouth, she hoped the loud thudding would cover up her gasps. Not one strayed from their ordered destination. They heard them slamming their feet into the floor all the way down the hallway. This wasn't the clean up crew.

The three of them grabbed their bags, looking back to one another, then at Ra'Ella.

"See..." Tallin whispered tersely. "No hesitation."

They heard more steps. These ones came with gun shots. There was nowhere to hide here. Needing to get out of this space, they scattered in different directions. D looked over her shoulder and caught a glimpse of Doc pushing Tallin through a doorway.

MEMORIES

No one followed her. The lights blinked ahead. She thought it was the black alert but the further she ran through the flashing lights, the more she realized she had gotten herself lost. The lights flickered in a dirty concrete cell.

"And this is where you shall die," she said out loud.

She stopped, taking time to look around. Something about this area felt familiar. It looked familiar. But she couldn't quite tell what. Closing her eyes to keep herself in check, she resisted the urge to scream. This was frustrating.

Slowly stepping further into the area, she saw scorched walls and caught a whiff of stale air, making her choke for a moment. She saw the tables and broken glass. Then she kicked something, sending it floating into the air.

Gingerly, she reached out her hand and caught it. Examining it, she removed her glove to feel the melted wax. One of her favorite colors of pink. A picture. She remembered the picture. Moving to the other side of the room, she saw the busted window that looked into another room.

Propelling herself over the wall, she sat in the tiny chair. And it happened. A flash. She remembered something of her life before her parent's death for the first time in years.

As she sat, she heard them.

"D...D...time for class," her mother said.

"Oh, mom. Do I have to? It's not fun. Can't I play with Erack?" she asked.

"Now, you know you are very special. The things you do in class will help everyone one day. Don't you want to help people?" Her father scolded lightly.

"Besides, aren't you and A supposed to have activities together. He's one of your friends right?" her mother asked.

"I suppose so. Erack is a bigger friend. Why can't I be in the same class as him?" she asked.

"Well...Because he is bigger, I mean older than you. That would make him feel bad," her dad reasoned. "Ready to go?"

"Okay," she relented, taking them by the hand as they lead her across the hall.

She set the picture down on the table. There were no crayons available, but she was so engrossed in her mind's eye, she picked one up anyway and began to color the picture. For the first time, she remembered that day. She watched it like the movie reels in history class. She hadn't wanted to go to class that day either. She was in her room, playing with something.

A knock at the door came once. Then again. It felt urgent. The man on the other side sounded familiar but she couldn't place him. He was hustled into a side room before she got a good look. Then, they told her classes were canceled. She needed to find Erack and play. Without a second thought, she skipped down the corridor. She felt tears on her cheeks. Feeling overwhelming fear and sadness caused her to breath in deep, as if coming up from underwater. Suddenly, she was in the present.

There was no way her parents could have known what happened to her in class and still sent her in there. She hated it. An intense fear came over her again as she stood up.

Walking out the door and down the hall a few steps, she found her quarters. She hadn't been here in years. *Why were we so close to the lab?* she thought.

She scoured the walls and rooms. There were three rooms but she didn't remember having any siblings. Three bedroom bunks were for families of five or six. Her brain flashed with memories, overwhelming her. Teetering then stumbling backward, she ended up in her parent's room. There was a picture of her in here, a very young her. Sitting on the bed to regain her composure, she grabbed the picture and put it in her pack. Unable to explain why it felt important. She sat for a while, forgetting her rush, forgetting her friends, forgetting the bunker would soon be in pieces.

Then she took off her pack and laid back. She had tried to find answers for so long and if she waited here long enough, she was sure to find them. Her brain filled with memories of sleeping here and classes. She hated remembering the classes. Spinning in good feelings, she sat up, feeling the bed unmade. Confused, her parents always made their bed, she turned to see why.

Brown. She saw the sheets stained in brown. She jumped up, recognizing the alkaline smell. Blood. She grabbed her pack, looking around, seeing the trail on the floor. But the door, she didn't remember the door. Part of her classes had been to explore the back corridors without supervision and manage to find her way back to the lab. She remembered. That's why she knew her way around so well. But what were they trying to teach her.

She pulled back the door in the wall. Someone had left it open. *Has this door always been here?* she thought. It must have as the blood lead right through it. She retraced the same steps Xayres had earlier. Out into the lab. She realized her parents weren't just scientists. They must have been studying her. But why? Did they know about her abilities?

The thoughts brought her back to the present. She heard the mechanical voice far away. Now she was determined to forget again. There was a reason her brain buried these secrets. For now, she wanted to keep it that way. Running out of the lab, she needed to find her way out of this area before she did actually get buried here.

"All hands, evacuate immediately. Destruction sequence set for 30 minutes. No override. All hands, evacuate immediately. Last verbal notice until countdown." The voice chimed as she made her way through the ventilation shaft.

D could hear the alert through the walls. If she wasn't outside soon, she wouldn't be far enough away to avoid the blast. This was going to topple this mountain.

She stopped for a quick sip of the water skin when she heard voices. Scrambling, there was nowhere to hide. Lifting her weapon, she saw the first of the voices come around the corner. It was a little girl who stopped at the sight of her. More followed, a little boy, an older couple and an elderly couple. The elderly man approached her with his hand outstretched.

"We're all a little tense down here dear. But I don't think you need that," he said, lowering her weapon.

"Why are you still here?" D asked, holstering her weapon.

"Dad wouldn't evacuate without grandpa and this is the first day he's felt well enough to move," the boy said.

"Well, let's get you out of here," D said. "Follow me."

She motioned them forward. When they arrived at the open hatch, she assisted them all through. The mother and children ran straight away in the direction she indicated. But the father was more concerned with his parents.

D went straight for the man, grabbing him by the shoulders. She turned him away from his parents.

"You have a family you have to worry about," she said.

He opened his mouth to protest but she didn't allow it. "You have two children who need their father, especially now," she walked him toward the forest. "You need to go with them. I will take care of your parents."

He looked at her, sadness in his eyes. This decision was a difficult one.

"Go!' she shoved him forward.

He turned to look at her again, torn.

"GO!" she shouted, not worrying about anyone hearing her.

He looked stunned. She pointed and stomped her foot. Stumbling backward, he headed in the direction of his family.

The elderly couple looked thankful, as she turned around, she noticed they were already sitting under a small tree.

"We told him to go without us. We've lived our lives. Those kids need a chance to live theirs," the old man said.

D knelt down next to them. He took her hand and touched her cheek.

"You deserve to live a life too. Don't let us keep you here," the woman said.

The old man began to scan her face, as if trying to remember it. This made her uncomfortable. She tried to change the subject.

"I have morphine which will take the edge off but it's not the quickest way to go. Or I have caffeine, but if I don't administer enough, you'll still be alive and you'll suffer from horrible withdrawal," she explained.

"Withdrawal in less than 30 minutes. Highly unlikely young lady," the man said. "I was a doctor."

He motioned for her to come closer. Then he moved her hair off her ear and gasped. The mark was there. She jerked back.

"What are you..." she asked.

"It's as I thought. You're one of the special ones," he

said.

D deflected, "I'm nothing special. Just me," she shrugged.

"One of those ones. Are you A, B, C, D, E or G?" he asked.

"Why can't I be F?" D asked sarcastically.

"F died early," he replied. "They couldn't handle it."

D stood up, pulling the morphine out of her pack. She wanted the caffeine to get back to the city, just in case.

"Yes, morphine will do. But please, humor an old man. What is your name?" he asked.

"I don't remember. Everyone calls me D," she answered dryly, now anxious to get away from him.

She leaned down and administered the first dose to the woman. Smiling, she thanked her quietly. The man grinned as she pushed the needle into his arm.

"That mark behind your ear. Don't let anyone see it. Trust no one," he whispered.

She looked at him, hand touching her ear unconsciously. Her hand moved to protect it instinctively, pulling her hair over her ear.

"But why?" she asked.

He didn't answer, motioning for her to go. Picking up her pack, she stood up, seeing twilight was falling. She had to get back to the ruins before nightfall.

Stopping only once to look back, she could still see the old couple. Shaking her head, she turned on her heel. Then she heard it. The pre-blasts they were warned about shook the ground so hard she fell to her knees before running as fast as she could away from the bunker.

BACK TO HERE

Boom! Boom! Boom!

With each blast, the ground shook more fiercely. She knew she didn't have enough time. As she ran, she grabbed the needle, pushing it into her arm. The caffeine kicked into her system, helping her legs to move faster.

She heard a loud crashes and felt the heat of fire on her back. Ground shaking, she struggled to keep her balance. Then the blast wave ripped her off her feet, propelling her forward, slamming into the tree hard.

Standing up clumsily, a steady stream of tears rolled down her cheeks. Feeling her head, it was wet and the liquid it transferred to her hand was red. Her ears were ringing and her balance was off, but she knew she had to press forward.

Her extensive injuries didn't stop her from reaching the ruins before it got too dark. The search crews would be out and she needed a place to hide. Her abdomen protested most of her movements and her head pounded. She tried to remember what the effects of mixing caffeine and morphine were but she was finding it harder and harder to think coherently.

The ground shook again. The bunker explosion was causing some residual ground tremors. This was not part of their training, but it was studied in other bunkers. *Erack probably knew about it too,* she thought. She worried they had done a lot of irrevocable damage, that the tremors would never cease. Although the fallout was not nuclear, she wondered if there were other effects they hadn't accounted for in the blasts.

Arriving at the rendezvous, she found it abandoned. Not a trace anyone had been here. She knew to expect that but for some reason, her heart ached a little at the idea of being abandoned. She kept her mind busy, trying to forget all the pain of the last few hours. Then she saw the lights.

Luckily she knew this area so well, the dark did not inhibit her and before long, she found a small conclave near her. Crawling up inside it, she knew trying to sleep was pointless. Her body protested the tight space. Her injuries were much worse than she imagined. But she was well camouflaged and she needed to try to rest.

Regardless of how tired her body and mind were, sleep would not find her this evening. She was overcome with anger, hatred and despair. Her mind flooded with angry thoughts about every thing. Her parents. Ra'Ella and Micha. Then the gurgling German. She wanted to scream but she couldn't. How could she turn this off?

Then the lights were right outside. She covered her breath in the cold. Thunder crashed outside. Then lightening. The storm had arrived. She knew they were close, reading their emotions without issue. One was very angry. Something about losing his son in the blast. The others just wanted to kill someone. So much hate. She'd never felt so much hate. They didn't find her fox hole.

She released her tense muscles. Pain rippled through her body. She knew she had to work through this. Until the sun rose, she couldn't move. Deciding the morphine was worth the risk, she gave herself a very small dose to take the edge off the pain.

Her thoughts were less coherent and her stomach churned, unable to eat any rations. It made her head a little more dizzy. She'd forgotten about the possibility of concussion. She wrapped herself up and sat, waiting for the light.

It was still raining when it rose. She waterproofed herself as best she could in the small space. As she exited, she wasn't as careful as she normally would be. The drugs were making her sloppy. She noticed it but she couldn't convince herself to care for some reason.

Backing out of the entrance, she lugged her pack across the ground. As the sun hit her back, she thought she heard someone, but ignored it. No one was out here except people who escaped at this point. Then...*Click. Click.* Quick. Like the cocking of a weapon.

The voice was deep. Cursing at her to turn around. She tried to keep him quiet, to prevent him from alerting others. But as she turned, she saw he already had back up. There were two of them.

"Hande hoch!" he spoke tersely.

She tried but her body wouldn't allow her. Why hadn't they just shot her anyway? *Were they in the taking slaves stage now?* she thought unsure if it was silent or aloud.

When she didn't respond appropriately, the other came over and slapped her, causing the buzzing in her ears to almost overwhelm her. Hoping to hold in any verbal response, she bit her tongue. She should have stayed in the bunker. Then she wouldn't have to be tortured more than necessary. A little blood trickled out of her mouth.

Thwerp! The man next to her fell. ***Thwerp!*** The one holding the gun dropped to his knees, then face first into the leaves. The soldier next to her had a hole between the eyes. The other not quite so. She scrambled to grab her pack. Looking around only for a moment to find the shooter, she decided not to waste this chance, taking off through the back side of the ruins.

When she safely reached cover, she stopped. It was only long enough to wrap her abdomen and head to help with the pain. *Compression helps,* she kept thinking as the initial wrap exacerbated the pain in every movement. Dressing her wounds did help as she took off toward the city.

The weather was turning worse. She was far from her

destination and it was becoming more clear she most likely needed help to make it all the way back. Although she had been warned about the use of the caffeine, she couldn't help herself.

As she ran, the rain worsened. The ground became heavy on her boots. She heaved as she took on water and continued. She had to get to the city. Everything was a blur. The sun came up. The sun went down. She wasn't sure if it was day or night. The cloud cover kept things mostly twilight the entire way. Her abdomen screamed at her. The morphine continued to make her sloppy having internal battles with the caffeine.

She started to trip over her own feet, let alone the wet brush. The rain poured down harder as she found herself getting more wet and colder. Dangerously cold. If she stopped, she may not survive. Suddenly, she saw the tall buildings ahead of her. The cold concrete shined in her mind. Close enough to slow down a little, but too far away to stop. She needed to get there.

She approached the familiar cave. Her legs heavy. Dropping to her knees, hands shaking through her pack, she desperately searched it for lighting sticks. No idea how to start a fire in this drenched place without them, she just had to hang on long enough to get a fire started. She'd come too far to freeze to death now.

Pulling out her water skin, then the morphine, she felt she could afford to be a little sloppy here. If the Germans saw her now, they would just shoot her anyway. A welcome end. But her stomach relented. The acid forced its way up her throat. Coughing uncontrollably, she looked up. No lights. No voices. She couldn't be that far behind the others.

Lightening flashed illuminating an outline of the city. Thunder boomed and crackled. She saw her breath turn white in the cold. The world went dark.

AWAKE

D breathed in hard, sitting straight up. She was dry, which was all she could determine.

"Where..." she croaked, her voice not answering to her commands.

"It's okay D. You're safe," Erack soothed her.

"Take it slow," she heard Doc say from across the room.

She grabbed Erack in a tight embrace, taking him by surprise. All she wanted was to hold him. To see him okay. He had been so ill. If she held him long enough, she may be able to tell if this was real or a dream. Since the training with Tallin started, she had even more trouble distinguishing the two.

"Oh – it must've been a dream. What a horrible dream," it all poured out of her mouth as she hugged him. "You will not believe everything I saw. It was crazy. I don't know where to begin."

Erack pulled out of her embrace. Holding her by the shoulders, looking deep into her eyes, "What was a dream D? Did you see something we need to know?"

"There was a traitor among the survivors. People died. You were so sick and I rescued you with Xayres' help. And Tallin died but then he wasn't dead. The bunker is here. It wasn't destroyed. And you're well," words came tumbling out in an illogical jumble of mixed up sequences. "My parents weren't murdered." Mixing what she wanted with what was reality so fast Erack couldn't understand most of what she said.

Her eyes came into acute focus. This was the med bay. Thinking she was taken by some sickness. Causing her to have hallucinations or dreams that felt so real. But she reasoned all this was too wild to be real.

She heaved a sigh of relief, having been under the watchful eye of Doc during her fits. Apparently, now she was getting better. She was lucid.

"I know it all sounds so crazy. So there's no way it could be true. No way it was real...right?" she smiled looking for reassurances.

All she saw were the confused and concerned looks on everyone's faces.

"D..." Erack looked at her sternly.

As she looked at everyone, the room seemed off. It was different. The equipment was different. The layout...different. This wasn't Doc's med bay. Her mind raced to find a reason. A reason it was different.

She jumped off the table, almost falling over. Why didn't her legs respond? Erack helped her back up. She fought back fear as she tried to reconcile her emotions, her eyes and her memories.

"D" Erack tried again. "I was sick, very sick. I almost died. Tallin's people made the antitoxin and you brought it to me. Do you remember?"

Her eyes widened as he spoke. She didn't want to hear. it. She tried to cover her ears but Erack had her firmly by the wrists. It was all too terrifying. Too awful to think this was their world and she was in the middle of it all. She squeezed her eyes closed, hoping to wake up. She needed to wake up. But it wasn't working. The world spun for a moment. Then she took deep breaths, remembering all the training.

"I helped blow up the bunker..." D pushed the words out with all her energy but could barely manage a whisper. "The Nazis, the tracker. The children. The poor dead children," her mind still swirling, she grasped at any real memory. "This can't be my reality. I left children to die. I blew people up. I killed people! The gurgling...oh the gurgling."

Erack released her wrists. She grabbed her head. The sounds of the gurgling German, of Trey, the blood sprayed across her face. The old couple, their children. They waited as it all raced through her head and she seemed more calm. Tears tumbled down her cheeks at the sight of it all in her head. Every horrible thing she had done to save her friend.

"D, we're at war. You did what you had to...to survive," Erack's voice was soft and even, almost sweet. "And to save me."

"But now what?" she asked, looking up at him. Now what do we do?"

"We keep surviving," Erack answered.

"How can I ever get over all these bad things? How can I..." D cried out.

"We focus on now. We do what we have to do in the now. There is nothing we can do about the past," Xayres answered, as softly as his voice would allow.

The change in tone shocked D. Her system registering he was here but her mind still somewhere between.

"Where are we now?" she felt desperate to understand her lost time.

"We're in the city now D," answered Erack.

"Yes, the city D," Xayres repeated.

"Why? How long..."

"We're here waiting," said Erack.

Her mind swirled around all the information, "Waiting...Waiting for what?"

"To find a new bunker." Now she saw Xayres standing

in the doorway, "To make a new home somewhere." He smiled at her.

"How long have you all been waiting?" D asked.

"Eh, about six months," Xayres said, moving to the other side of her table.

"Is that how long I've been here?" she asked.

"Yeah, we found you outside. Pretty broken and bruised. Unconscious," Erack explained.

She was responding more confidently forcing herself to sit up straighter.

"Good thing we found you when we did. We were worried we wouldn't be able to save you," Doc said.

"You shouldn't have saved me. I didn't deserve it," D replied.

"You can talk to the Shrinker about those feelings later," Doc said, going on about her work.

"Besides, we had to save you. You're important," Xayres said, but D didn't hear or notice the comment.

"But you've all been waiting here for six months. Why? Not for me, I imagine," D said.

"Actually yes. We've all been waiting for you," Erack said.

D looked surprised. She couldn't understand why they would wait for her.

"Why me? I'm nothing special," she warded off all the weird feelings the idea gave her.

"Well, as survivors showed up here, we took them in. And between Tallin and I, we explained your...your..." Doc was uncertain what to call it.

"The specialized things you can do," Erack assisted.

"Yes, that. They've seen the science and they have now seen the leadership stand confidently behind the science," Doc paused to think.

"So now they understand and accept...well...your" Erack struggled as well. "Your stuff," he motioned to his head.

"So they don't intend to burn me at the stake?" she mused.

"No, no stakes here," Xayres chuckled, relieved she was relaxing enough to be sarcastic. "And you're not the only one. Many more like you have come forward. They've been working with Tallin."

"Stringing you up was in no one's best interest at that point," Tallin walked into the room. "How you feeling kid?"

She gave him a weak smile. He nodded in understanding.

"It's a lot to take in, but we need you to try and get your head wrapped around it," Doc said, pushing past Tallin to see to another patient.

"Why? Why do I need to wrap my head around it," D asked.

"Because we've all been waiting for you D," Erack reiterated.

"For me? For me to what?" she was getting weary with the circular conversation.

"To find a new bunker D," Erack explained. "You need you to use your skills to find a bunker out there that will take us in. You've proven you can do it already with your work outside," he tone was optimistic.

"You're the special one who can," Tallin assisted. "My skills are not quite as attuned as yours."

She blinked uncontrollably. Shaking her head.

"Wha..." D forced the world to stay still, to stay grounded, to stave off the overwhelming feeling.

Xayres walked to the foot of the bed. "We've waited for you to wake up so you can take us there," he smiled.

Erack lifted up her chin with his finger, looking deep in her eyes again. "D, you're the only one who can."

Kenny B Smith

D-Evolution

D found it cumbersome. Someone had to carry her everywhere she went. So far, she opted to just stay in bed and subject herself to extra physical therapy exercises. They kept telling her it would get better with time. But she was becoming more skeptical. One thing that had improved dramatically were her extra sensory abilities. She no longer needed pain to kick start them. But she had little control over volume or when she wanted to turn them off. Both those functions were controlled carefully through meds administered by Doc. With the change, her dreams also changed.

D and her physical therapist finished a set of leg exercises as her carrier waited in the doorway.

"Okay, now, try to push on my hand," instructed the therapist.

D's forehead dripped with sweat as she tried desperately to make her leg respond. Then she felt it. A twitch. The therapist smiled and picked up her other leg, signaling for the same.

"I felt that. You're getting stronger. Your muscles are starting to respond on a more regular basis," she tossed D a towel for her forehead and massaged her legs a little. "Pity your special abilities don't involve healing yourself. But, what do I know. Maybe you can and you just don't know how yet."

"Great, she's one of those," she heard the whisper in her head, an unfamiliar voice.

Looking around, she noticed the carrier was someone

she had never met. The others must be busy or in chambers. She tried to get Erack or Xayres or even Tallin, Doc...sometimes Kaya made her feel more comfortable than a stranger. But she was headed to the council. So she imagined none of them were available.

"I guess I should get ready to go," she pushed herself into a sitting position while the therapist placed pillows behind her to hold her up.

"See, much much better. Won't be long now before you won't need a carrier," picking up her things, the therapist gave a quick good bye over her shoulder as she slid past the carrier in the doorway.

She felt the carrier's hesitation. Maybe they thought she was contagious. D tried to clear her mind to listen again.

"I'm D," she held out her hand. "If we're going to get up close and personal, we may as well be introduced. What's your name?"

"Sariah," the carrier mumbled, not taking D's arm to shake.

"Nice to meet you," she let her arm fall. "Should we go now?" D asked.

The carrier huffed as she moved across the room and picked up D. She was not as muscular as she had been while training, In fact, she felt much too skinny and knew it could not be healthy. But it did make her very light. Doc told her she had dropped to under 100 pounds while unconscious and now Doc shoveled more food at her than she would ever be able to eat in a lifetime.

As they approached the private session chamber, the guard opened the door. Sariah and the guard grimaced at one another. D was so busy trying not to bounce out of her arms, all she could hear was, "I can't believe I am touching one of them."

Her body filled with disgust, obviously the emotion was overwhelming the carrier. She literally dropped her into the solid wood chair offered and quickly escaped her object of disgust. D never experienced something like this. Before she just assumed people did not trust her. Now she could confirm things and while she was mostly correct about certain people, she'd never experienced someone finding her so disgusting. At least not without getting to know her first.

She shook off the feeling and continued to focus on her level of control. The guard shot her a fake smile as he closed the door. Xayres and Tallin sat at the center table facing one another. A rush of distrust and annoyance swept over her. Trying to shake it off, she focused on the other members of the council. She saw Kaya, a nice familiar face and about half a dozen others who she didn't recognize. One sat in the far corner from her. When she looked at him, he smiled just as the guard did.

"Can't wait to rid us of *them*..." she heard his thoughts.

She looked away. He looked down, forcing all thoughts out of his mind. All she heard was white noise.

"Well, this is awkward. Boys, you mind if we get this show on the road?" D asked in a bored tone.

"I suppose," Xayres stuttered as he moved his seat to the other side of the table to face her. "Did Kaya explain why you are here or did she just invite you?"

"No, we talked about it. You know I don't get dragged around against my will for no reason," she replied imitating a sweet tone.

"Good, then we can get started," Tallin huffed again, arms folded as if he were sulking.

"We need to know if you would be willing to work with others like yourself," Kaya said. "As we discussed, you would need to find a way to bring out the best of their abilities. Teach them to control them and the like. We know you have a long physical recovery ahead of you, but we were hoping you could start right away. With the scans Doc has managed to complete, we have been able to find a few more like you and would like to see if you all would be an added tool for use in the resistance."

"I'm not sure I like the idea of being known as a tool," Xayres said.

"As if you didn't know people already see you that way," Tallin replied.

"Gentlemen! It's like you've reverted back to being toddlers. And in front of the council," Kaya scolded, walking up behind them.

"Oh, but they make this bore of an activity worth showing up for," D faked a whine.

Kaya seethed at her. The look on her face is one D knew well. It meant shut up and quit messing around. This look meant what was happening between Tallin and Xayres was becoming serious. Her suspicions were confirmed when Kaya cleared the council out of the room.

"You don't have that kind of authority," Tallin said.

"Yes she does," Xayres said. "It's part of her position. If she finds the chair out of line, she is obligated to act and has the power to do so until she finds us fit to make decisions again," Xayres shook his head at Tallin while looking sheepishly at his feet. "You really didn't read anything in the charter, did you?"

"I only read the parts that concerned me. I did not have the privilege of serving on a council in a bunker," replied Tallin.

"All the parts of the charter pertain to you Tallin," Kaya quipped. "You need to go to your quarters and read it all. Every word...at least twice."

"What is with you two? The last time we were here, you were thick as thieves and now you can barely stand to be in the same room together. I mean, I found it as annoying as anyone else but I have to wonder what crazy shit happened while I was unconscious," D asked.

"Politics makes close friends enemies. It's a normal thing. They will adjust...quickly," Kaya commanded.

"Don't you guys remember that?" D asked.

"Of course I remember. But I also remember the training he subjected you to and now he wants to do it to the others like us. Whether they choose it or not," answered Xayres.

"Tallin, you can't force people to develop this stuff. Not everyone feels as we do about it. Some people don't want it," D said. "Hell, I'm pretty certain this was not my first choice," she paused, not sure if she could explain. "I didn't really have a choice. I am certain I was designed not to have a choice, although I am not sure what all that entails exactly. I will not train people who did not make the choice. Whether you like it or not Tallin."

She tried to get up but only stumbled. Xayres rushed to help her back onto the chair. For a moment, there was an awkward silence.

"Everyone deserves a choice," she said meekly. "With your history Tallin, you should know that more than anyone."

Tallin's look softened. "There are few people who can make me feel sheepish and put me in my place." Tallin said softly. "You are in rare company D."

"It's settled then. No forced training," Xayres concluded.

"I don't completely agree but I see what you are saying. And I know everyone deserves the choice. At least in the beginning stages," replied Tallin.

"We'll never get you to see it completely our way," D said. "But I will not allow you to force people Tallin."

"And neither will I," Kaya agreed sternly. "It goes against everything we stand for. It makes us like the Germans. We cannot become like them in our efforts to defeat them."

KENNY B SMITH

Spending over a decade working as a freelance ghostwriter, content writer and editor, she decided she had spent enough time creating works of art for others. While most of her professional work revolves around academics and curriculum, her passion is creating stories and worlds. Now she attempts to incorporate her love of history and creative writing into one with alternative history stories that address current issues we face today.

When she's not writing, she wants to assist other authors in creating their own works of art. She generally specializes in unpublished first time authors and those who may have published works, but haven't managed to make a splash in the market. Believing traditional publishers are risk averse and vanity/small publishing houses focus too much on their bottom line, she wants to create a new way to publish that is more supportive than self-publishing. See more information at teapotsawaypress.com

Kenny B Smith is a mother of three and lives in Utah with her husband. She enjoys crochet, quilting, reading and homeschooling her kids. One day, she hopes to world school and her domestic passion is travel. She enjoys history, learning about serial killers and crime procedurals.

I want to extend a special thanks to everyone who has supported me in my adventures and read the book. I love you all. Even if we have never met, you hold a special place in my heart.

CPSIA information can be obtained
at www.ICGtesting.com
Printed in the USA
FSHW012331120419
57211FS